LIVINGSKY

Stonehouse Publishing Inc. is an independent
publishing house, incorporated in 2014.

Cover design and layout by Elizabeth Friesen.
Printed in Canada

Stonehouse Publishing would like to thank and acknowledge
the support of the Alberta Government funding for the arts,
through the Alberta Media Fund.

Government

National Library of Canada Cataloguing in Publication Data
Anthony Bidulka
Livingsky
Novel
ISBN 978-1-988754-47-5
First edition

LIVINGSKY

A NOVEL BY

ANTHONY BIDULKA

n public but trouble in private. On this occasion, he was
who'd been drinking. Could he trust himself? "What's this

bout Merry. I think she's in trouble."
was all it took. Sharpe stepped aside and motioned the
to come inside. It was a move he'd regret.
ntil about a year ago, Merry Bell had been his employee,
his top investigators. But their relationship went beyond
ey'd been through a lot together and, like one of those un-
imal friendships you see on You Tube (cat and duck, rhi-
and chicken), a bond had formed. If there was anyone Na-
arpe, self-proclaimed lone wolf, would ever come close to
ng as family, it was Merry Bell. He wasn't sure if she felt the
it that didn't really matter.
pe switched on lights as he followed the woman into the
om where he invited her to take a seat on the couch. "Can I
something to drink? Water? Beer?"
nk you, no. I won't stay long."
pe lowered himself into an armchair across from the couch,
and slightly uncomfortable one he used when he wanted
without risk of falling asleep. Dispensing with polite nice-
jumped right in. "You said Merry is in trouble. What's hap-

you hear about the murder in Yaletown?"
own was an upmarket neighbourhood running along
th side of Vancouver's peninsula where decrepit CPR
ses had been converted into chic residential lofts, high-
tiques, trendy restaurants, and chill lounges promoting
culture. Not exactly the part of town anyone associated
lent death.
I didn't." After running errands in the morning, he'd played
ith his regular troupe of Saturday buddies followed by din-
drinks. Lots of drinks. There'd been no time for local news.
looked surprised. "It was all over the TV and internet.
anstone was killed, *Dr.* Elliott Vanstone, in his apartment."

FOR HERB

CHAPTER 1

"Do you remember me?"

Nathan Sharpe inspected the unexpected [...] for any clue that might tell him why the w[...] his front door at a time of night far beyo[...] consider polite. "You're Merry's friend."

She nodded. "Her roommate. Julia."

"Julia, yes," he said, his tongue still thic[...] her a couple of times at the office when sh[...] lunch, back when Merry was still workin[...] lived alone. "How can I help you?"

"May I come in?"

He looked at his watch. Almost midnigh[...] "It's quite late, Julia."

"I know, I'm sorry, I just don't know w[...] responded, her face pleading.

As a private investigator, Sharpe was no[...] night visitations. They were often accompa[...] tions, followed by desperate pleas for help. [...] work was done after hours, when people w[...] guards down from fatigue or having had [...] falsely protected, as if what was talked abo[...] possibly bite them in the ass come dayligh[...] let the woman into his apartment. Ms. Tur[...] and, as he stood there in pajama bottoms [...] processed vague memories of flirtatious ban[...]

be fun[...]
the on[...]
about?"

"It's[...]
Tha[...]
woman[...]

Up[...]
one of[...]
that. T[...]
likely a[...]
nocero[...]
than S[...]
describ[...]
same, t[...]

Sha[...]
living [...]
get you[...]

"Th[...]
Sha[...]
the firr[...]
to read[...]
ties, he[...]
pened?"

"Di[...]
Yale[...]
the so[...]
wareho[...]
end bo[...]
cockta[...]
with vi[...]

"No[...]
soccer[...]
ner an[...]

Juli[...]
Elliott[...]

The name sounded vaguely familiar, but he couldn't place it and said so.

"Vanstone," she repeated, as if that should somehow jog his memory. "Merry's doctor."

Sharpe's ears perked up. "Merry's doctor? He was murdered?"

"In his apartment. They think it happened a couple of nights ago, Thursday, but no one found him until, like, yesterday."

"I'm sorry to hear it." He stared harder at the woman. Was he missing something? "But I don't see what makes you think Merry might be in trouble."

"Mr. Sharpe," she said slowly, eyes wide. "Merry killed him."

Nathan spent a torturous Sunday mulling over how best to approach his former employee and friend about what he'd learned from Julia Turner. The woman had made him promise not to tell Merry about her visit, afraid of how it might affect their own friendship. Nathan was freed from part of his decision when he received a text from Merry at the end of the day asking for a meeting at Sharpe Investigations Monday morning. Merry hadn't been in the office for almost a full year. This could only mean one thing: she was going to take him into her confidence. Which led him to contemplate an entirely different set of worries: How much of what happened would she tell him? Would she tell him the truth, or a redacted version of it? How should he respond?

If it was anyone else, he'd know exactly what to do, without question. But this was Merry. She knew his reputation as a gruff, lantern-jawed, tough-as-nails, granite-hearted detective was nothing but a cover for a gruff, lantern-jawed, tough-as-nails, teddy-bear who, against all odds, had developed father-like affection for his former employee.

Merry arrived at Sharpe Investigations at 8:00 a.m. sharp, looking…not great. Still, the moment they saw each other their faces cracked into matching ear-to-ear smiles. They weren't huggers, instead Merry handed him the Starbucks she'd brought for him.

He took a sip of the extra-dry, triple-shot, tall cappuccino. "You remembered."

"Of course. I haven't been gone that long."

Actually, you have, Nathan thought to himself as he led her into his office and closed the door. They sat, he behind the desk, she in front, as they had so many times in the past; ready to discuss cases, solved or to-be-solved, or just shoot the shit. Today's conversation would be much different.

"I was surprised to get your text last night."

"I know," Merry said, taking a careful sip of her own multi-titled coffee.

Sharpe noticed Merry couldn't quite look him in the eye. That bothered him.

"I'm sorry I haven't been better about staying in touch," she said. "I've had a lot going on, but you know that, and it's no excuse."

"No excuses or apologies necessary for me." That was the truth.

"I know."

Nathan studied Merry more closely. She looked exactly the way she described herself, like someone who had a lot going on. It wasn't that she looked unwell, actually quite the opposite—her skin glowed, her eyes were bright—it was more how she'd pulled herself together, there was something…off…like she'd tried too hard to look good and missed the mark. None of this, however, was surprising. After the monumental changes she'd been through this past year, and now this mess with Vanstone, he was surprised she was standing upright.

"Merry," he began carefully, "I want you to know I'm here to help you in whatever way I can."

She let out a nervous laugh and added, "You may be sorry you said that."

"Never."

"Nathan, I've made a decision."

He pulled in a deep breath, knowing that whatever came next was probably going to change things forever.

And then she said the last thing he expected.

"I'm leaving Vancouver."

"What?" he responded, a choking sound escaping his throat. *She's making a run for it.* "You're leaving? Why? Where are you going?" As a detective he knew better than to ask several open-ended questions in a row, but she'd taken him by surprise. He was expecting her to spill the beans about what happened the night of Elliott Vanstone's death. He was certain she'd set up this meeting to come clean about her part in it and ask for his help in figuring out what to do next.

"I know it's not what you were expecting to hear."

Was she reading his mind? "No, it's not."

"I know I promised you I would come back to work, but, well, I've decided to go home." She let out another mirthless laugh. "Back to where I came from."

Nathan's eyes, the colour of a cool lake, grew wary with concern.

"Merry, you don't have to go. I can help you. I will help you."

She'd never know how much he already had. His visit with Julia Turner had ended in a way he could have never expected. His only hope was that he did the right thing. Was hiding out on the prairies Merry's version of doing the right thing?

Merry gave him a wry look halfway between a smile and nervous frown. "There you go again, making an offer you might regret." She stopped to lick her lips. A look flitted across her face as if the taste of lipstick surprised her. "Actually, I do need your help."

"Okay, shoot."

"I can't stay in Vancouver."

He gave her a hard look. This was becoming one of those frustrating conversations where he was left wondering if she knew that he knew but wanted to pretend she didn't and wanted him to do the same. Or, did she think he knew nothing about Vanstone's murder and wanted to skip town before he and the rest of the world found out?

"Why not?" he asked, watching her face carefully for any telltale sign that she was about to lie to him.

"I've given this a lot of thought. I can't do this anymore. Not in Vancouver."

More double talk? "Can't do what?"

"Everything. Live here. Work here. Pay my bills."

"Like I told you before, whenever you're ready to come back to work, your job is waiting for you."

"I know. I can't tell you how much that's meant to me. But it's not just that."

Here it comes.

"This has been a long, hard road for me. It's taken a toll in every way imaginable, not the least of which is financially."

"If this is about money," he knew it wasn't, "I'll advance you whatever you need until you…work things out." As Nathan said the words, he wondered what he was really suggesting. If Merry never admitted what happened with Vanstone, if the police failed in their jobs and the truth never came out, was he willing, given what he knew, to bankroll her living with a lie? A huge one.

This was happening so fast his head was spinning. On the one hand, Merry was his trusted colleague and long-time friend who, in her own screwed up way, was asking him to support her, no questions asked. On the other hand, this was a person who was very likely responsible for the death of another human being. How could he possibly ignore that? How could she ask him to?

Thanks to its founder, Sharpe Investigations enjoyed a sterling reputation. Nathan Sharpe looked like the kind of guy you'd trust with your problems. He was tall, robust, handsome in a Liam Neeson way, not a Liam Hemsworth way, with thick dark hair turning grey in all the right places, perfectly befitting his sixty-one years. He relied on a well-earned status as a charming tough guy who got the job done for a fair price. People immediately liked him, unless they were on the wrong side of his investigation, in which case they feared him. Nathan Sharpe rarely failed in his professional pursuits. Admittedly, there were times when he'd had to skirt the edges of honesty and integrity to get the results he was after, but in the end, he could always hold his head high. What about now? Had he gone too far?

"Of course it's about money." Merry's smile was more of a mask than anything else. "But I refuse to take charity, from you or anyone else. Besides, you need all the money you can get to buy a replacement for that pug-ugly suit."

Nathan grinned. It *was* an ugly suit and only Merry would tell him so. He was about to return the volley but hesitated. A banter of light insults was nothing new between them, it was a staple of their former relationship. It worked because they both knew that whatever was said was cushioned by an abundance of respect and affection. Normally he would have disparaged her right back, but the fact of the matter was that Merry did not look great and saying so would only hurt her feelings. He wasn't sure she could take another blow. Instead, he asked, "Are you ready to come back to work?"

Merry sighed. "It's time for me to put on my big girl pants and face facts. I am ready to work, but I can't do it here. I can't afford this city anymore, Nathan. With all the expenses I've racked up the past couple of years, I've had to move three times, each time into someplace smaller and crappier than the place before, and now I can't even afford that. I've been sleeping on Julia's couch for the past six months. I can't do it anymore. I have to go somewhere where I can start over again. I have to go somewhere where it's cheaper to live. I have to go home." She leaned forward in her seat. "Nathan, I need a favour."

Nathan hesitated, but only for a fraction of a second. "Name it."

"You took a chance on me all those years ago when I didn't know what the hell I was doing. Your Help Wanted ad was the only one I'd seen in months that didn't require years of education or experience I didn't have."

Nathan grunted by way of a laugh. "You came in here with a one-page resume with nothing on it but spelling mistakes. But you had a whole lot of confidence and sheer guts. It was the guts I needed. It was the guts I hired. You've never proved my instincts wrong."

"Investigating is the only thing I know how to do. It's the only way I can think of to make money. I need to make money so I can come back here one day."

"You'll come back?"

"Of course I'm coming back." She said it like she believed it. Nathan wasn't so sure. "My life is here. I just can't afford to live it. I need to start over, earn my way back."

Nathan searched Merry's face without knowing what he was looking for. This was it. He was either with her or against her. The answer wasn't hard. He'd made the decision the night Julia Turner showed up at his door. "What do you need?"

"Your name."

"I don't get it. You want to get hitched?" he asked with a tinge of the familiar playful tone they'd often used with one another. It felt good. "Just so you know, I only take out the garbage when I feel like it, and weekends are reserved for drinking beer and watching sports, no antiquing or visiting museums."

"Misogynistic much?" she shot back in the same teasing tone. "I'll take a beer over a museum any day. But no, I don't want your last name. I want your business name. I want Sharpe Investigations."

"I still don't get it."

"I want to open a satellite office of Sharpe Investigations. In Livingsky."

"Livingsky? Saskatchewan? Your hometown? You want to open a P.I. office in the boonies?"

Merry rolled her eyes. "It's not like I'm moving to Antarctica. Saskatchewan is not the boonies. Livingsky is not some sleepy village with nothing but a butcher, a baker, and a candlestick maker. Livingsky has a population of over three hundred thousand people. Several investigation firms already operate there. Most focus on security work, but," she admitted, "there are a couple that offer personal investigative services."

He nodded, appreciating the research she'd done—probably most of it from Google—but he was doubtful. He decided to say nothing for the moment. A good detective always encouraged the other party to do all the talking.

"I can't afford to go into the market cold," Merry told him. "I need clients and I need them fast. Associating myself with a recognizable name and good reputation can do that for me. 'Merry Bell, P.I., with paint still drying on her shingle, isn't going to get a second look, but people will hire an experienced Sharpe Investigations agent. I don't have the time or money to come up with a professional-looking website or an advertising campaign, but I can pull together a web page, and if that web page is linked to the Sharpe Investigations website with all its bells and whistles and testimonials and whatnot, I can hit the ground running."

Nathan regarded Merry with a practiced eye. It was Merry who'd convinced him to invest in a website in the first place, a decision that had proven fruitful. Regardless of what was going on in his brain, his heart was telling him one thing: *Sharpe, if you're in for a penny, you're in for pound.* He may as well admit it, he was fully prepared to help Merry any way he could, for whatever reason. Lending his name, his firm's credibility, was a no brainer. He only hoped she wasn't overestimating the clientele-generating power of the Sharpe Investigations brand in an untested market. His answer was yes. Still, he waited. Was there something more she needed to tell him? According to her friend Julia, there was plenty.

"You know I do good work. You've always said so. I promise I won't do anything to harm the reputation of Sharpe. Who knows, maybe I'll add to it. And just think, once I open my doors, you can officially refer to the business as a national firm."

Nathan didn't think he'd be amending his business cards and logo to include the phrase "With offices in Vancouver and Livingsky" just yet.

"I promise not to ask for help on cases…unless I really need it."

Nathan sipped his coffee slowly to give himself time to form a response. It was obvious Merry had made up her mind. Without her giving him anything to either refute or support Julia's version of what happened the night of Elliott Vanstone's death, and with his hands tied on bringing it up himself, all he could do was rely on Merry's instinct on what was the right thing to do.

Nathan leaned forward, resting his forearms on his desk, and smiled. "You know you can always ask me for help, whether it's with a case, or anything else. Actually, I insist on it."

Merry's mouth opened. Then closed. Opened again. She stood up, Sat down. Stood up again. "You mean…is that a yes? You'll do it? I can open my office under the name Sharpe Investigations?"

Nathan pushed back and reached down for something. Keeping a bottle of hard liquor in the bottom drawer of his desk was a stereotype of an old-timey private eye that he enjoyed perpetuating. "This calls for a celebration. You still drink scotch?"

Merry fell into her seat, looking elated. "Only if the glass is dirty."

CHAPTER 2

"What have I done?"

It wasn't the first time Merry Bell had muttered those words since arriving in Livingsky. Gingerly she stepped onto the slippery sidewalk, bracing for the attack of the same arctic wind that had hounded her like an ice-breathing dragon on her way to the coffee shop. She sipped her beverage and winced. Once upon a time her coffee of choice was a grande, quad, nonfat, one-pump, no-whip mocha, possibly one of the most obnoxious drinks on the Starbucks menu. She didn't care. She loved it. But no more. Now she was reduced to making do with a small, original blend, dark roast from Tim Hortons. The Timmies drink cost a buck fifty-nine. Starbucks required the sale of a kidney.

Trudging down the street, collar high, toque low, begging the steaming cup of coffee to infuse her gloved hands with warmth, Merry mulled over her time in Livingsky. So far, things had not gone exactly as planned.

In Merry's estimation, if she wanted people to take her seriously as an investigator, it was paramount that the Livingsky offices of Sharpe Investigations be located in the city's downtown business district, alongside the lawyers, doctors, accountants and potash mine executives. Online research of real estate offerings had revealed lease rates a fraction of those in Vancouver, still, downtown office space did not come nearly as cheap as she'd hoped. In fact, prices were so high she didn't know how she was going to afford both an office and a place to live. There was only one solution.

Before leaving Vancouver, Merry struck a deal on a new office space. The price and location were acceptable. It came furnished with the basics, compliments of its recently deceased former occupant and, most importantly, it was two rooms. Until she got on her feet with a paying client or two, she planned to live in one room and work out of the other. She neglected to mention this brilliant scheme to the landlord when finalizing the paperwork. What he didn't know, she reasoned, couldn't hurt him.

In truth, the location wasn't exactly prime. Finding a place in her meagre price range meant having to give up her dream of setting up shop in one of the glitzy high rises lining the riverbank and boasting enviable views. Instead, she settled on a turn-of-the-twentieth century house repurposed at the turn-of-the-twenty-first century for business and commercial use. 222 Craving Lane was in an area the landlord cleverly referred to as "downtown adjacent". Instead of a river view, the online ad described the view as "urban chic", which turned out to mean: back alley.

But the location wasn't Merry's biggest disappointment. When she arrived at her new office (and home), direct from the Livingsky airport, she was surprised to find that, although there were two rooms, as promised, they fell rather short of expectation. One of the rooms was little more than an antechamber, a miniscule waiting area where, at most, two clients could squeeze together on a cracked leather loveseat, as long as maintaining personal distance wasn't an issue. A coat rack, shoe mat, and a surprisingly stylish floor lamp filled any remaining space. There was room for nothing more, other than a bit of air, certainly no living space for Merry and all her worldly possessions. The second room, although adequate for an office, wasn't much bigger. Merry's heart sank. How on earth could she both work and sleep here?

Merry's new landlord was an accountant named Alvin Smallinsky. Aside from a shared tenant kitchen and public restrooms, his office took up the balance of the main floor of the building. The second and third floors were divided into smaller offices rented to a variety of tenants. After showing Merry her new space, reviewing the rules of the building (parking, garbage services, etc.) and handing over the keys, Smallinsky had gone back to work, unaware of her distress over the inadequate illegal squatting potential.

At 5:00 p.m. sharp, the front doors of 222 Craving Lane were locked for the night. After five, anyone wishing to enter would have to utilize a security panel at the front door to request access which could only be granted by a tenant still inside the building. Under the guise of checking out her new environment, Merry wandered the hallways as she watched her fellow tenants lock their office doors and depart the building. By 5:57 p.m. she was the only one left. Time to make her move.

Piece by piece Merry transferred all her personal belongings from her rental car into 222 Craving Lane. This consisted of three suitcases, an overnight bag, and two large plastic totes. If she'd known how heavy the totes would be, she might have thought twice about leasing an office on the third floor of a building without an elevator.

Once everything was inside, Merry fell into the chair behind her new desk to catch her breath and take stock of the situation. It seemed hopeless. As paltry as her mound of possessions were, there was simply not enough room to put everything, never mind conceal it so no one would know she was living where she worked. Rummaging in her overnight bag, she found the gas station sandwich, Coffee Crisp chocolate bar and, most importantly, the bottle of red wine (a gift from Nathan) she'd been saving for this occasion. She'd imagined this moment in great detail. She'd open the wine whilst enjoying an expansive view that somehow encompassed both the stately South Saskatchewan River and glittering lights of downtown Livingsky. She wore a plaid power suit, her nails were painted blood red, and diamonds glinted at her ear lobes. On a mahogany desk would be an impossibly huge bouquet of fresh flowers from, well, someone special. She felt triumphant, confident, happy.

Merry felt none of those things.

Instead of the river and bright lights, her office window looked out on a rusty fire escape precariously pinned against a graffiti-splattered wall across the back alley. Instead of couture she was wearing stained jeans, her nail polish was chipped, and diamonds and flowers were nothing but words. She cracked the wine anyway. Thank goodness for screw tops and plastic cups.

Half a sandwich, an entire Coffee Crisp, and two plastic cups of wine later, things were looking up. She'd pulled a set of filing cabinets away from the wall, creating a space wide enough to hide the suitcases and totes. Since she didn't have any clients yet, she didn't have files, which left room in the cabinets for clothing, toiletries, a blanket and pillow and anything else she'd need easy access to. Everything else remained packed.

Prior to leaving Vancouver, Merry had arranged for Wi-Fi and let out a quiet "woo hoo" when she confirmed access to the internet. Sitting in front of her laptop at the definitely-not-mahogany desk and raising her third glass of wine to toast the occasion, Merry tapped the button that would cause the Livingsky Sharpe Investigations webpage to officially go live along with its link to the main Sharpe Investigations website.

With pride, Merry stared at the page she'd painstakingly created (with the help of a YouTube tutorial). There it was, staring back at her with sharp images and rich colours: her future.

The page was simple but professional. It announced to the world that Sharpe Investigations, established in 1988 in Vancouver, British Columbia had now expanded its national presence with an office in Livingsky, Saskatchewan. Livingsky Sharpe Investigations or LSI (an acronym Merry was trying out and liked because it might remind people of the multiple TV shows with CSI in the title) offered a wide range of investigative services. Local lead investigator, Merry Bell, was experienced in: missing persons/property cases, child custody matters, premarital checks, caregiver surveillance, spousal surveillance, biological parent & relative search, stalker reveals, bullying and other harassment issues, child abduction, property vandalism, mystery shopper activities, employee background checks. Merry knew it was important to cite as many examples as possible of what she could do. Sometimes people didn't know what they needed until they saw it in black and white.

She felt triumphant, confident, happy.

Finally.

It might have been the wine.

She waited.

And waited some more.

Days passed. She obsessively checked her phone for messages and to confirm the ringer was turned on. She used a computer at a public library to search the internet for her website, just in case she'd done something wrong and it hadn't gone live after all. But there it was. *Livingsky Sharpe Investigations. Lead Investigator Merry Bell.* She accessed the website's analytics to check the number of hits. Three.

"What have I done?" she uttered.

By day ten the situation hadn't improved. No calls. No emails. No texts. No messages on any social media platform. Even more pressing and just as depressing, the time had come for Merry to stop bunking in her office. Although no one had directly confronted her, loaded silences and sideways glances convinced Merry that some of her neighbours were beginning to get suspicious. Why was she always the first one in the building in the morning and the last to leave at night? Were the kitchen and washroom being utilized for something more than regular daily use by clients and building tenants?

Merry sprung for a one-month membership at a nearby YWCA so she could use the shower, but the 222 Craving Lane facilities were too handy to pass up for evening ablutions. Unfortunately, someone had found a tube of toothpaste she'd inadvertently left behind and displayed it in the coffee room the next day with a note that read: "Found in bathroom???" Three question marks. *A bit passive aggressive*, Merry thought as she swiped back the toothpaste when no one was looking.

Every day she scoured the rental listings. Cost of living in Livingsky was considerably lower than in Vancouver, but with no clients, no money coming in, and her savings disappearing at an alarming rate, affordable options weren't plentiful. With search parameters restricted by how little she had to spend, Merry's hopes plummeted.

Finally, while scouring the "Apartments For Rent" section of the local newspaper (who knew those still existed?), Merry spotted a new ad that held promise. Sort of. It advertised a one bedroom with bathroom, but no price listed. Merry googled the address. On the pro side, it was not an entirely unreasonable distance from the office, if she wore flats. On the con side, it was in a neighbourhood she knew to be less than desirable. Hopefully the price would reflect that. She called the contact number, set up an appointment, and made a beeline for Tim Hortons. She hoped an infusion of cheap caffeine would dull her desperation, sharpen her negotiation skills, and help her land a place to call home.

CHAPTER 3

22nd Avenue was one of Livingsky's busiest thoroughfares, beginning in the heart of downtown and shooting straight west for anyone wishing to ride away into the sunset. Merry located the faux-brick apartment complex facing the bustling street, and decided it looked like a squatting buddha. With heavy traffic passing by day and night she knew the building would be noisy, but she didn't mind that so much. She was a big city girl after all. By comparison, the structures on either side of the buddha, also multi-unit rentals, were shabby and looked like good places for murder. So that was a win. A path had been shoveled through accumulated drifts of snow clearing a way to the front entrance, which, to Merry's mind, was the sign of a landlord who gave a shit. Another win. So far, so good.

Having made quick work of her coffee on the long, wind-whipped walk from Tim Hortons, she wished she'd sprung for a larger size. Staring at the building from the sidewalk, she adjusted the collar of her pitifully inadequate coat and did her best to stay hopeful. She needed a place to live. If this one didn't work out, she might find herself in line at the local women's shelter.

The front door to the building swung open and a tall, wiry man beckoned her inside. Kindly or creepy? She wasn't quite sure which. "It's only temporary," she muttered to herself as she made her way up the walk. She stopped at the door and studied the man's face. Kindly *and* creepy? She stepped inside.

Gerald Drover introduced himself as the building's owner. He was not what Merry expected. He was very tall, six-and-a-half feet at least, and slender as a streetlight. He wore a Heavy Metal band t-shirt, skinny jeans that still required the assistance of a belt to stay up, one of those wallets with a chain that hooked onto a belt loop, and crusty cowboy boots that'd seen one too many rodeos. Merry guessed him to be about her age, late twenties, or maybe a bit older.

Even more bizarre than the man's wardrobe was everything above the neck. Atop Drover's perfectly oblong head was a full-on mullet, ginger red. His cheeks were puffy, his chin pronounced, his ears and nose were super-sized. But it was his eyes and lips that Merry couldn't stop staring at. They were…stunning. The eyes were like nothing she'd seen before, the colour of an aquamarine sea sprinkled with specks of sand, rimmed with lashes so thick Merry wondered if he was some kind of mutant with double sets on each lid. Like many of his other features, Drover's lips were far too big for his long narrow face, but they were so pleasantly plump and cherry-pink they looked like a chewy chunk of double bubble. Maybe he wouldn't be so bad.

Then he opened his mouth.

"Well, aren't you a tall piece of hard candy?" Drover proclaimed, showing off a generous gap between two large front teeth and an unapologetically lascivious smile.

Merry moved as far back from the man as the confines of the small foyer would allow. *What a loser*, she thought to herself. Too bad. She liked tall guys. Being tall herself, they made her feel more feminine, especially when she wore high heels. She loved wearing high heels.

"You're here to look at the apartment, right? You gotta move fast on this one, babe. Probably be rented by end of day. You want it, you have to tell me now, righto?"

"Righto." Seemed like the best response.

"Come with me, sweetheart."

Ugh.

Merry followed the lanky landlord down a short flight of stairs. She was disappointed to learn the apartment was in the basement. On the bright side, basement suites were typically less expensive than main floor units. Three matching doors lined each side of the hallway. Drover stopped at the last one on the right. He knocked. *Does he think someone might still be in there?* Selecting a key from about a million others on a ring hanging off his belt, Drover opened the door. Stepping aside, he gestured with a grand flourish, encouraging Merry to enter. For a second, she hesitated. Then, deciding she could easily take this skinny guy in a fight if she had to, she moved into the apartment.

The first room was modest in size, a living room-dining room-kitchen combo. For a basement suite the windows were surprisingly large, letting in plenty of natural light. He showed her a bathroom, simple but clean, and one bedroom, also clean but barely big enough for a double bed and small chest of drawers. The furnishings were garage sale quality, the appliances worked (or so Drover claimed) and, aside from a few suspicious carpet stains and gouges in the wall, the place was not entirely horrible. This could work. Temporarily.

"The last tenants moved out on the weekend. My cleaners were in here yesterday. Looks super good, right? All spit and polished for you. Is it just you, or who all's moving in here?"

She stepped into the centre of the living room and stared out the windows. Not unlike her new office, the view offered nothing but the building next door. Even so, this was definitely a lemon she could make into lemonade. She could add a few colourful cushions, strategically-placed area rugs would cover the carpet stains, pretty drapery and prints on the walls would hide the gouges, candlelight would take care of the rest of the room's shortcomings. Sure it was small, but still way bigger than the last place she'd rented in Vancouver before moving in with Julia. She'd noticed a bus stop less than a block away, for the days when walking to the office wasn't an option. This was not the best part of town; it was loud, transient, probably had a high crime rate, but she had to start somewhere. This could work, it really could. "It's just me," she turned to answer the man. "How much is it?"

"Six hundred a month, first and last up front. That's twelve hundred poppers. You got a steady job, or what?"

Merry's mouth fell open. Six hundred a month. Twelve up front. The last time she checked (which was every day), she had less than seven hundred dollars left in her bank account, with no immediate prospects for a top up. Her heart fell. There was no way she could afford this place. Or any place for that matter. It was time to face facts. She'd screwed this up. Not just this. Everything. She'd screwed up life. How did this happen? How had she failed so spectacularly? How had she allowed herself to get to this point?

People talk about taking a risk, following your passion, doing what makes you feel good, being true to yourself, being who you are. That was bullshit! The only people who said those things were the ones who did some or all of those things and, by some crazy stroke of luck, succeeded. But what about everyone else? The ones who took a chance, made a big change, invested in themselves—the ones who sacrificed everything—and then ended up on 22nd Avenue realizing they couldn't afford the basics of life? What becomes of them? What would become of Merry Bell?

Drover eyed up Merry with a look that said he suspected the panicked eyes and quivering lip were a ploy designed to sway him on price. "Something wrong, Hot Lips? You ask around," he suggested, "six is cheap for a place this nice. A one bedroom, you kidding? Other one bedrooms you see around here go for seven, eight hundred, and way more than that in other parts of town."

Merry knew that by "other" he meant better. Still, she was crestfallen. The place was perfect. Well, not perfect, not even close, but good enough. Now she knew. Even good enough was out of her price range. Pitiful. Now what? She'd been kidding about needing a women's shelter; suddenly it wasn't so funny. Was this how it happened? One day you're opening a new business in a new city with a kickass website and high hopes, and the next you're lining up for free food and a cot to sleep on?

She should have stayed put in Vancouver. She should have taken Nathan up on his offer to help. In the five years she'd been an active investigator for Sharpe Investigations, Nathan Sharpe had been much more than a boss to Merry. He was teacher, mentor, father-figure. He'd never have allowed her to end up in Vancouver's eastside as a homeless person. He'd have saved her. That thought made her even more upset. Was she so pathetic she needed to be saved?

Turned out, going home is not as simple as it sounds. Her gut had warned her. After she'd made the final decision, every time she said the words *going home* out loud she'd felt something hard and prickly, like a laundry ball, rolling around inside her stomach. Yet, no matter how she looked at it, going home was the only move that made sense. She'd loved living in Vancouver. The energy, the kinetic motion, the promise of opportunity around every corner, all set against a backdrop of sea and majestic mountain peaks. But new beginnings come at a hefty cost—financially, spiritually, emotionally—and for Merry, it was time to pay the piper.

Ultimately, every decision Merry had made led her here. She regretted none of them.

Drover looked confused. Merry knew her less than enthusiastic response to his sales pitch was probably both disappointing and perplexing.

"You okay, sweetheart?" he asked. "You look a little pale."

"I just moved here. I…this is the first place I've looked at. I'm just…surprised."

"What's up? Too luxurious?"

One corner of her mouth ticked upwards.

"No? Too expensive?"

She nodded. Now that she knew she couldn't have it, the basement suite looked even better. She longingly ran a hand along the cool, cracked laminate of the kitchen counter as if it were precious marble; the stains were less noticeable, the questionable odour less bothersome.

"You know it's a deal, right?"

She shrugged.

Drover grunted and gave his wad of gum a good chewing while he thought a bit. Then: "How much you got to spend?"

Merry was jerked out of her wah-wah-poor-me stupor by the unexpected question.

"What did you say?" *Snap out of this self-indulgent crap*, she ordered herself. Couldn't she choose a better time for an existential crisis than right now, right here, in front of this guy? Sure, things didn't look good, but she didn't need saving, not by Nathan Sharpe or anyone else. If she was going to fall apart, fine, but she should do it on her own terms and preferably when it was just her and a bottle of wine, not in front of this red-headed flamingo.

"How much you got to spend on a place?" he repeated.

What could she say? There was no money. Not now, and if she didn't get a client soon, not in the long run either. But it wasn't as if she'd come here today thinking someone was going to rent her an apartment for free. Leaving a little for food and incidentals, she figured she had three hundred dollars to spend. So that's what she offered.

He laughed, sort of a heehaw, showing off those crazy teeth and too much gum (both kinds). "That's gonna get you a nice lunch, not an apartment. At least not a prime-o piece of real estate like this beaut."

Merry's shoulders slumped and a lump blossomed in her throat. She should have known better. She couldn't blame Gerald Drover. She wanted to. She really did. He looked like the sort of guy it would feel really good to blame stuff on. But this wasn't his fault...or was it?...no, no it wasn't. It was hers for making bad decisions. She'd have to figure something else out.

"Hey! Hot Lips!"

The jarring words crashed her pity party.

Hot Lips. Why did he keep calling her that? Maybe what the mirror had hinted at that morning was more accurate than she'd allowed herself to believe. Her lipstick was too bright. But it was the only one she had. Her eyeshadow was uneven. Who had the patience to start again? Her hair looked too puffy. *But so what*, she thought to herself, feeling her engine revving up. Maybe the Tim Hortons was finally kicking in. Her makeup and hair, today or any day, was nobody's bloody business. Her choices were her choices. Her mistakes were her mistakes. Her decision not to fix them was her decision too. Nobody need comment on any of it one way or another. She turned on Drover with a glint of fire in her eye.

"My name is Merry. Enough of the Hot Lips, babe, or any other name you think of to call me. They are all unacceptable."

Drover backed up, palms up. "Okay, okay, don't get your innards in a knot. I just thought you were falling asleep over there or something." An extra toothy grin sent his oversized ears reaching for the mullet top.

"Oh. Sorry." Maybe she'd gone too far. He was right. She had been in another world. "I was thinking about something else."

His eyes narrowed as he studied the woman. "You alright or what?"

"Sure."

Drover's mouth scrunched into a fleshy knot. He shrugged. "You said you got three hundred to spend, that right?"

She looked up. Those damn eyes. Drover was ridiculous looking, but those blazing blues got her every time, like laser beams intent on pulling her closer. "Yes."

"You sure? In cash? You can show it to me? Cuz I'd hate to have to punt you."

Merry was stunned. What did he just say? What was happening? "You mean I can have this place for three hundred? Really?"

Drover responded with his donkey laugh. "Of course not."

Merry's face darkened. *Asshole*! What was this guy playing at?

"I didn't mean this place," he clarified. "If you're interested, I can show you what I do got for three. To be paid in cash," he stressed. "You okay with that?"

Merry sucked in her cheeks and said, "Let's go."

CHAPTER 4

Gerald Drover's vehicle was as peculiar as the man himself. The 1978 Chrysler Cordoba two-door coupe was the shade of out-of-date chocolate. It assertively took up the same amount of space as any two modern-day cars, and the engine roared like a biplane about to make an unexpected nosedive.

"This thing is huge!"

Merry had never been in a car like this before. She liked that the front seat was wide enough to allow a comfortable distance between herself and this cuckoo bird of a man. The only reason she'd accepted the ride to the second apartment was because she'd arrived for their appointment on foot and if there was any way of avoiding another long walk in high heel boots battling Jack Frost's bad breath, she was going to take it.

"You are mistaken, Hot L...Merry," he responded, confidently maneuvering the beast toward their destination. "She is not *huge*. If anything, Judi Dench is considered a luxury-sized automobile. She..."

"Wait. You named your car Judi Dench?"

"Uh, yeah," he said as if it were the most natural thing in the world.

"Why?"

"She may be a little older than some of her colleagues on the street, but Judi is extra special."

"Oooookay."

"This particular model was only available between '75 and '83.

It was specially produced by Chrysler to be *smaller* than full-size. Hugely exclusive. She's a real dame. Just like Judi."

"So you're gay?"

"Not the last time I checked."

Merry thought about that for a second. "Did you say they made this car to be smaller than full-size? You mean there were cars bigger than this back then?"

"Of course."

"How did they get them down normal-sized streets?"

Drover elected to ignore the question. Instead, he went with: "Judi's got a 400 cubic inch engine, 3-speed A727 automatic transmission, she's 215.3 inches long, 77.1 inches wide."

Merry rolled her eyes. Why do guys always assume people want to hear about their precious little—or in this case, not so little—car? They go on and on, in excruciating detail like what they're saying is the most important thing in the world. It was time to see how this guy liked the same in return.

Lifting one booted foot, angled just right so Drover could see its red sole, Merry grudgingly admitted that only in a car the size of Judi Dench was there enough room to pull off the feat without being a gymnast.

"These are Christian Louboutins." One of Merry's most prized possessions, a wildly expensive parting gift from the person she used to be to the person she was always meant to be. "Do you know how Louboutins got the idea for painting the soles of his shoes red?" Merry was quite certain there was no need to await an answer. "From his assistant. One day he saw her wearing this super bright red fingernail polish. He loved how flirty the colour was. He thought every woman who bought his shoes should have the opportunity to feel flirty if they wanted to, so he painted the soles the same bright red."

She glanced at Drover, prepared to see his eyes glazed over. Instead, Gerald nodded thoughtfully, then inquired: "What if you don't like red? Could you paint them another colour, like blue or pink, to match what you're wearing?"

Merry found herself staring at Drover. *Damn*, she realized, this emu actually had a stupid, completely unworkable, but interesting idea.

"For sure four hundred's all you got to spend?" Drover asked, changing the subject as he directed the spaceship on wheels down another street. "Not sure I can let this place go at that price."

Reneging on his deal? No way. "Of course not," Merry replied sweetly, on to his bargaining game. "I said I had *three* hundred to spend. That's the price you'll let it go at."

He let out a that's-pushing-it whistle from between the gap of his two front teeth. "That ain't a lot of money, honey. You got a job, don't you? I asked you before and you never answered me. I'd hate to get you all moved in then have to kick you out because you got no money for next month's rent."

Merry's cheeks grew warm. Given the deafening silence in response to her website, she wasn't at all confident she'd be able to pay rent for more than a single month.

She gave Drover an assessing look.

Nope. This was not the guy you shared your sad sack story with then asked for mercy. She had to find another way to keep him on her side and reassure him (and herself?) that she wasn't going to be a deadbeat tenant. Three hundred dollars was not a lot of money for an apartment. If Drover was for real and actually had a place that was livable, she couldn't afford to let it slip away. There were times as an investigator when Merry had found it necessary to play fast and loose with the truth. Now was one of those times.

"I don't have a job, Mr. Drover, I have a career. I'm starting a new business. As I mentioned, I just moved here. My head office is expanding their operations into Saskatchewan and I'm in charge of opening the Livingsky location. Which is why I don't have a great deal of disposable income to spend on an apartment at the moment. As the face of the Livingsky venture, I need to make a good impression on clients, and that's expensive, not to mention the overhead."

"By overhead you mean things like Christian Louboutins?" He pronounced it Lah-buttons.

For a brief moment Merry thought Drover was making fun of her, but the look on his earnest face said otherwise. He was totally buying what she was selling.

"What kind of business are you in?" he asked.

"I'm a private investigator." This usually impressed people, or at least stoked their interest. Most people know P.I.s from TV and movies. Meeting one in real life is, generally, kind of cool. Merry could see the announcement had its desired effect on her potential new landlord.

"Wow," Drover whistled again, this time with admiration. "I've never met a real detective before. You said the company you work for is national? All across Canada? Would I have heard of it?"

Damn. Even though it was in her best interest to sell it as such, Sharpe Investigations wasn't exactly a name on the tip of everyone's tongue. That bitter truth had become patently obvious over the past ten days since she'd put up her webpage, the one no one seemed interested enough in to visit. She shrugged. "Only if you've ever needed one."

"Oh yeah, that makes sense. What's it called?"

"LSI. Livingsky Sharpe Investigations."

Drover nodded enthusiastically. "LSI. Yeah, I think I heard of it."

Merry smiled inwardly, guessing he was probably mixing it up with CSI.

"So, if you're in charge of this new office, does that mean you're the boss? Do you have a bunch of private eyes working for you? How many?"

She cringed. Suddenly this guy was Anderson Cooper? How far was she willing to spin this tale of a successful professional career? She wasn't exactly lying, but she wasn't telling the complete truth either. The most important thing was to convince this guy she could afford rent. "Most of our operatives work out of the Vancouver office." Sort of true. Nathan never called his employees operatives. "LSI is a little smaller, but yes, I am the lead local investigator."

"Righto. Cool beans."

"Uh, yes, it is the coolest of beans." *This guy is bizarre.*

Drover appeared to mull over the new information.

Merry thought it best to change the subject. "Exactly where is this apartment?" She'd been away from Livingsky for several years, but she knew the city pretty well, and Drover was turning down streets she'd never even heard of.

"Not too far. Just a few more blocks. Little deeper in the hood, y'know."

She didn't like the sound of that. "How deep?"

Most Livingsky residents, except those who actually lived there, referred to this part of town as Alphabet City. It was directly adjacent to downtown but incontrovertibly separated from it by the steel beams of a CP Rail line and a number of less visible but just as rigid cultural and economic barriers, leading many to also call it "the wrong side of the tracks".

Defenseless against a powerful self-fulfilling prophecy, Alphabet City, beginning with A Street hugging the rail line, and ending at a freeway that sliced through the city's west end at Z Street, was debatably the least desirable place to live and do business in Livingsky. Efforts to gentrify or resuscitate pockets of the neighbourhood, especially those closest to downtown, historically experienced questionable degrees of success. Over time the worst areas, those least visible pockets that many considered beyond help, descended into near slum conditions. Rundown tenement buildings and deteriorating houses were overcrowded, inhabited by immigrants from other countries, First Nations reserves and abandoned rural communities, people who'd fallen on hard times and couldn't find a way out. Merry remembered being warned as a teenager to stay away from Alphabet City, parts of which no outsider with a lick of sense would ever dare venture in after dark. Fortunately, it was daytime.

"Don't worry, it's fine," Drover assured her.

They rode in silence for several minutes. Merry knew something was up by the way Drover kept sneaking peeks in her direction. It bothered her. Mostly because she wanted him focused on the road. With a car this size she was amazed Judi Dench wasn't scraping the side of buildings or knocking over pedestrians.

"What?" she finally barked at him when the side glances kept coming.

"I think you're nice looking, that's all," he said matter-of-factly. "I know you're way outta my league, that's for sure. So the way I figure it, alls I can do is take a good look while I got a chance."

Merry blushed, angry and bashful and grateful all at the same time. How was that possible? To cover for her confusion, she pulled out her phone and flashed its face in his. "I've got 911 on speed dial. You do anything but look, I'm calling the cops. Then I'll roll down this window and scream." She clicked a photo. "And I'll send your picture to my best friend who knows exactly where I am and who I'm meeting with." That sounded like it covered all of the bases.

"Yeah, yeah, Sweet Thing, no need to get all pissy and stuff."

"What did I tell you about name-calling?" she shot back.

"Sweet Thing is a bad name? Since when?" he asked with astonishment. "I meant it as a compliment."

"Since this is the twenty-first century, and I don't know you and you sure as shit don't know me. Since this is a business meeting and not a hookup in a back-alley bar. Since calling any woman Sweet Thing is just, I dunno, corny as shit."

Although she would never admit it, despite her tirade, Merry believed him. Gerald Drover was weird enough to truly believe that calling a woman Sweet Thing was a nice thing to do.

"You'd hook up with me in a back-alley bar?" he responded with a mischievous wink and matching grin. "That what you saying?"

Merry stifled a laugh. This guy was too much. She knew she should be offended, maybe even smack him one, but something about the stupid smile that never left his stupid face convinced her not to. Not to mention those eyes and crazy thick eyelashes.

Gerald turned down a street Merry had never been on before. Then again, most of Alphabet City was unfamiliar to her. At first it appeared to be a benignly unremarkable suburban neighbourhood, lined with mature trees with weighty boughs stretching across the road like arms reaching out for one another. On closer inspection, the reality was something quite different. Whatever pavement was visible beneath layers of cruddy snow and ice was cracked and crumbling. Sidewalks, lined with bushes in dire need of a pruner's shear or executioner's axe, heaved and buckled in a winless battle against overgrown roots. On one side of the street were small, humble homes, on the other, no-frills businesses operating out of ramshackle, one-storey buildings. Not, Merry concluded, the most sought-after part of town to live in.

She was about to protest when Judi Dench unceremoniously scudded to a halt in front of a padlocked gate. A chain link fence mostly hidden behind a gnarled caragana hedge effectively camouflaged whatever lay on the other side. Prominent signs posted on the gate made three proclamations: Private Property. No Trespassing. Beware of Dog.

"What is this place?" Merry asked, inching—quickly—towards nervousness. "I thought you were taking me to see an apartment."

"Yeah, Doll, I am. This here place is extra special because it's in what you might call a gated community. Very secure. Someone like you would probably want that, right?"

Her head was too full of other questions and concerns to wonder what he meant by that. "Uh, nothing about this looks like a community, gated or otherwise. Where are the people?" Merry hadn't seen another car, human, or any sign of the "Beware of Dog" since they'd arrived on the disintegrating street.

"Jes' wait 'til you see it. You're gonna love it. Wait here." With that Drover hopped out of the car.

Merry watched through the windshield as the scarecrow searched his colossal keyring and, after a couple tries, found the one he was looking for. He unlocked the padlock, pulled aside the gate and jumped back into the car. With growing confusion (and not a little consternation) Merry registered the giddy look plastered across Drover's face, as if he could barely wait for her reaction to what she was about to see.

Carefully maneuvering the vehicle through the gate with barely a millimetre to spare on either side, Drover again stopped the car and hopped out to secure the gate behind them.

Having her first look at what lay inside the "gated community," Merry gawked in bewilderment. In the centre of the space was a single stump of a building, dwarfed by what looked like stack after stack of massive metal carcasses, like creatures from a *Transformers* movie (after the war).

"What is this place?" she asked again when Drover returned, puffing clouds of frozen breath and rubbing his hands together to coax warmth into them.

He shifted into drive to inch the car further into the lot. "It's a scrap metal yard. Business hasn't been too good lately, so we're, well, I guess you'd say we're taking a break. That's why I can offer you such a great deal. It's a steal, really. Get it? Steal. Steel. Scrap metal. Get it?"

She did but refused to confess it.

Braking a final time, Drover leapt from the car before Merry could press him for more details.

Taking a deep breath and questioning her sanity, Merry stepped out of the car and followed the giraffe-in-a-coat to the front door of the structure. Shivering in the wretched cold she watched, irritated, as he again fiddled with the ring, trying to find the correct key. Settling on the one he thought might fit, he inserted it, only to discover the door wasn't locked after all. His attempt to hide the unsettling fact was met with eyerolls.

With exaggerated fanfare, Drover stepped aside, inviting Merry to behold the interior. She stepped inside.

The space was surprisingly large. The first thing she noticed was that there were only two windows. A tiny one in the door they'd just come through and, to the right, an oversized picture window that took up most of that wall. Merry moved closer to inspect the view.

It was not the typical view one might expect from the window of an apartment, or what in this case turned out to be more of a…little house? Shack? No street view, no back alley, no trees, no neighbours or roadways or sidewalks of any kind. Instead, Merry found herself gawking at dozens more of the same misshapen cenotaphs she'd spotted on arrival, sky high piles of rusted metal and rutted steel, as if abandoned there by some kind of alien or arranged by a funky conceptual artist. Tearing her gaze away from the unusual sight, she slowly took in the rest of the room.

Situated below the large window was a desk and chair, and to the right a collection of time-battered filing cabinets. To the left was what Merry guessed Drover wanted her to believe was a kitchen. There was a microwave, coffee maker, a bar-sized fridge and a sink. No stove. Between the desk area and kitchen area was a round Formica table with three mismatched chairs. On the opposite side of the room was a low-slung leather couch, two more chairs, and a collection of TV trays arranged to face an ancient cabinet-model television set. Badly faded laminate flooring was in desperate need of cleaning. Torn wallpaper had given up any attempt at disguising the splotchy wall behind it. Overhead lighting consisted of four bare bulbs, only two of which worked.

Sucking in her cheeks and swallowing a few colourful curses, Merry gave Drover an incredulous look.

He grinned. "Sweet, right? And down there," he motioned towards a forebodingly dark hallway, "is the can and a stor...uh, the bedroom with room for a full-size cot. Only four hundred. Can you believe it?"

"Three hundred!" Merry spit out the words, then just as quickly wished she could take them back. The only thing more unbelievable than this jerk trying to pass off what was obviously an abandoned office building in the middle of a junkyard as a rental unit, was that she was negotiating the price. There was no way she could live here.

Apparently unfazed by withering looks and tone of voice, Drover said: "Okay, okay, three. In cash. When do you want to move in?"

"Uh, well, Mr. Drover..."

"No!"

Merry lurched backwards, surprised by the harsh sound. The man's silly putty face had turned rock hard.

"Don't call me that," he said, nostrils flaring. "Call me Gerald. Or Drover. Not Mr. Drover."

Jeez. "Okay, Gerald," she said, giving the man a wary look.

As quickly as he'd become upset (for no discernable reason), Drover reverted to his customary goofball countenance. As odd and wacky as he was, something about this guy had found a soft spot in Merry's heart. Instead of telling him exactly what she thought of his so-called sweet deal, she decided to let him down easy. "I have a few other places to look at. I'll let you know."

"Really?" He seemed hurt.

Couldn't this doofus just appreciate that she was lying to him to avoid hurting his feelings? Didn't matter. She needed to get out of here. Away from him. Away from this sketchy part of town. Away from this desperate hellhole pretending to be a home that too closely reflected the current state of her life. "Yes, really."

"You'll never find a place this size and this nice for cheaper."

"Maybe. Could you please unlock the gate? I can walk to my next appointment from here." A lie. But she didn't think she could manage another car ride with this guy, icy streets and high heel boots be damned.

"Really?"

Why is this guy looking like I just took away his ice cream cone? "Really."

The Louboutins looked great, but they were maiming her feet, punishing her for promenading in the snow as if they were nothing more than common Mukluks. She only got as far as 20th Avenue, Alphabet City's main commercial street (such as it was). It was just beginning to get dark and between her snow-averse boots and the biting cold, Merry could go no further. She checked her phone for the cost of an Uber and decided it was worth it. She wanted to get back to the office and begin a new search of rental listings for anything she might have missed. Anything would be better than a run-down shanty in the middle of a scrap metal yard owned by Big Bird's scuzzy cousin, Gerald Drover.

The Uber dropped her off in front of 222 Craving long past closing time. From the street she could see that most of the office windows were dark. Although there were no rules against coming in after hours, the fewer times her fellow tenants saw her coming and not going at night, the better. She'd picked up a submarine sandwich while waiting for the Uber and was looking forward to chowing down on her first full meal of the day while finding the perfect apartment she'd somehow overlooked. Merry Bell was an optimist, even when she had little reason to be.

Letting herself into the building she was met with darkness and quiet. With any luck, everyone else had gone home. Did they know how lucky they were to have a place to call home? Probably not.

She scaled the steps to the third floor. Except for an overhead Exit sign, the hallway was unlit. Another person might have been spooked. Not Merry Bell. She had nerves of steel. Without them she wouldn't have made it as an investigator, or through the past year of her life.

Following her phone's flashlight, she reached her office, unlocked the door and stepped into the waiting room. And then she froze.

The light had landed on something unusual, something unexpected.

She stood perfectly still and listened.

Was there someone inside her office?

She heard nothing. On silent tiptoes she moved to the door that connected the tiny waiting room with her office. Placing her ear against the door she listened. Still nothing. She slowly turned the knob and pushed.

Murky light from the back alley filled the room, casting every surface in a grey, hazy version of itself.

"Who's there?" she shouted, at the same time flipping the light switch.

The room was empty.

A quick inventory revealed nothing missing or disturbed. She returned to the waiting room and bent down to pick up the piece of paper the iPhone's gaze had found. She stared at it and gasped.

On a plain white sheet of paper was a single sentence: "I know it's you."

CHAPTER 5

It was a warning shot. One of her fellow 222 Craving Lane tenants had figured out she was living in her office. But which one?
And why had they sent a scrawled note slipped under her door instead of simply confronting her face to face? Were they giving her a
chance to remedy the infraction before revealing her disregard for
the rules to Smallinsky, the landlord? Or was this something more
diabolical, some kind of threat?

All Merry knew for sure was that she needed to make money fast
and use it to find a place to live as soon as possible. Which was why
when Gerald Drover emailed her the next morning to say he might
be interested in hiring her she couldn't turn him down. Working for
Sharpe Investigations in Vancouver she'd dealt with her fair share of
bizarre clients. Gerald Drover would just be another in a long list.
She could handle him easily enough, she just wasn't sure she wanted
him in her office. It wasn't that she was afraid to be alone with him,
she just didn't want the memory of her first official client meeting
as the proprietor of her own private investigation firm to be with
someone as icky and sticky as him.

Livingsky Plaza was the city's largest shopping mall and Merry
decided its busy food court was the perfect spot to meet with Drover. There'd be plenty of other people around should he decide to
make an inappropriate move on her. Not that she'd need anyone's
help to fend him off, it was just way more fun to put jerks in their
place in full view of the public.

Irrationally, Merry found herself taking extra care getting ready for their meeting. She fretted over the wrinkles in her outfit—bright red skirt (a little too short), pale pink blouse (a little too tight) and a bright orange belt (a little too everything)—and getting her makeup just right, which was always a frustrating ordeal. No matter how many magazine pictures or Instagram pictorials she tried to emulate, the end result was never quite right. What looked high fashion on screen ended up low rent when translated through the filter of Merry's meagre budget and skill level. It didn't help that her temporary home offered nothing but poor lighting and a wardrobe crammed into a filing cabinet drawer.

She arrived at the mall twenty minutes early. She wanted to select the best table in the food court from where she could spot Drover's arrival from any direction. Once settled, she spread out an impressive collection of paperwork, file folders, and pens to make it appear she was a hard-working professional with little time to dawdle. Just when everything was perfect, her hand swiped the lip of her paper coffee cup, knocking it over and sending its contents sluicing over her perfectly constructed paper landscape.

Dabbing at the mess with a few flimsy paper napkins, Merry was grateful when a food court employee arrived with cloths and began working the spill.

"I hope these aren't important," the woman commented as she dabbed the brown liquid from the assortment of papers.

"Not really," Merry said. They really weren't. Most of the papers were blank and the folders empty. "I'm so sorry about this. Thanks for helping me. I'm just waiting for someone. It's an important meeting."

The woman looked at her with a lazy smile. "Good luck," she said as she moved off with a pile of sodden napkins and rags.

Ten minutes late, Gerald Drover appeared at the far end of the food court. Merry was both surprised and irritated by the smile which bloomed unbidden on her face when she saw the man's silly face. She quickly did away with that and waved to get his attention. He saw her, delivered his trademark happy-gopher look and ambled over. She'd forgotten how tall and lean he was. She'd also forgotten the terrible cowboy boots, dangling wallet chain, and massive ring of keys that hung from his belt. She couldn't quite put her finger on it, but as he came closer she noticed something different about him. Had he slicked back the mullet?

"Mr. Dr…" Merry stopped there, remembering how the man did not like to be addressed as Mr. Drover. "Gerald, thank you for meeting me here." She straightened up still damp papers in an effort to look officious.

"Is this where you usually meet clients?" he responded, folding his lanky figure into the seat opposite. "I thought you'd have an office or something."

"I do," she said, prepared for the comment. "As I mentioned to you the last time we met, I just moved here. The office is still being renovated. I thought you'd prefer this to paint fumes and listening to nail guns."

He shrugged. "I like the smell of paint, but this is fine. Just happy to see your pretty face."

There he goes again. Does this guy never learn? Merry crinkled her nose and was about to give Drover another lesson in boundaries when he held up both paws like a squirrel facing a mountain lion. "Sorry, sorry, sorry! I shouldn't have said that. It's just what was on my mind. Sometimes I have a hard time keeping stuff inside, that's all."

She instantly forgave him. She couldn't help it. In some ways he was like a child who meant well but needed to be taught good manners. The sooner they moved on to business, the better. "You said on the phone you might need my help. Do you have an issue that requires an investigator?"

"Right to business, huh? Not even gonna let me buy you a coffee or nothing?"

"I've had my fill of coffee today, but thanks anyway. Would you like me to buy you a coffee?"

He grinned. "As in like a date?"

Steam blew out of her ears. "What can I help you with?"

To his credit, Drover shifted easily into a more serious manner as he began to recount his situation. "I own an apartment building, a rental property, that caught on fire last month. There's an ongoing investigation, but it seems to have stalled."

"Why is there an investigation? Was this a suspicious fire?"

"Yes. At least according to the police and fire department people."

"Arson? They think someone started the fire intentionally?"

"Yes."

"They think you started the fire?" she guessed.

His left eyebrow shifted upwards ever so slightly. "I may be a person of interest," he admitted, quickly adding, "but the investigation is still in progress. No cause has been officially identified. The problem is, they're trying so hard to pin this on me they're not bothering to look elsewhere. Unless they find proof that I did it—which they won't because I didn't—the investigation is going nowhere and they won't close the case or rule the fire accidental. That's bad for me and for my business."

Merry's brow wrinkled as she thought this through. "Why are the police so sure you did it?"

Drover shrugged. "Who knows? That's why I need you. I want you to prove I didn't do it. And if the fire was set intentionally, I want you to find out who's behind it."

Merry's hopes for a paying job plummeted. "Gerald, I'm not a trained fire investigator. I don't have the skills required to determine the cause of a fire. That's not what I do."

"I know that. But you can investigate everything else, right? The fire happened, that's a fact. It was either an accident or it wasn't. If it was an accident, no problem, the cops will figure that out eventually. If it wasn't, that means there's somebody out there who did something shady. And I'm telling you it wasn't me. Prove I'm telling the truth. And if someone else isn't, prove that too. You can investigate the hell outta that, can't ya?"

"Yes, I can," Merry agreed, feeling the familiar excitement of a brand-new case burbling up inside of her, like getting your hands on a mystery grab bag. You had no idea what you'd find inside but, good or bad, it was going to be fun finding out. "If there is something more to this fire than meets the eye, I will find out." Nathan Sharpe had drilled into her that confidence in front of clients is step one in successful case management.

Drover slid back in his chair, partly to stretch out his long legs which were beginning to cramp under the restrictive food court table, and partly to get a better look at Merry Bell.

"Our standard fee at LSI is $100 per hour, plus out of pocket incidentals." She'd adjusted her charge-out rate way down from what she was used to in Vancouver to something she felt would be more palatable in the Livingsky marketplace.

Without blinking an eye, Drover responded with, "I pay minimum wage."

Merry was sorry she'd spilled her coffee. If she hadn't, Drover would have found it in his lap. She was pretty sure minimum wage was something in the range of $12 an hour in Saskatchewan. So, they were a little far apart on price. Too far to expect reasonable negotiations.

Pasting a half-smile on her face, Merry began collecting her soggy paperwork and pens and stuffing them into her purse. "I see. Well, I wish you good luck finding a reputable agency at that price." Having done her research, she knew damn well he wouldn't.

"Hey, hey, hey wait a second," the words tumbled out of Drover's mouth like marbles from a mason jar. He laid a big hand on top of her smaller one. "Ooh," he marveled, "you are soft!"

She growled at him, and although his hand on hers felt disarmingly nice, she yanked it away.

"Sorry, sorry, sorry. Listen up, Merry Bell, you can't expect a businessman to pay the first price you give him, can you? This is a negotiation."

"No, it's not."

"And besides, we're friends."

"No, we're not."

"Sure we are. Besides, don't you think you should give your new landlord a break on your usual price? Don't I deserve a deal for finding you the perfect place to live?"

"Perfect? Ha!" She studied his face and wondered if maybe he really did think the junkyard house was a perfect place to live. And maybe Gerald Drover wasn't all wrong. After an abysmal evening scouring the most up-to-date Livingsky rental listings for something that just wasn't there (a decent place to live at a price she could afford) she'd come to the depressing conclusion that perhaps the Junk House (the name she'd come up with in reference to Drover's property) might be her only option (other than rolling out a sleeping bag in some dark, dank corner of 20th Avenue). Even so, she wasn't about to give in so easily. "That perfect place isn't fit for rats on crack."

Drover looked aghast. What Merry couldn't figure out was whether the man's astonishment was sincere. Did he truly not know how bad the Junk House was?

Is it so bad? Really? Couldn't I make do, at least until I find something better or scrape together enough money to move out? Merry shuddered at the thought. Then she remembered the mysterious note slipped under her door. *I know it's you.* She had to make a move, and this, she realized as an idea formed in her head, was it.

"Seventy-five an hour, applied against rent and damage deposit," Merry told Drover.

"Seventy."

"Deal." She'd have settled on sixty-five. Maybe sixty.

And just like that, LSI had its first client. And Merry had a home. She didn't allow herself a smile until the last of Drover's ginger mullet disappeared from the food court.

It wouldn't last long.

"You know that man?" The same woman who'd helped her earlier was standing nearby, listlessly clearing trays from a recently departed table of messy eaters. "That was your important meeting guy?"

"Yes, it was," Merry replied with unbridled pride. "Mr. Gerald Drover, local businessman. He just hired me."

"Gerald Drover hired you?"

"Yup."

The woman raised an eyebrow and rolled a shoulder. "Well, all I gotta say is, you better be careful, girl," the woman offered in a cautionary tone.

"Why do you say that?"

"Maybe you don't know it yet, but your new boss is one of the lowest forms of life in all of Livingsky.

CHAPTER 6

Apartment owned by controversial Livingsky landlord involved in fire

Six residents were displaced from a westside apartment building, owned by Livingsky property owner Gerald Drover, after a fire Monday morning, the third in five years at the same address.

At 4:30 a.m., firefighters responded to a blaze at the four storey building. The fire was contained to an occupied suite on the third floor and was under control within 20 minutes. Although the fire was confined to only one suite, fire marshal Amanda Gordon-Young deemed the building unfit for human habitation. The building was not insured, and damage is expected to cost between $50,000 and $100,000 to repair.

Drover, a longtime controversial figure in the city, has accumulated in excess of 100 convictions and tickets for violations under the Fire Prevention Act and the fire bylaw. His properties have also been cited by fire inspectors with 62 improvement orders under city bylaws and the Fire Prevention Act.

Drover Inc. properties have been ivolved in multiple fires, includinga blaze that killed a 78-year-old man and another in which two young girls perished. Drover spent a year in prison after he was convicted of obstruction of justice in connection with the latter fire. He denies there is a pattern of fires and maintains there was nothing wrong with the latest suite to go up in flames.

Drover controls a growing inner-city empire of at least 33 apart-

ment buildings and houses representing 200 units. Drover was not
available for comment late Monday afternoon.

Merry's mouth hung open as she read the Livingsky Tribune article,
Google's number one hit when she typed in Gerald Drover/Living-
sky/landlord. She was sitting in her office, dark except for whatever
sullen light the back-alley window allowed. She cringed, realizing
the food court employee was right. Her new client truly was "one of
the lowest forms of life in all of Livingsky."

She scrolled through the article one more time, noting that the
fire took place on the third floor. The fire he'd hired her to investigate occurred in a basement suite. All that told her was that this was
not his first fire and, quite possibly, not his last.

My client is a slum landlord. Terrific.

During her time working for Sharpe Investigations there'd been
plenty of times when Nathan Sharpe had accepted less than reputable clients and assigned them to Merry. In his mind, P.I.s operated in the same arena as lawyers who defended alleged criminals.
Everyone deserved help if they asked for it. But lawyers adhered
to a creed which presumed every client was innocent until proven
guilty. Was Merry supposed to presume Gerald Drover was innocent of the newspaper's claims and merrily continue to help him?

She knew about the kind of buildings described in the article,
predominantly within Alphabet City; rundown, dirty, often without heat or water, garbage strewn everywhere, overrun by rodents
or bugs or both. The 78-year-old old man, the girls who died, it
was almost a guarantee they were people of colour or recent immigrants, and undoubtedly poor. They had nowhere else to go. Were
they dead because Drover took advantage of them and the kind of
lives they were forced to live, seeing them as nothing more than
easy sources of income?

Merry knew what it meant to be discriminated against because
of who you were and the circumstances you were in. Did Drover

rent to her because she was poor? Or was it something else? The man had flirted with her. Outrageously. Maybe it was all part of his game. Maybe that was why he'd been staring at her so intently during their drive to the junkyard. Was he trying to figure her out, and the best angle to take advantage of her?

Merry flinched at the thought that Gerald Drover had so easily pegged her as a transgender woman, yet another category of people he undoubtedly considered easy to exploit. After all the sacrifices, the prices she'd paid, physically, financially, emotionally, after all the surgeries—genital, facial feminization, tracheal shaping, implant— to think she still couldn't pass in front of a complete stranger was devastating. If Drover saw it so easily, did everyone else see it too? Over the past year her mirror rarely complimented her, but had it been outright lying? *FUCK!* She repeated the word out loud for good measure.

According to the article, Drover was, at best, a renown slum landlord and, at worst, quite possibly criminally negligent in the deaths of multiple people. But he was a paying client, her first, and he was asking for Merry's help. It was because of Gerald Drover that she'd soon be saved from squatting in her office or the indignity of living on the street.

Like it or not, for the moment, she needed him more than he needed her.

Which made her feel all the more guilty.

Was it simply too convenient to brush aside the atrocities written about in a newspaper article in favour of her own comfort, her own needs? Shouldn't she stand up for the voiceless, powerless people he apparently routinely took advantage of, including, quite possibly, herself? By helping him was she silently condoning his behavior? Acting as an accomplice?

Without this job, Merry would be lost. Not only would she have nowhere to live, she'd have no work, no money coming in. It was becoming clear that a P.I. business did not bloom overnight just because of a fancy name, decent website, and plenty of gumption. It was going to take more than a downtown(ish) office and business cards to attract clients. She'd have to earn her stripes, pay her dues, and all those other unromantic cliches about having to work hard before reaping the benefits.

There was only one thing to do. She had to solve Drover's case as quickly as possible and, hopefully, move on to more reputable paying clients. As far as moving into the Junk House, conceivably another of Drover's highly combustible buildings, well, for now she had no choice.

Merry dove into research mode. Something she'd excelled at while working for Sharpe Investigations. She had more than a passing familiarity with all the databases, search engines, online catalogues, bibliographies, keywords and filters she might need to find what she was looking for. She even knew how to tiptoe around a few of the less than reputable, unregulated, unsecured, sometimes hazardous, deep dark places hidden within the guts of the interweb where most people feared to tread (and rightfully so).

Locating information about the recent fire that occurred at one of Drover's rental properties took very little of her skill. The apartment building was at the corner of A Street and Redberry Road which ran alongside the banks of the South Saskatchewan River as it spliced through Livingsky heading east. Official records showed the property having thirty-four rental units spread across six floors including a basement level. The fire was reported to have started in an unoccupied basement suite. A resident from a neighbouring suite happened to be coming home late at night and smelled smoke. He alerted the fire department who were successful in extinguishing the blaze before it spread. No one was hurt and the only damage beyond the originating suite was from smoke on the basement and first floors, both of which were temporarily evacuated.

A full month after the fire there was still no further information released to the public about the fire or its cause. Merry knew that city fire investigators typically investigate fires only when there is

significant property damage, injury or death, or if the fire is considered suspicious in nature. When the cause of the fire is determined
to be arson, the police are called in. The Livingsky Police Service,
LPS, currently categorized the event as being under "active investigation." Obviously, somebody somewhere believed the fire at Drover's property was no accident.

After a few telephone calls, Merry discovered the lead police
investigator for the Redberry fire was a Detective Sergeant named
Veronica Greyeyes. A couple more *I'll direct your call*s later she
reached the detective in person. In short order, Merry was invited to meet with Greyeyes at the Livingsky Police Station. Greyeyes'
amenability to an in-person meeting didn't come as a surprise to
Merry as she may have intimated that her purpose was to give information rather than collect it.

The newly constructed police station was an imposing six-storey
building sitting on the unofficial dividing line between downtown
Livingsky and Alphabet City. The structure appeared to be made
entirely of glass. As Merry scaled the Rocky-Balboa-worthy set
of steps leading to the main entrance, the building loomed over
her as if about to swallow her whole. Once inside, she was officious-
ly escorted upstairs and invited to wait in one of a string of identical meeting rooms. She didn't have long to wait before Greyeyes
appeared.

"Thank you for coming in."

The detective's tone was friendly but not too friendly. Police
business was serious business. The whole friendly neighbourhood
cop thing was fine for casual interactions, but when it came to formal interactions with citizens and investigations of wrongdoing,
Greyeyes believed rules of engagement for professional lines of
communication should be etched in cement right from the get-go.

Taking a seat in a purportedly ergonomic chair across the table from her visitor, Greyeyes noted with an imperceptible crin-

kle of her nose that the interview room still smelled of fresh paint. There were many things about the new precinct she did not like. Everything was too bright, too shiny, too new, right down to the garbage receptacles and pencil holders. Too much glass let in too much light and too many eyeballs. Even on the upper floors you could never be completely certain someone wasn't looking in. Just last week a drone was spotted flying around the building. The pilot was unaware of Bylaw No. 5729 which states that no person shall fly a remotely piloted aircraft (commonly known as a drone) in, on or above property owned by the City of Livingsky except as permitted by the City. He claimed only to be interested in getting photographs of the new building. A stiff fine was levied.

To Greyeyes' mind, the building's brilliant facade was the opposite of what actually happened inside. On a daily basis, police deal with every kind of dirt and grit and depravity humanity is capable of. Why disguise it behind a cloak of spit-polished glass? The blaring incongruency and insensitivity to reality hurt her eyes and her head.

The improvement Greyeyes did appreciate were the interview rooms. The ones in the old building were poorly lit, cramped, and always smelled bad. The room where she'd arranged to meet with Merry Bell was bland but palatable; with its clean, off-white walls and sturdy, scratch-and stain-resistant furniture.

As the two women settled in, Greyeyes noted that Bell was assessing her in much the same manner as she was assessing Bell. This was a red flag. *Keep sharp with this one*, Greyeyes advised herself, *she may not be what she appears to be.* Actually, she already knew Merry Bell was not what she'd pretended to be during their brief telephone conversation, a call that was as auspicious as it was unexpected. Beyond that, the woman sitting in her interview room was maybe thirty, certainly attractive but—Greyeyes hated the superficial judgment in her head—Merry Bell looked cheap. Of course, none of that mattered. The only thing that mattered, Greyeyes concluded as she mentally licked her lips in anticipation of the interview, was what happened next.

"I appreciate your taking the time to meet with me," Merry Bell said, shifting to find a comfortable position in the stiff chair.

"You said on the phone you have information about the fire that occurred at 101 Redberry Road," Greyeyes began, referring to notes she did not need.

"No," Merry politely corrected, "I said I wanted to discuss the fire that occurred at 101 Redberry Road."

Greyeyes tensed. Her suspicions were correct. Bell was going to surprise her. Interesting. "My mistake. Can you tell me a little about your relationship to that property?"

"I recently moved here from Vancouver. I was about to sign a rental agreement for one of the suites in the building when I learned about the fire. As you can imagine, that raised some concerns for me."

Greyeyes nodded. "I can imagine."

Neither woman spoke for a few seconds. Greyeyes thought she detected Bell hiding a smile. Perhaps she wasn't the only one in the room who knew the tactic: first one who talks loses.

Merry was the first to give in. "I called the fire department. They told me the incident was still under investigation by the police."

"I see."

"That's why I called you. Is it safe to move into that building?"

Greyeyes narrowed her eyes. The Redberry investigation was supposed to be open and shut. She'd have it off her desk in no time; that's what they told her. None of that proved to be true. Was Bell yet another unanticipated player in a game she didn't yet fully understand? How did the fire tie in to what she already knew about this woman? She could feel layers of complications multiplying by the second. She hated complications. "That sounds like a question you should be asking your landlord, Ms. Bell, not the police. Have you spoken to Mr. Drover about this?"

"It's just so awkward, isn't it? Asking someone if the building they own is a firetrap. What's he going to say: *Yes it is, you really shouldn't rent from me*?"

Good point, Greyeyes conceded, without actually saying so.

"Livingsky Police Service does not get involved in the personal rental decisions of its citizens. I'm sure you can understand that."

"But isn't the Livingsky Police Service involved in the safety of its citizens? If a building is unsafe, shouldn't we know about it?" Merry responded. Her eyes narrowed as she moved on to her next questions. "Isn't there anything you can tell me about the fire? What caused it? Do you suspect Mr. Drover? Or do you think someone else caused the fire? Because if so, I'm sure you can understand, I'd feel a lot better about moving in."

Greyeyes sat back, straightening her shoulders in a way she knew made her look imposing. She chewed the inside of her bottom lip, a habit, had she been aware of, she would have broken. "I understand your concerns." She did believe the concerns were real. She did not entirely believe the reason for them. There was something about this woman she didn't trust. Was the cheap floozy look actually a disguise meant to distract her? To what end?

"I really need a place to live," Merry added in a plaintive tone, as if sensing her ploy was verging on failure. "Especially with it being winter and all. It's a tough rental market out there and I was hoping this place would work out for me, but I don't want to be in danger. Can you help me?"

As the woman nattered on, Greyeyes formulated a plan. Bell was hiding something, she was sure of it. It was time to find out what it was. Veronica Greyeyes hadn't risen through the ranks for nothing. If asked, her colleagues and supervisors would describe her as smart, tenacious, and uncompromising when it came to matters of the law and dealing with lawbreakers. The question here was: is Merry Bell a lawbreaker? She decided the best route to finding that out was to give the suspect some rope. *Let's see if you hang yourself.*

"There have been indications that arson is a possibility." Greyeyes almost smiled when she saw the reaction to the revelation on Bell's face. "Possibility, I'm sure you know, Ms. Bell, is a far cry from certainty. The police deal in proof and evidence."

"Indications? Like what?"

Greyeyes chose her words carefully. "The door to the suite involved in the blaze may have been tampered with. The presence of an accelerant has not been ruled out." The two comments described half the scenes of the eighty fire investigations LPS did each year. She was revealing much less than Bell probably assumed. The most revealing thing would be what this woman did with the information.

"That doesn't sound too good," Merry said.

Greyeyes shrugged noncommittedly.

"Thank you for telling me this. I shouldn't take up any more of your time."

Greyeyes watched carefully as Merry Bell gathered her things, then made her move: "Perhaps you'll allow me the same courtesy?"

Merry stopped what she was doing and stared at the cop.

"Do you have a few more minutes to spare?" Greyeyes asked. Her tone was flat, but her eyes flashed in a way that screamed: Get ready. "I'd like to ask *you* a few questions."

"Oh," Merry replied slowly, drawing out the word. "I don't know if there's anything more I can add to what we've talked about."

"Probably not," Greyeyes agreed, preparing to pounce. "I was thinking we'd talk about something else."

"Oh? What's that?"

"Dr. Elliott Vanstone."

When Veronica Greyeyes had accepted the telephone call from Merry Bell, she could not believe her luck. She'd heard the name before, only days earlier, when a request from the Vancouver Police landed on her desk. They were crossing their t's and dotting their i's on a recent murder case, checking alibis and conducting interviews with any persons of interest, looking to exclude as many as possible in order to narrow their list of viable suspects. It was an often lengthy but necessary part of the process. One of their persons of interest, Merry Bell, had recently left Vancouver and been tracked to Livingsky. They wanted LPS to ascertain Bell's exact whereabouts and check her out. Half the job was solved by Merry's phone call.

"What was your relationship with Dr. Vanstone?" Greyeyes asked.

Merry crossed then uncrossed her legs. "He was my doctor."

Greyeyes stared at the other woman and wondered if she'd begun to notice the tables turning in a meeting she herself had initiated? "Is that all?"

"Yes," she responded quickly. "What's this about?"

"Are you aware that Dr. Vanstone was recently found murdered in his apartment?"

Merry's mouth fell open.

"I take it that's a no?"

"That's a no. When did this happen?"

Greyeyes made a show of pushing aside the file she'd been referencing during their discussion of the Redberry fire, beneath which was another, much thicker file. In truth, much of what typically filled a police file was now stored electronically and easily accessed from a computer, but Greyeyes still preferred going old school, the visual of a file often striking fear in the hearts of whoever sat across from her. She inspected a few papers then looked up and gave Merry the date of Vanstone's death. She then flipped a few pages, studied something, then said: "It appears you suddenly left Vancouver soon after he was killed."

"It wasn't sudden," Merry protested the sly wording. "I'd been planning to leave for some time."

"Why is that?"

"A lot of reasons. There've been…things are complicated. My life has been topsy turvy for a while now. Which is probably why I didn't hear about Dr. Vanstone's death. I've been so myopic about my own shit, I haven't paid much attention to the world around me."

Greyeyes nodded. It was a good answer. But she was far from satisfied. "Complicated how?"

Merry hesitated, as if considering whether or not to reply. "To make a long story short, I couldn't make a go of things in Vancouver. My bills were piling up and I couldn't survive there any longer. It was time to come home, time to start over."

Greyeyes abruptly shifted gears. "Where were you from 8:00 p.m. to midnight the evening of Thursday, January 12th?"

Merry sat upright upon realizing she was seriously being considered as a suspect in her doctor's murder. "I was at home, watching TV."

"Was anyone with you?"

"I was alone."

"Is there any way you can prove you were at home? Did you see a neighbour? Order takeout? Something like that?"

Merry's cheeks reddened. "I'm sorry, I can't think of anything. I don't know why I'd be a suspect. Are all of Dr. Vanstone's patients being treated like this?"

"Treated like what?"

"Like we're guilty of something."

"I'm sorry if that's what you think," Greyeyes responded, her face giving nothing away. "Are you feeling guilty about something?"

Merry bit her lip. She'd fallen right into that one. "Not at all. I'm just surprised by this, that's all. I didn't even know Dr. Vanstone was dead and suddenly I'm being asked for an alibi."

Greyeyes agreed the conversation had taken a turn her guest might find startling. That was just good police work. She'd zigged, and now it was time for a zag. "Do you know of any reason why someone might want to harm Dr. Vanstone?"

"I don't."

"I have one more question before I let you go," Greyeyes said with a benign smile. Merry Bell may have called this meeting, but she wanted the woman to know this interaction was fully under her control. "I assume you have a cell phone?"

"I do."

The detective pushed a blank piece of paper and a pen across the table.

Merry wrote down a number and pushed it back.

"Thank you for coming in."

For a second time Merry gathered her belongings and rose from the butt-numbing chair. With a nod of farewell, she headed for the exit.

Greyeyes stood. She waited until the woman opened the door and was about to leave before asking, "So tell me, Ms. Bell, will you be moving into 101 Redberry Road?"

Merry glanced back at the detective.

Greyeyes kept her face impassive, knowing this wasn't the last time she'd be seeing the woman.

"I don't think so."

Merry slipped the key into the lock of her office door. Even though it was the middle of the day, by force of habit she surveilled the hallway for prying eyes before opening it. The other two doors on the floor were closed. Good. Just the way she liked it. Her meeting with Detective Sergeant Greyeyes had been mentally exhausting and more than a little worrisome and the last thing she wanted was to run into another tenant or Alvin Smallinsky and have to participate in small talk. She was also distracted thinking about Gerald Drover. He told her he would call as soon as the Junk House (not his words) was ready for her to move into. Who knew what he'd have to do to make the place habitable, but she guessed exterminators would likely be involved.

Stepping inside the waiting room, she immediately saw it.

Another message slipped under her door. She leaned down to pick it up and smiled. This one she'd been waiting for.

Flipping the light switch she hurriedly opened the card and studied it's contents. There it was. She stared at the words and whispered: "Gotcha."

CHAPTER 7

Sitting at her desk, Merry signed into her computer and pulled up the online directory for businesses operating out of 222 Craving Lane. What she was looking for should be a simple matter of cross referencing the directory to the name written on the birthday card slipped under her door.

The plan was simple but ingenious. The original note slipped under Merry's door with its cryptic message "I know it's you" had been handwritten. Rookie mistake. Anything handwritten could easily be used against you. Which is why ransom notes are typically anything but. How each writer forms their letters is unique and Merry was confident she could spot telltale characteristics. The challenge was to find an innocent way of obtaining a handwriting specimen for comparison from every 222 Craving Lane tenant without raising suspicion. But how to do that? Who even used cursive anymore? The last time Merry handwrote something longer than her signature she was shocked by how her penmanship had degraded from lack of use. There were only a few remaining situations she could think of where humankind still used their dwindling handwriting skills, like signing a cheque or birthday card. Getting her neighbours to each write her a cheque would solve a great many of Merry's current problems, but going the birthday card route seemed the most likely to succeed.

Other than Smallinsky's accounting practice on the main floor, there were six other offices in the building, including Merry's, three per floor. The ruse was straightforward. Attached to a birthday card, Merry prepared a note explaining to the other tenants that it was their landlord-in-common's birthday. She requested each write a short birthday message and sign their names before passing it on to the next office. The last person was to return the card to Merry. The only wrinkle in the plan was if someone knew it wasn't actually Smallinsky's birthday. If that happened, Merry would play dumb and claim that as the newest renter in the building she'd gotten her facts wrong. The deception had the added benefit that if she was found out, her thoughtfulness could only serve to endear her to her landlord and maybe some of the other tenants. Deception didn't always work out that way.

The trick was a success. Merry was delighted to see that one of the signatures was noticeably similar to the handwriting on the original note slipped under her door. In big loopy letters, someone named Brenda wished Alvin a "Happy Birthday and many, many, many more". Very sweet.

Scanning the directory, Merry let out a triumphant whoop when she spotted an entry for "Designs by Brenda". The mouse had been snared. The same mouse who'd slipped the creepy note under her door. And probably the same mouse who'd discovered Merry's toothpaste in the public washroom then displayed it in the coffee room, probably in the hopes of catching a mouse of her own. But Merry Bell never played the role of mouse.

Sitting back in her chair, Merry considered her discovery. What was Designs by Brenda playing at? Was her intent merely to warn Merry, letting her know she'd been caught contravening building rules and would report it if the sleepovers didn't stop? Or was she simply being a nasty bitch?

By the business address Merry could see that Designs by Brenda was right next door. Damn it. There was nothing worse than conflict with a neighbour. Especially when you're the newbie in the neighbourhood. She swiveled her chair one-hundred-and-eighty degrees and gazed out the window. She stared at the colourful graffiti emblazoned across the wall of the building across the back alley.

It was a view she shared with Designs by Brenda. Merry considered hiring a graffiti artist of her own, asking them to scrawl something like: *Sorry. Moving soon.* Maybe add a happy face for good measure?

Not knowing any graffiti artists and intent on averting discord, Merry decided the preferable action was to address her neighbour in person. The plan was to artfully convey, without outwardly admitting any wrongdoing, that her living situation would soon be changing. And if that didn't work, she'd kill her with kindness. Unable to come up with a reason to put off to tomorrow what she could suffer through today, Merry hopped up from her desk and headed straight for the office next door.

Standing at the door with its bejeweled pink sign that read: Designs by Brenda, Merry hesitated. She was never sure of the correct protocol in situations like this. Do you knock? Do you walk in? She made a mental note to add a sign to her own office door inviting clients to "Please Come In". Seeing as it was after hours, she decided a knock was the best way to go.

She waited.

Maybe Designs by Brenda had gone home and left her lights on by mistake. Merry was about to turn away when the door opened, revealing a medium-height, fit-looking woman with shoulder-length blond hair impeccably styled to look messily casual. Her outfit, an upscale tracksuit with strategically positioned rhinestones matching the colour of the sign and hugging her body in the perfect places, clearly announced "I'm stylish but approachably casual too". Merry guessed they were roughly the same age, in the late-twenties, early-thirties range, but that's where any similarities ended. She saw women like this every day. Effortlessly beautiful, looking completely put together no matter whether they were coming out of spin class, picking their kids up from school, or stepping out of a board meeting. They probably weren't going to be friends. Which was going to make what had to happen next a bit more challenging.

Merry threw out her hand. "Hi, my name is Merry B…"

The woman smiled sweetly as she pointed to sparkly pink buds in her ears then held up a finger meant to say: "Hold on just a sec."

Merry nodded, slowly lowering her hand.

"Yes, that's right, Marcello. I need those Venetian tiles *immediatamente*," Designs by Brenda said into an invisible receiver, while giving Merry a subtle head-to-toe surveillance.

Merry smiled. As it happened, she was very familiar with the exact brand of phone buds her neighbour was using. She'd used the same ones (albeit not in sparkly pink) working at Sharpe. She knew that, when in use, a tiny green light was visible near the outside tip of the earpiece. Design by Brenda's light was red.

"Of course, I realize it's a big order, but I've got big clients, Marcello." Pause. "I knew you'd understand. I'll look forward to the shipment. *Ciao*, Marcello!" She tapped a bud to end the fake call.

Once again, Merry extended her hand. "Hi, I'm Merry Bell, your next door neighbour. Sorry to interrupt your phone call."

"Oh, don't you worry about that. I'm Brenda, Brenda Brown."

Merry tried not to grimace at Brenda Brown's chosen handshake style. Instead of her palm, Brenda inserted only the tips of her fingers into the shake, exerting the pressure of a sickly kitten.

"I'm dealing with an international supplier in Rome," Brenda explained.

Merry did some quick math. It was the middle of the night in Italy, an unlikely time for an Italian supplier to be doing business. *Poor girl*, Merry thought, *Brenda Brown needs to work on her fibbing skills*.

"He's extremely handsome, but a bit of a cad when it comes to business. Especially when dealing with women. I'm sure you know the type."

Merry answered with a noncommittal shrug.

"Come in, please," she chirped, stepping back to make room for Merry to pass by.

Brenda's office was twice the size of Merry's and had roughly one trillion times the number of things strewn about, albeit artfully, across tables and desks and chairs and shelves, as if having been deposited there by scores of discriminating clients making discriminating selections, but in a way that looked gorgeous. There were fabric swatches, tile samples, beading and ruffled things, pillows and feathers, and lots and lots of coloured jars in a seemingly infinite array of sizes and shapes, some filled with beads, some with sequins, others with glittery items not immediately identifiable. Diffusers filled the air with just the perfect nuance of citrus and mint, while hidden speakers emitted what Merry thought of as spa music: no words, no dramatic highs or lows, with the occasional babbling brook or songbird solo.

"Wow, this is…something," Merry commented.

Brenda beamed. "Sorry it's such a mess. I've had several clients in and out of here today and I haven't had a moment to clean up. I'm sure you've had those kind of days?" she asked, with a look in her eyes that was either expectant or hopeful, Merry couldn't decide which.

"Sure." Merry wondered why this woman started so many of her sentences with "I'm sure you…" Perhaps it was her way of trying to find common ground. *Good luck, sister.*

"Never mind all that. Welcome to the building, Merry! I'm sure you've already realized what a close-knit group we are here at 222 Craving Lane. Everyone is super friendly. More like family than people who happen to work in the same building."

Ugh, Merry thought, but kept it to herself. She made a point of throwing another appreciative gaze around the expertly staged room. "I can see Designs by Brenda is a thriving business," she commented, knowing it's what Brenda wanted to hear.

"Oh, I do okay," Brenda laughed coyly as if bashfully wanting to underplay her obvious success.

"It's so good to finally meet you," Merry said. "I would have come by sooner, but I just moved here from Vancouver and things have been hectic. I'm sure you can understand. New business. New people. Trying to find a place to live." She let that last sentence sink in for an extra second. "But, thank goodness, I finally found the perfect little house to rent." The words caught in her throat like a dry chicken bone. The junkyard? Perfect? Ha!

Brenda was suitably happy to hear the news. "Oh, how nice. What part of town will you be living in?"

Crap. If she told Brenda where the Junk House was, the woman would probably start a Merry Bell Go Fund Me page. Fortunately, Merry was a much better liar than Brenda. "Close to downtown." Fibs followed up with deflection always worked. "It looks like there are a lot of great restaurants and cute shops downtown. I'm sure you've been to all of them. I hope you'll give me some recommendations."

Brenda petted her ultra-trim tummy as if she regularly wolfed down dozens of burritos. "There are some excellent places, and some you'll want to avoid. I'll prepare a list for you."

Merry could picture it now, a Designs by Brenda's restaurant guide would be collated within a bejeweled pink binder with colour-coded tabs and smiley face/sad face rankings. "I'll be moving into my new place very soon," Merry stressed. There it was, the message had been delivered. Time to double down with some well-placed but noncommittal compliments. "I could probably use the expertise of a successful, professional designer like you…" Truth. "…but I don't think I can afford it right now." Big ass truth.

Brenda's ears perked right up. "You know, good design doesn't have to cost a lot. I bet I could spruce up your new place in the wink of an eye for a very reasonable price." She stepped over to a table hidden beneath bolts of colourful fabric and a large glass bowl of gold finials. "I'm sure you'd be super amazed at the difference a few small details can make."

Oh, oh, had she gone too far? She'd just gotten Brenda on her side. She didn't want to hurt her feelings by not hiring her. She went with a nervous laugh and said, "You'd be super amazed how little money is in my bank account."

"Oh," a momentarily deflated Brenda said, laying down a Burberry swatch. "Tell me, Merry, what is it exactly that you do?"

"I'm a private investigator."

Brenda caught her breath, stared at her neighbour, and clasped an invisible pearl necklace.

"Are you okay?" Merry was used to unusual responses to her career, but this one seemed a little extreme.

"Are you fluffing kidding me?" Brenda blurted out.

Merry blinked. Did she just say "fluffing"?

"Okay, okay, okay," Brenda enthused, rushing over to stand directly in front of Merry. "You have to come home with me tonight."

"Uh, we just met. Maybe dinner first?" Merry joked, desperately hoping the levity would break the trance Designs by Brenda seemed to have slipped into.

"You have to, you just have to. My husband will die."

"You're husband is dying?" *What is going on here?*

"No, of course not. He's fine. He's an electrician. Roger. You have to meet him. It's his birthday."

"Well, that's very nice, and please pass Roger birthday wishes from me but…"

"You don't understand."

Understatement.

"It's Roger's birthday. Of course I've already bought him a very nice gift, a beautiful, hand-tailored Luigi Borrelli shirt, but you, you would be the most perfect gift I could ever give him. You have to do this, Merry, please, you have to come over tonight and meet him. Say seven o'clock? Drinks and nibblies?"

"I'm sorry, Brenda, I'm a little confused here. Why would I be the perfect birthday gift for your husband?" Merry sucked in her cheeks, hoping this wasn't about to get kinky.

"Oh," she snickered. "Did I forget to tell you that part?"

"I think you did."

"Roger's an electrician by day. He and his business partner, Kevin, who's a plumber, run a very successful business called Spark Plug. Get it?"

"I do."

"I came up with it. Spark as in electricity, plug as in plugged sinks."

"Mmhmm. Clever."

"Thank you. Anyway, that's what Roger does during the day,

but at night he's a crime junkie. TV shows, movies, documentaries, books, satellite radio, online chat rooms; he loves them all, always has, long before we met. A few years ago, he began hosting a true crime podcast at night. He covers all the high-profile and celebrity cases everyone wants to hear about, but what he really loves to do is talk about local crime, stuff that happens right here in Saskatchewan. Maybe you've heard of it? A couple of years ago—although the police will never admit it—Roger's investigation into a string of Livingsky burglaries led them to finding the bad guy. The podcast really took off after that."

"He investigated the burglaries?"

"Yes, no, well sort of. He's not a real detective like you, but he knows his stuff. That's why you are the perfect birthday gift, Merry. He will be so excited to meet you. Please say you'll do it! Please? Pretty please with sprinkles on top."

"I like sprinkles, but…"

"Please don't say no. Please do this for me. I'll do anything. Oh wait! I know, I know, I know what I can do! I'll give you a free interior design consultation for your new house."

Merry's mouth grew dry as she began to realize she'd dug herself into a hole that was quickly becoming impossible to get out of. Not unlike her meeting with Greyeyes, this meeting was not going as she'd planned. She certainly did not want Designs by Brenda setting foot in the Junk House, but she suspected the woman would be put off if she didn't accept her offer, and she couldn't afford to offend her, at least not before she moved out of Craving Lane.

"Tell you what," she began slowly, worrying that what she was about to say might be a horrible mistake. "Instead of a home make-over, how about you teach me how to do that."

"Of course!" Brenda nodded enthusiastically before knowing what she was agreeing to. "Do what?"

Merry felt as if breath was leaving her lungs faster than it was being replaced. "Your makeup. You look really nice. I don't. Can you help me?"

There it was. Admission of failure combined with asking for

help. Some psychotherapist somewhere was leaping for joy. Merry's experience with Gerald Drover had shook her. Even though she knew it shouldn't matter what anyone else thought about how she looked, she also knew she hadn't given her outward appearance the attention it deserved, the attention she wanted to give it but was... afraid?...to.

Brenda beamed. Holding out her fingers for another wet noodle handshake, she squealed, "You have got yourself a deal."

CHAPTER 8

Newton Heights was one of several Livingsky neighbourhoods that did not exist when Merry left the city to move to Vancouver. A GPS-assisted Uber driver expertly navigated the trip and deposited her in front of Brenda and Roger Brown's home. It was a brightly lit modern building with interesting angles and plenty of glass, the kind of house that once would have seemed more suited to a California beach than a prairie suburb, but times were changing.

From the moment she'd agreed to the visit, during which she was expected to indulge Roger Brown's amateur interest in crime detection and partake in a makeup tutorial, Merry fretted she'd made a big mistake just for the sake of avoiding conflict with Brenda Brown. Her illegal tenancy status was about to disappear (as soon as Gerald Drover gave her the thumbs up to move into the junkyard), so did she really need to go to this extreme just to make nice? Probably not, but it was too late now. She'd grin and get through it. Besides, she was in no position to turn down free food and drink.

A pleasant looking man opened the door with an expectant look on his face. He was conservatively dressed in tan khakis and denim shirt, not at all what Merry was expecting of someone married to Designs by Brenda.

"Hello, can I help you?" the man asked.

"Hi, I'm Merry."

"What can I do for you, Merry?"

"Oh, uh…" Not quite the welcome she was expecting. "You must be Roger? I think your wife is expecting me."

"That's funny. She didn't mention…"

"Surprise! Happy birthday!" an overly exuberant cheer erupted from behind the confused man.

The next moments were consumed with Brenda explaining Merry's role as human birthday present. To give her credit, Brenda knew her husband well. Once he understood who Merry was, he was demonstrably excited to meet her.

They invited her inside and together settled in a large formal living room beautifully appointed with high end furniture that probably cost more than several years rent on the Junk House. Merry noted that whereas she was wearing the same clothes she wore to work, Brenda had somehow managed to find time to change her hair and outfit (pale green palazzo pants with a matching flowy blouse). Roger poured wine while Brenda presented a platter of beautifully appointed homemade canapés that looked too good to eat.

Roger could not wait to play with his birthday present and dived right in. "So, you are a real detective? People actually pay you to solve crime?"

By the look on his face, Merry guessed she could admit to nothing more than knowing how to spell the word crime and he'd be ecstatic. "Yes, I am and yes they do. Most of my experience has been in Vancouver. I just moved back to open a satellite office of the firm I worked with there. It's called LSI."

"Sounds like CSI. People will like that."

Merry grinned. She liked Roger Brown. "I sure hope so. I'm just getting started."

"That's how Merry and I met," Brenda jumped in, making it sound like they'd been besties for years. "Her office is right next door to mine. I just knew meeting a real private eye would be the best birthday present I could ever give you."

Roger smiled at his wife with undisguised affection. "You always know the perfect thing to get me." He turned back to Merry and said, "Isn't she great?"

Merry nodded, not bothering to voice her doubts about exactly where on the great spectrum Designs by Brenda really sat.

"Brenda's probably bored you to death about how much I love true crime detection. If I wasn't an electrician, which, don't get me wrong, I love that too, I would want to do what you're doing. Of course, I don't know anything really, I'm just an amateur in all this. But I know enough to know that to be a successful detective you need to be smart, patient, and inquisitive; and you've got to have guts. I am in awe of you, Merry."

Merry blushed, surprised by the sentiments and how sincerely they were delivered. It felt good to be complimented like this. Roger Brown was a fan. She had a fan. She needed one. "Thank you. That's very nice of you to say."

"I mean it, I really do. Can I ask what kind of jobs you're working on right now?"

Jobs. Plural. If only. "I can't go into detail." She felt compelled to give her biggest fan something juicy. "But I can tell you that my biggest case at the moment," AKA only case, "involves a potential arson."

"The 101 Redberry fire."

Merry blanched. How the hell did he pick up on that? Brenda wasn't kidding when she claimed her husband knew his stuff. "Yes, that's right." Unlike other professions where confidentiality was a must, with private detection, the reverse was true. One of the most useful ways of digging up information about a case was to talk about it. "How do you know about the Redberry fire?"

"Livingsky may be growing leaps and bounds, but it's still a relatively small city. Things like Redberry get around, especially in the true crime community. The investigation seems to have stalled. As far as I can tell, it's sitting inactive on desks at both the fire department and LPS. I've been discussing it on my podcast for a while now. Did Brenda tell you I host a podcast?"

"She did."

His eyes lit up. "Would you like to come downstairs and look at my studio? We can exchange thoughts about Redberry. You could be a guest on my next show!"

"No!" Brenda jumped in, quickly and loudly.

Merry watched the couple exchange an unusual look. She couldn't quite figure out what it meant.

In the flash of an eye, Brenda replaced a look of concern with a broad smile. "I promised Merry some girl time in exchange for her coming here to meet you. We have to get to it before it gets too late. This is a school night, you know."

Merry looked at Brenda, surprised and touched by the woman's gracious lie. She didn't say anything about her part of the bargain being a 911 makeup lesson.

"Oh," Roger said to his wife, disappointed by the abrupt loss of his birthday gift, like a kid who'd just broken his favourite toy. "I understand. Girl time's important." He turned to face Merry. "Merry, I know this may sound a bit crazy and please forgive me if I'm being too forward, but I think you could use my help."

"Roger—" Brenda began, making moves to clear away the appetizer tray and his wineglass.

Undeterred, and knowing his time was limited, Roger kept on at a faster pace. "You said yourself you're new in town. I know you lived here before, but the city has changed a lot in the last few years. We have a mayor who is keen on growing this city and her plans are working, but you probably know better than anyone, the bigger the city, the bigger the crime. I don't claim to know much, but I know some. I think I could really help you."

"Roger—" Brenda tried again, but Merry cut her off this time.

"I really appreciate that, Roger, and if there's anything I think I could use your help with, I'll certainly give you a call." She was lying, but it was a nice, pearly-white lie. She liked Roger and didn't want to hurt his feelings.

"Come on, Merry," Brenda said standing up and pulling Merry with her. "I've got us set up in my dressing room. Roger, honey, would you mind cleaning this up? Don't forget, the crystal does not go in the dishwasher, it must be hand-washed. And make sure the leftovers are put in sealed containers. And…"

"Yes, I know," he said, rising. "I won't bother you two until girl time is over."

Brenda blew her husband a kiss. Tying her arm into Merry's, she led the way out of the room saying, "Isn't he great?"

Passing the Brown's kitchen, Merry noticed a woman sitting quietly at the island, lazily stirring a cup of tea. Brilliant white hair and reading glasses dangling from a delicate gold chain around her neck were the only hints that she was well into her seventies. Despite the time of day, she was fully made up as if awaiting a photo shoot, and wore a soft mauve sweater set that perfectly complimented her eye shadow. This was odd. Had everyone gotten dressed up for her visit?

"Hi," Merry ventured a greeting even though Brenda showed no signs of slowing down.

The woman looked up, startled.

Brenda stopped in her tracks, looked at the woman, then at Merry, then back at the woman. "I thought you'd already gone to your room for the night, Mother. This is my friend, Merry."

Merry thought "friend" was overstating things more than a little, but said nothing.

"Hello," the woman said. "Nice to meet you."

"Merry, this is my mother, Doris."

"Hi, Doris. Nice to meet you too."

"Are the children in bed?" Brenda asked her mother.

Designs by Brenda took time out of her extraordinarily successful career to have kids?

"They are."

Merry spotted an unusual look pass between the women before Brenda asked, "Do you need help with anything, Mom?"

"Of course not," Doris replied. "I'm just having my tea."

Brenda marched into the sparkling kitchen which was the size of the entire Junk House, headed straight for the counter where someone, likely Doris, had left an open box of Twinings tea bags. "Mom, I asked you to use the teabags in the tea cannister." Reaching into a drawer, Brenda pulled out a roll of scotch tape and resealed the offending box. "You know I like us to use up the older teabags before we open a new package."

"I'm sorry, dear. I forgot."

"It's okay. I'm sure you'll remember next time," she said, inserting the Twinings box into a Glad plastic storage bag then reaching up to store it in the highest shelf of a nearby cupboard. "Enjoy your tea."

Done with that, Brenda clasped a hand around Merry's forearm and pulled her out of the kitchen.

The dressing room, Brenda explained, was a converted bedroom they'd decided they didn't need. It was large, sumptuously decorated in much the same way as the Designs by Brenda office, with the added glamour of several racks of high-end clothing and a wall solely dedicated to shoes and handbags. The closet was over-the-top in a way that convinced Merry that Brenda would be a shoe-in as a castmate should Andy Cohen ever decide to create a show called "The Housewives of Saskatchewan".

Placing a hand on each shoulder, Brenda directed Merry into a high back chair tufted with pink faux fur and situated in front of an oversized mirror and makeup table which was covered with enough cosmetics to stock a store.

As soon as Merry was positioned, Brenda ignited a halo light so bright Merry thought they were about to witness the landing of an alien spacecraft. With practiced flourish, Brenda pulled open several of the table's drawers revealing even more beauty products and related accoutrement.

"This is amazing," Merry said, truly in awe. "I can't decide if this feels like a department store makeup counter or Area 51."

"Area 51? I don't know it. Is that the salon you used in Vancouver?"

Merry smirked. She couldn't remember the last time she used a salon. "What I mean is that your dressing room is very impressive, out of this world."

"Thank you. This isn't just for me," she quickly added. "I do my mother's makeup every morning and… sometimes other people's too. I love it. If I wasn't a designer, I would be a makeup artist. My mother was a beautician at The Bay before she retired."

"Your mother is very beautiful. I can see where you get it from."

Brenda hesitated as she assessed the comment, then said, "That's nice of you to say. Makeup does a lot of the work. If it's done right. You'll see that after tonight. Now just hold on a sec while I set up the iPhone to record this."

"What?" Merry was startled. Was Brenda some kind of podcaster, like her husband? If so, she was outta there.

"After you see what I do to your face today, you're definitely going to want to replicate it, but you'll get home and realize you forgot half of it. If we film it on your phone, you can use it as a tutorial whenever you want."

Merry wavered as she considered how to proceed. She'd only just met Brenda Brown. Did she trust this woman with her face? Did she trust her with the truth? "I suppose that makes sense. I'm sorry I'm being weird about this, it's just that this is all so out of my comfort zone." The easiest thing to do, Merry knew, would be to jump out of the chair and get the heck out of there. But nothing about her path had been easy, so why did she expect this to be any different? She'd not only agreed to do this, she'd suggested it. It was time.

Brenda frowned, as if trying to figure out why Merry was acting so skittish. "Did your mother teach you how to put on a face?"

Merry shifted in her seat, trying unsuccessfully to find a comfortable spot. She cleared her throat. "Brenda, before we begin, I should…I want to tell you something. I am a transgender woman."

Brenda's eyes grew wide, her lashes fluttered so fast Merry wondered if they might fly off.

"Are you okay?"

After fumbling for words, she replied, "Yes. Yes, yes. I am okay. It's just that I've never…I don't know…I'm a little surprised, that's all."

Merry could not hide her smile. *Take that, Gerald Drover.* If she could pass as a woman in front of Designs by Brenda—who was, in

Merry's mind, as girly-girl as a female could get—maybe she wasn't so lacking in the feminine department after all.

Standing over Merry's shoulder, Brenda caught her eye in the makeup mirror. "Can you tell me exactly what that is, uh, what you are? Oh crap, I'm messing this up…can you…what is a transgender woman? I'm sorry, now it's me who's out of her comfort zone."

"It's okay, we'll figure our way through this together. Besides, I did kind of spring all of this on you. I'd rather be asked the question than have people assume they know the answer when they probably don't. A transgender person is someone who has a gender identity that differs from the sex they were assigned at birth. In my case, I was born a boy but I'm actually a girl. So, for me, I needed, and wanted, to make changes to align the two in order to feel comfortable in my body." She added with a titter of laughter, "And now I'm perfect."

Brenda nodded but said nothing.

"To answer your question, no, my mother did not help me, nor did I experiment with makeup with girlfriends in high school. I was born a boy. I became a girl much later in life. So, my experiences are probably quite different from those you might have had."

"That must have been very difficult for you."

"When you finally decide to transition, there are so many things to think about, to learn, so many things to worry about; surgeries, how to afford them, figuring out how to tell people, how to walk, how to talk. Sometimes, well, most times, it felt overwhelming. It was more than I could handle just to get myself through the medical stuff, never mind the mental adjustments, the financial strain and social challenges," Merry admitted, surprising herself with how honest she was being with a complete stranger. "I figured I'd deal with learning how to dress and do my hair and makeup later. To be honest, I didn't think the aesthetics were all that important in the grand scheme of things. I'm still not sure they are."

Brenda jumped in. "Oh Merry, aesthetics are very important. Maybe not for the reasons you think."

"What do you mean?"

"Women have a right to look however they want without being judged or sexualized or demeaned or shamed. If I want to look cheap, that should be okay. If I want to run around town without a stitch of makeup, that's my right. It's not about needing to look pretty or natural or professional or sexy, it's about wanting to. Once you figure out what you want, all you have to do is figure out how to do it. Easy peasy."

Merry silently disagreed. There was nothing easy or peasy about this.

"I know I'm not a professional or anything, but I get a sense about women, Merry. I don't know what it is, but when I look at a woman, I can usually tell what they really want to look like, just by watching how they move, how they sit, how they talk to me. I'm usually right. When you walked into my office today, I saw someone who didn't look like herself."

Clenching her teeth, Merry recoiled at the words. What was this woman saying? Was Designs by Brenda saying she'd made a mistake, that she shouldn't have become a woman because it was so obvious it wasn't who she was? How did she get here? How did she let this happen? How did she allow herself to be sitting in this chair at the mercy of this horrible person?

"Do you know who I saw, Merry?"

"Who?" she could barely get the word out.

"I saw Wonder Woman. I saw a Superhero who doesn't know she is one yet."

Merry felt blood rushing to her cheeks, her heart thumped faster. *Wonder Woman? Like Gal Gadot Wonder Woman?*

"Was I right?" Brenda pushed.

Closing her eyes, Merry pulled in a long, deep breath through her nose, allowing the light floral sent that accompanied it to calm her. Sitting in this stranger's dressing room, bathed in light, surrounded by vials and jars, lipsticks and feathery brushes, as treachery removed its mask to reveal compassion, she realized something unexpected. She felt seen. She felt safe.

Slowly at first, then with more vigour, Merry nodded assent.

"Good," Brenda whispered. "What do you want, Merry?"

Merry knew the answer. She'd known it for a long time. "I want something different than what I see in the mirror." It was a sentence she'd used many times as a boy, then a man. Now the words took on a whole different meaning. "When I put on makeup, or I'm in a store trying on clothes, I feel like a country butcher pretending to be a pastry chef. I'm shooting for pretty and feminine, but it always ends up a mess. Every time. To be honest, I don't know exactly what I want to look like. I'm not sure it's Wonder Woman, maybe it is, I'm just not sure."

"Perfect!" Brenda exclaimed.

"What?"

"That's why we're here, isn't it? Step one. We're going to figure it out together. First the face, then," she hesitated, "I'd like to talk about wardrobe." Without waiting for a reaction, she added, "As long as you're open to trying, I am too. This is going to be fun!"

Merry groaned, again not sure she agreed with Brenda's assessment.

Laying her perfectly manicured hands on Merry's shoulders, and reaching into the reflection in the mirror, Brenda added, "But Merry, you have to promise me one thing."

"What's that?"

"Roger has told me that I, not always but sometimes, can come off a tad too…blunt. I'm sure if you knew me better, you might think the same thing. So please, if I say something that hurts your feelings, don't let it."

Merry's cheeks tightened with a small grin. This woman was something else. She wasn't promising not to be blunt, not to hurt her feelings, only that Merry shouldn't let it hurt her feelings if and when she did. Fair enough. This woman knew herself. Merry knew herself too. Well, mostly. She was tough, she was strong and brave, but was she ready for Designs by Brenda? Were her nerves too raw, her skin too thin?

"I'll try. But you have to promise me one thing too."

"For sure. What is it?"

"If I forget not to get hurt and say something to hurt you in return, don't let it."

For five seconds the room was silent as a tomb. Then they laughed.

✠

Three hours later, as Merry prepared to leave the Brown house, Roger emerged from the basement to say good-bye.

"I know it's frowned upon for a random man to comment on how a woman looks, but would it be okay if I complimented my wife on her outstanding skills?"

Both women smiled. Brenda hugged her husband while beaming at Merry's new face. When she was done with Roger, she embraced Merry with a hug that was a little long for Merry's taste but was graciously accepted. Her opinion of Brenda Brown, although not entirely changed, had certainly shifted. When it came to applying makeup, the woman knew what she was doing. She'd gamely applied, cleaned off, reapplied, cleaned off, then reapplied again face after face after face. Merry guessed that if she hadn't finally called a time-out, Brenda might have kept on until morning.

The final iteration was a dramatic difference from the Merry who'd arrived hours earlier. She'd need time with the new look, to allow the transformation to sink in, to answer the question: is this what I want? Brenda insisted the experimentation was far from over. Merry wasn't so sure.

"I just thought of this," Brenda said when she released Merry. "If your new house isn't ready yet, where are you staying?"

There it was. The little pinprick disguised as an innocent question that burst the bubble. She just couldn't let it go. If Merry was contravening the Craving Lane rules by sleeping in her office, Designs by Brenda wanted to know about it. "I've rented a motel room for now. Nothing fancy, but it does the trick," Merry fibbed, pasting a fake smile on her new face.

"Oh good. Make sure you check for bed bugs. I've heard horror stories."

Roger stepped forward holding out his hand. "Merry, I want to thank you for being my birthday present."

Merry grasped Roger's hand to shake it and felt something being pressed into her palm.

"It was a thrill to meet a real detective," he said, his face betraying nothing, a skill he and his wife seemed to have in common. "I hope we can talk again."

As Merry headed down the front walk to her waiting Uber, she had one thought: *There is something very strange going on in the Brown household.*

CHAPTER 9

As soon as Merry settled into the backseat of the Uber for the trip home from Brenda and Roger Brown's, she unravelled the piece of paper Roger Brown had covertly slipped into her palm when they said goodbye. It was obviously something he didn't want his wife to know about and Merry was dying to find out what that was.

The note was short and to the point. It read: "A guy who heard another guy bragging about setting the Redberry fire owns $$$ Now Pawnshop." She re-read the poorly structured sentence three times. Was this the type of hard-hitting, unofficial, unsubstantiated, chicken-clucking information that fuelled the true crime podcast industry? By the time she was halfway home (AKA her office), she began rethinking her reaction. Who was she to turn down a potential lead, as obtuse as it and its source were? It's not like she was overrun with them.

Back at the office she booted up the computer and looked up $$$ Now Pawnshop. Other than an address and two 0 out of 5 stars Yelp reviews, there was little to learn. It was too late to call Roger, and she wasn't sure how she could do that anyway without raising Brenda's suspicions, especially since his helping her was obviously something he didn't want his wife to know about. Having neglected to ask him the name of his podcast, Merry searched the more popular podcast platforms using: "Roger Brown," "Livingsky," "True Crime," and "Saskatchewan" as parameters, but came up empty.

First thing the next morning she placed a call to Spark Plug, the electrician/plumber combo business where Roger worked. A friendly receptionist informed her that Roger was busy all morning and would return her call in the afternoon. She didn't have time for that. Her plan was to get to the bottom of this case and dump Gerald Drover as a client as soon as possible. Taking matters into her own hands, she headed for Alphabet City to find $$$ Now Pawnshop.

Alphabet City's commercial district began with A Street, just across the tracks from downtown, and petered off somewhere around F Street where low-income tenement housing and apartment buildings took over. The A and B blocks were home to several decent restaurants (most of them labelled "ethnic" by people who pretended they weren't), several cannabis providers, a "Made in Saskatchewan" knickknack store, and a diverse assortment of other independent businesses with historically high turnover rates. The further you got from downtown, the sketchier the businesses became. At C block the pawnshops and second-hand stores began to appear. By F block you could find Triple X video stores and head shops, most of which were thinly veiled covers for more nefarious or stimulating enterprises, depending on your point of view.

Painstakingly navigating a hopscotch design of ice patches, Merry made slow progress down several blocks of 20th Avenue, Alphabet's City's main commercial street, eventually locating the pawnshop. It was impossible to see inside with the windows entirely used up as exhibition space for a sampling of the multitudinous items on offer within; used furniture, VCR tapes, CDs, vinyl records and the machines to play them on; all manner of electrical appliances, artwork and exercise equipment, all of it previously owned and of questionable quality and provenance.

Stepping inside, Merry was surprised to hear the chime of an overhead bell. She knew it was meant to alert the owner that someone had entered the store, but to her the innocent tinkle conjured up simpler times; visiting an ice cream shop on Sunday afternoons with her parents, the corner grocery store down the block from their house. None of the stores she frequented in Vancouver had a bell.

The pawn shop was long and narrow, dominated by four rows of overloaded shelving, a vast collection of bulky furniture, and plastic-wrapped mattresses piled to the ceiling. Any space left was filled with weighty silence and cobwebs. Sitting behind an expansive counter at the rear of the store was a solid bulk of a man with heavy eyebrows and a corona of dust motes circling his head. The counter and the shelf behind the shopkeeper had glass fronts, showing off goods apparently so valuable they were kept under lock and key. The man nodded at Merry, Merry nodded back, then he went back to reading his paper.

Merry leisurely proceeded down the centre aisle, casually glancing at merchandise as she passed by. The place smelled strange, not bad really, just strange; a blend of musty fabric, old newsprint, and mothballs.

"You looking for something in particular?" the man asked when Merry ran out of aisle.

Merry stepped up to the counter.

"Windy out there?"

Merry scowled, ticked off that the man made absolutely no effort to pretend he wasn't looking at her hair. She knew it had fluffed up like a puffer fish during her journey from Craving Lane to Alphabet City. "A bit."

"You buying or selling?"

"I might be buying."

"Tell me what you want. I got pretty much everything. If I don't, I can probably get it for you."

"That's great," she said with a broad smile. "I'd like to buy some information."

The man pushed back from the counter and crossed heavily tattooed arms over a barrel chest. "You a cop?"

"Do I look like a cop?"

He grinned, once again eyeing up Merry's hair in what she considered an impolite manner. "No, you really don't. But I still want an answer to the question."

"I am not a cop. I am, however, a private investigator." She pulled a card from her purse and handed it to the burly, dark-haired man. "My name is Merry Bell. I work for LSI."

"Never heard of it." He tossed the card onto the countertop, probably a temporary stop on its way to the garbage can.

"Livingsky Sharpe Investigations."

"If you say so."

He was obviously not one of the thirteen hits her website had received since going live. "I was hired to look into the fire at 101 Red-berry Road. Not too far from here, actually. It's a building owned by Gerald Drover. Maybe you've heard of him?"

Tattooed veins twitched.

"Like I said, I don't work for the cops. Nothing you tell me will get back to them."

"Oh yeah? Why should I tell you anything?"

She smiled and winked. "Because I'm asking?"

He grunted.

Merry put his staunch resistance to her wiles down to a bad hair day.

Sighing, she dug around in her purse, swearing under her breath the whole time. She pulled out a wrinkled bill and took her time flattening it out on the countertop. "Maybe this will help?" This was exactly the type of situation where money talked. She'd done it before. Plenty. The only difference was that when she worked for Nathan, bribes were reimbursed. Now they were coming straight out of her own anorexic piggy bank.

The man looked at the denomination then back at Merry. "Lady, get the hell out of my store."

Merry swore some more. Inside voice only. She had correctly predicted ten bucks wouldn't do it, but it was worth a try. She pulled out another bill. *There goes dessert with dinner.* Then another. *There goes dinner.* Then another. With each bill the shaking of her hand grew more pronounced. The game had to end somewhere. Hopefully somewhere between her running out of cash and the man's willingness to talk. Of course, pawnshop guy would be no help in figuring out when that was. It was up to her to guess. Fortunately, Merry had a good eye for tells. Like amateur poker players who unconsciously convey when they're bluffing, bribe-ees often had a tell that communicated when the amount of money on the table was enough to loosen their tongue. The pawnbroker's tell was a slight tick of a faint scar hidden beneath the five o'clock shadow at the left corner of his mouth. Spotting it, Merry gathered up the accumulated stack of crumpled bills, shrugged, and turned to go.

"Wait, wait, wait. I might know something."

Merry replaced a satisfied smirk with a blank face, then turned back. She laid a ten-dollar bill on the counter.

"Uh, uh," he said. "All of it, or I know nothing."

Merry dumped the rest of the bills and fastened her eyes on the man. "Tell me."

"I know the guy who did the fire you're talking about, the one on Redberry."

Merry narrowed her eyes, studying the man. He was not difficult to read. There was a good chance he was talking about himself. For the moment, she didn't care. "Why did he do it?"

The man's heavy shoulders heaved up then down.

"It's not a hard question to answer."

"He didn't care nothing about why he was doing it."

"What did he care about?"

"The money. Everything's about money in this part of town. You'd know that if you spent any time here."

There it is. The tip of the iceberg. "What's to say I haven't?"

"Those boots. It's my business to know what things cost."

Not only were her boots worthless in Saskatchewan winter weather, they were wreaking havoc on her game. In truth, it kind of made her love them a little bit more. "This guy, he was paid to set the fire?"

"Yeah."

"By Drover?"

"Nope."

Merry did her best to reign in her excitement. Scumbag that he was, maybe her client was telling the truth after all. Maybe the cops were wrong about him…this time. If Drover didn't set the fire, or pay to have it done, and it wasn't caused by his infamous habit of allowing his properties to become firetraps, that meant the fire at 101 Redberry Road was intentionally set by someone else.

Merry laid an extra bill on the counter. "Who was it? Who paid him?" She held her breath and waited for the answer.

CHAPTER 10

"How did you know about Nicky Sokolov?" Merry didn't waste time with hello when she answered Roger Brown's return call.

"The pawnshop guy? Did my lead actually lead to something good?"

"It did."

"Wow. That's terrific. I'm so glad."

"Roger, how did you know what you did?"

"I told you, I've been discussing the Redberry fire on my podcast for a while now. People love to share what they think or what they've heard."

"You mean people actually call in while you're...podcasting, is that a word?"

"Of course. That's what makes it exciting, getting like-minded people involved, everyone working together toward the same goal."

"Which is what, exactly?"

"Solving the crime, figuring out whodunit before the cops do, if they ever do."

"Let me get this straight. Nicky Sokolov called in to your show?"

"Not him, but someone who knows someone who heard something."

Oh my god.

"I know what you're thinking, and you're not wrong. Sometimes the theories that get tossed around on my podcast go nowhere. Well, a lot of times they go nowhere. But sometimes we hit gold, like I did with the serial burglary case a few years ago. Now that I'm working with a real detective, we can…"

"No, no, no, there is no you working with a real detective. You gave me a lead, I chose to follow it. Thank you. That's it."

"Come on, Merry, I was serious about what I said last night. I really think I can help you. I did help you. I know this city. I know its people. You're new to town, I've been involved with the Livingsky true crime scene for a while now. It's win-win."

"Why all the cloak and dagger slipping me the note without Brenda seeing?"

"I shouldn't have done that," he admitted, sounding a little sheepish. "It's just that Brenda isn't always one hundred percent supportive of…well, of what I do with the podcast. She seemed pretty intent on keeping you to herself last night, even though you were supposed to be my birthday gift. So, I figured it was the best way to do things without upsetting her."

He had a point there.

"I searched for your podcast last night, but I couldn't find it. What's it called? Can you send me a link?"

The line bowed with silence, then, "I'm at my next appointment, but before I go, I need to tell you something."

"Uh, okay."

"I hope it wasn't breaking a confidence or anything, but Brenda and I tell each other everything, and she told me about you being transgender. I wanted to be upfront about that and not pretend I don't know."

"That's not a problem for me." It wasn't. Merry knew some transgender people felt their status was nobody's business but their own, that they shouldn't be identified or labelled by it. She completely understood that. But she also wanted to encourage people not to be afraid to talk about it, or feel they have to lower their voices to a whisper when they do, as Roger just had.

"I'm so glad," Roger replied. "I don't know you, but I want you to know I think you're brave and wonderful."

Not expecting the words, Merry was left speechless.

"What's the next step with Sokolov?"

The podcasting electrician was right, he did help her. She owed him something more than a quick "Thanks, now get lost."

"Sokolov claims his 'friend' was hired to set the fire by a suit and tie guy, whatever that means."

"He means someone who doesn't live in Alphabet City. An outsider. Happens all the time. If somebody wants something bad done, their first stop is usually Alphabet City."

"According to Nicky, the guy approached his friend in a place called The Hole. According to Google, it's at the far end of 20th Avenue."

"You're going to The Hole?" It did not sound like Roger Brown approved.

"Tonight. He thinks there's a chance the guy might show up there again. If he does, he'll point him out to me."

"What's Nicky getting out of this? There's no way he's doing this out of the goodness of his heart."

Merry had to give the electrician kudos for his keen grasp of how things work on the other side of town. "I agreed to buy his drinks all night. I'm going to have to take out a loan if Sokolov doesn't stop costing me money."

"How does Nicky know what the guy looks like?"

Merry grinned. "My question exactly. A little suspicious, wouldn't you say?"

"So the 'friend' who started the fire is actually Nicky?"

"That's what I'm thinking."

"Merry, you have to be careful around people like him."

Merry did not disagree. Nor was she surprised. Of course Sokolov wouldn't be keen on implicating himself in a crime, but if he could make a few bucks and score a few free drinks from selling bits and pieces of the truth, why not? The only question was: did he actually know something or was he just stringing her along? With no other immediate leads on the horizon, Merry decided it was worth a night out at The Hole to find out.

"Do you know The Hole? Have you been there?"

"I've heard of it. It's not exactly the kind of place someone with an interior designer wife would go after work for cocktail hour. Mostly it's a biker bar, the kind where you go if you don't want to be seen. If you're fooling around, looking to score pretty much anything, or recently escaped from prison, The Hole's the place for you."

"Sounds like fun. I can hardly wait."

"I'll come with you."

"No."

"Merry, I really th…"

"Isn't your client waiting for you?" With that, Merry hung up.

In the back seat of the Uber on the way home from the Brown's, Merry had snuck repeated peeks at Brenda's handiwork using her iPhone's selfie-mode. The reflection was unrecognizable. Could it be? Did she spy a resemblance that was maybe an itty bitty closer to Wonder Woman than a RuPaul's Drag Race cast off?

Brenda began by wiping off the layers Merry had conscientiously painted on that morning, a process she called "naturalization". Once that was done, she meticulously inspected Merry's skin under a very bright light, then began a lengthy process of comparing Merry's face to a colour wheel of cosmetics, probably in the same way she compared fabric swatches to paint chips. After two false starts which ended with dissatisfied "humphs" and a full-face wipe-off, Brenda finally settled on a colour palette she was satisfied with and expertly applied selected products which she unapologetically described as "not the circus colours you were using". *Bitch*.

The entire procedure was liberally narrated by Brenda in the hopes that the resulting iPhone video could be used by Merry to duplicate the procedure on her own. Merry kept her eyes and ears open, more so in the hopes of identifying workarounds that would streamline the seemingly interminable process. Spending hours applying makeup was never going to be her idea of fun. Grudgingly, Merry did come to appreciate the woman's skill. More importantly, she began to understand how she'd gone wrong in the first place.

Physically, Merry had transitioned from man to woman; her doctor, the recently deceased Elliott Vanstone, had declared her a triumphant success. Mentally she hadn't caught up. Despite months of therapy and absolute certainty that it was the right thing to do, when it was all done and the healing complete, Merry looked in the mirror and saw the same face she'd started out with. To her, the reflection had male features that required as much feminization as possible in order to pass. Embarrassed by what she considered a failure, instead of accepting the assistance of others—assistance which was certainly on offer—she loaded up on makeup from online retailers who promised miracles she was desperate to believe in. She contoured, shaped, shadowed and painted her face to hide its many imagined shortcomings. What Merry didn't know and couldn't see, was that what she thought was feminization had crossed the line into exaggeration. To her mind, the redder the lipstick, the thicker the eyeliner, the more blush, the more bronzer, the better. What Merry realized as she watched Brenda work on her face was that it wasn't the mirror that had been lying to her, she'd been lying to the mirror.

No one until Brenda, a complete stranger, had bothered to tell her she'd become a caricature of the woman she was (which, in all fairness, wasn't surprising.) Who would have the balls to tell her something like that? Certainly not Nathan Sharpe. From the moment pre-Merry told her then boss what she planned to do, he'd admirably dedicated himself to supporting his employee as much as a hopelessly straight guy could muster. The last thing he was going to do was tell her she looked like a clown. As for most of her friends, by the time she really needed their help, they were gone, having either run away or been run off.

On the morning post magical makeover, after her morning YWCA shower which removed every last brush stroke of Brenda's handiwork, Merry returned to the office and rewatched the video over and over again, marvelling at the miraculous transformation. Mustering up her courage, and gathering the makeup she had on hand—no doubt much less expensive and of poorer quality than

Brenda's—Merry painstakingly attempted to recreate the look. As expected, it was not easy and rather time consuming. On more than one occasion she'd been one blot away from throwing in the makup-smudged towel, but persevered. She rated the end result one-point-five stars out of five. Not bad.

Although they didn't have time to work on hair and wardrobe, Brenda pointedly suggested Merry consider toning down the volume of her hair and the brightness and tightness of her clothing choices. The hair was the easier of the two. Mercifully, all she had to do was spend less time on it, and voilà, flat hair. Clothes would be more of a challenge.

When Merry was physically male, trying on clothes for a body that wasn't meant for her was akin to torture. Whereas most people looked for clothing that fit well and made them look or feel a certain way—relaxed, sexy, professional, casual, whatever—Merry's goal was to cover, conceal, obfuscate. Once she was physically female, after going so many years being confused about how to dress her body, she suffered paralyzing anxiety over what to wear, what looked good, what was in style, what was not. People talked about classics versus trendy versus contemporary; professional attire versus formal wear, clothing for travel, clothing for sports, clothing for lounging at home. It was all too much.

But she couldn't very well go about her days naked, she had to make choices. On her first foray into a womenswear department, she'd devised a hasty Plan A: if it's expensive it must look good. Which was how she ended up with the Louboutins. She'd paid almost two-thousand-dollars and they were worth every penny, a gift from him to her for becoming a woman. They were also the reason Plan A was exceedingly short-lived. With medical and other bills piling up and finding herself unable to return to work for abundant reasons (how she looked being one), shopping like a Kardashian was unsustainable. Plan B was not quite so lofty and, she now knew, just as inaccurate: *if a piece of clothing was bright and cheap or tight and cheap it must look good.*

A much-debated and fretted-over Plan C went into effect this morning with a visit to Value Village, where if you looked hard enough you could get an entire wardrobe without breaking even the most fragile piggy bank. The trick was knowing what to look for. She tasked herself with finding clothes that matched her new face and flat hair. Committed to ignoring fashion labels and confusing wardrobe categories, she focused on three things: stuff for work, stuff for going out, and stuff for hanging out at home. Simple as that.

With time to spare before her night out with Nicky Sokolov, Merry locked her office door to ensure she wouldn't be interrupted and stationed herself in front of the full-length mirror she'd hung behind it. It took an agonizing hour to adjust what she saw. Finally, critically evaluating her overall appearance, Merry whispered to the tired mirror's reflection: "I. Am. Wonder Woman."

CHAPTER 11

The Hole was located so far down 20th Avenue, city planners had ran out of alphabet to name cross streets and inexplicably started naming them like hurricanes—Arthur, Bertha, Cristobal. The Uber driver found the dicey-looking tavern at a dark end of Gonzalo Street. His worried look as Merry got out only fed her uneasiness.

The Alphabet City saloon's entrance was an unmarked door that, like the rest of the structure, was windowless. Even so, there were plenty of hints as to what was going on inside. A makeshift parking lot spilling into the vacant lot next door and extending behind the building resembled a Harley Davidson show room. The building's crumbling stucco pulsated in time with the deep bass thumping of Twisted Sister's *Live to Ride, Ride to Live*.

A little too on the nose, Merry thought as she carefully navigated a boot-stomped trail that led from street to sidewalk. She pulled in an ice cube's worth of chilled air and readied herself for an adventure.

Inside, The Hole was part abandoned warehouse, part dystopian underworld. Every lighting source was either flickering, strobing, or glowing neon. The main room was dark and murky like a slough at night and smelled of sunbaked leather and cheap weed. Merry didn't have a lot of time to look around. Mere seconds after arriving, Sokolov was at her side. He grabbed her elbow and directed—pushed?—her toward two seats he'd been saving at the bar. Evidently, he was anxious to get started on the promised free liquor.

"This is a good spot," he said once drinks were ordered. "If our guy comes in tonight, I'll see 'im no prob." Without waiting for Merry to respond one way or another, he swiveled in his seat to chat with the guy sitting on the other side of him, leaving her nothing but his wide back to look at.

Merry attempted to follow the conversation between the two men for about thirty seconds before deciding it wasn't worth it. Neither she nor Nicky Sokolov were here to make friends. She'd buy his drinks. He'd point out the guy who wanted Gerald Drover's building burnt to the ground *if* he showed up. That was it. Until the bad guy turned up, or Merry ran out of disposable funds (she'd budgeted for three drinks), she was on her own. Keeping one eye on the front door, she quickly settled into one of her favourite pastimes: people watching.

It didn't take long for Merry to decide that The Hole is to people watchers what The Louvre is to art lovers. The denizens of the dive bar were a peculiar and diverse bunch. Not surprisingly, given the number of hogs in the parking lot, there were plenty of leather jackets and tattoos on display. What was unexpected were the Stetson-ed cowboys and plaid-sheathed farmers who mixed seamlessly with a collection of skeletal druggies and recent parolees with daggers for eyes. Clean-cut businessmen in bad boy drag sidled up to women who'd coaled their eyes and teased their hair like bad-girl Sandy from *Grease* (or yesterday's Merry Bell), while failed rock musicians argued politics with inebriated slam poets. It was a tenuous United Nations of skin colour and spoken tongue, mixed with representatives of every age group from barely legal to nearly extinct.

As the night progressed, Merry began to sense a burgeoning tension and mounting unease blooming in the room like fertilized stink weed. The simmering aggressiveness was increasingly unsettling to her, but not, she suspected, to anyone who regularly darkened the door of The Hole. Danger routinely prowled the periphery of places like this, lurking in the floorboards, walls, back rooms and, when conditions were just right, sprung like a wolf, ready to arch its back and reveal its fangs. As the flagrant use of alcohol and illicit drugs flourished, so did the noise in the room, swelling in intensity, growing harsher, menacing, eventually overtaking the pounding music, irreversibly hurtling toward what could only be an inexorable eruption. In a strange way, Merry was impressed. A devil's labyrinth right here in Livingsky, Saskatchewan, her innocent prairie hometown. Things had certainly changed in the years since she'd been away. Or, she conceded, it was far more likely the darkness had always been there, she just hadn't seen it.

An explosion was coming. The question was, did she want to be here to witness it? If you knew a volcano was about to blow, did you stay to watch or run for your life?

Twice, over the course of the evening, Merry had tapped the hulking shoulder of Nicky Sokolov to ask if a new entrant into the melee could be the guy they were looking for, the one who'd paid to burn down Drover's building. Each time he stopped what he was doing, studied the face, shook his head, then turned away. Aside from telling her he was ready for another round, he never spoke to her. That was just fine with Merry. Judging by how often the poor schmuck who ended up sitting next to him got up and walked away, she concluded Sokolov was probably a bit of a blowhard.

Checking her phone, Merry saw it was just past midnight. She'd had enough. This was not working. Bringing her lips close to his ear so he could hear her over the ambient roar, Merry told Sokolov she was leaving.

For the first time that evening, the pawnbroker focused on her for more than a few seconds, dark eyes intently fixated on hers. If Merry didn't know better (and she did because she'd paid for three rye-and-cokes and could smell them on his breath), she'd have sworn Sokolov was stone cold sober. "I've been watching." His voice was deep, shredded around the edges but steady and clear. "Closely." He moved nearer, as if not wanting his latest buddy to overhear. "Tonight just wasn't the night."

Generally Merry could spot a liar a mile away. With blaring music, blackout lighting, explosive exchanges and raucous laughter coming at her from every direction, she found herself unsure about Nicky Sokolov. By nature she judged him to be a taker, not a giver. He was born to take advantage of people. But he was also someone to whom a deal was a deal. If he struck one, he stuck to it, not because he was principled, but because he knew if he didn't it wouldn't be good for him. For whatever reason (no doubt influenced by bribe money and the promise of free drinks) he'd made a deal with Merry. She knew it was a long shot from the start. He probably did too. In her books, a long shot was an acceptable thing, being hoodwinked was not.

"Do you want to do this again?" he asked.

"You buy drinks the next time?" she suggested.

He grinned, showing almost no teeth. "Fuck no."

"We'll see." She slipped off her stool. "I know where to find you."

The smile slithered off Sokolov's face as he watched the woman leave.

Outside The Hole, Merry welcomed the relative calm and quiet. Pointing her nose skyward, she took in the expansive canopy of black above her, smiling as countless wee dots of light twinkled a greeting. On a clear night like this, far from the ambient light of downtown, it seemed almost possible to reach out and touch one. It was hard to believe each star was trillions of kilometers away.

The night air was cold enough to redden cheeks but too warm for frost bite. Without a breath of wind to disturb their path, diamond flakes of snow fell silently, brushing against Merry's face on their way to the ground. It brought to her mind that thing Saskatchewan people often said when comparing their weather to Vancouver's, usually in response to a disparagement: "but it's a *dry* cold" they'd say. Having lived in both locations, Merry knew exactly what they meant. On many a dreary, sunless, soggy Vancouver day she'd suffered the bone-chilling effects of a *wet* cold that seemed to last forever. Even though the current temperature was probably lower than it ever got in Vancouver, the dry prairie air felt brisk, invigorating. Much preferable. Then again, Vancouver has the sea, and an incomparable skyline of impressive skyscrapers and magnificent snow-capped mountains. Could it be, Merry wondered not for the first time, that every place in the world is perfect in its own special way?

When she'd first arrived at The Hole, Merry had spotted a 24-hour convenience store across the street. The place didn't look like a major improvement over the bar, but at least it wasn't oozing thumping hard rock, illicit drugs and the promise of imminent peril. Whoever owned it had made a wise decision to stay open late. Business was undoubtedly brisk at night's end when inebriated Hole patrons staggered across the street having convinced themselves that a Jurassic-era rotisserie hotdog and cup of caffeinated sludge would be just the thing to sober them up before driving home.

After surviving a visit to the sketchiest bar in Livingsky, Merry felt she deserved an after-hours treat. If she timed the Uber just right, she could score a pint of Häagen-Dazs and make it back to Craving Lane before it melted (not that she minded melted ice cream, sometimes she actually preferred it).

Setting out on her errand, once again the Louboutins did her no favours. Whereas the boots fit in quite nicely at The Hole where leather and high heels were *de rigueur*, they showed irresponsible insouciance when it came to navigating the grime encrusted ruts of ice that crisscrossed The Hole's front lot like battle scars. She'd just made it to the sidewalk when the predicable occurred. The stiletto of her left boot caught the hardened edge of a mini-glacier in such a way as to cause her to stumble forward. Overcompensating in the opposite direction, she threw out her arms, propelling her weight backwards. This triggered her right leg to buckle and she dropped like a sack of flour into a handy snowbank; ass first, legs up in the air.

For several seconds Merry lay there, not knowing whether to laugh, cry, or test her memory of colourful expletives. Staring straight up, those damn twinkling stars suddenly appeared less cheery and more jeering, as if snickering at her misfortune.

"Are you okay?" a masculine voice reached her from somewhere beyond her field of vision.

Merry silently considered the answer. Was anything (other than her pride) damaged? The boots! Are the boots okay?

Suddenly the dark canvas of sky was immensely improved by the addition of a sinfully attractive face. Blond. Nice eyes. Forehead creased with concern.

To her shame, Merry released what anyone listening could only describe as a giggle.

The man's forehead creases intensified, no doubt wondering if the fall had knocked her senseless.

As Merry gazed up at Prince Charming, a medley of love-in-bloom visions waltzed through her head, backed by a soaring soundtrack; like a mashup of Hallmark romance movies, the kind she hated herself for loving. Each scene was a version of what was commonly known in the Hallmark-verse as a meet-cute, amusingly charming first encounters between main characters that inevitably lead to the development of a romantic relationship and, two hours later, a happy ending.

This was finally it! She was having her first ever meet-cute, rescued by a handsome stranger after falling flat on her ass leaving a biker bar. Good one.

"Are you okay?" the man repeated, ice blue eyes drilling into Merry's as if he was trying to decide if she was concussed or just a drunken idiot.

"If my boots are okay, then I'm okay," Merry informed him.

His eyes travelled down the length of her still prone body to the footwear in question.

"Give it to me straight," Merry pleaded. "Are they going to make it?"

He grinned, revealing two perfectly placed dimples. "I think they're going to be alright."

"Phew." She winked and added, "Leave me behind, just get them to safety."

"Stand-up comedian?"

"Nope, just a girl who lost her footing, along with her pride."

"You feel ready to stand up?"

"I do."

With great tenderness the man took Merry's hands into his own.

"Oh wow," he said. "Did you feel that?"

She had. There'd been a spark when his skin touched hers. This was a kick-ass meet-cute.

Carefully the man guided Merry into an upright standing position. He was a good two inches taller than her, even with her beloved boots on. She smiled, noticing he didn't immediately drop her hands.

"Are you sure you're okay? That was quite the fall."

She groaned. "Did you happen to see it?"

"Uh-huh."

"Are you feeling guilty because it kind of made you want to laugh?"

"No comment."

"Good call. I am okay. Thank you for helping me."

Ten seconds passed by in silence, neither one anxious to end the interaction.

The blond prince spoke first. "Can I help you to your car…or wherever? We don't want to risk endangering those boots again," he added with another dimpled smile.

Another woman might have strategically decided to leave her true purpose out of the conversation. Merry was not that woman. "Actually, I was heading across the street for ice cream."

"Won't it melt before you get home? Unless you don't live far from here?"

Merry smirked. This was fun. "Is that your way of asking me where I live?"

The man sputtered and reddened. "Oh, god, no, I'm sorry, that must have sounded so creepy."

"I'm kidding," she laughed good naturedly to show him she meant it. "As far as the ice cream melting, who are we kidding, it'll probably be long gone before I get home anyway."

He chuckled. "What's the point in waiting, right?"

"My thoughts exactly."

More silence.

The problem with meet-cutes, Merry now remembered, is that they almost always ended awkwardly.

"Well, thanks again," she said, nodding in the direction of the convenience store. "I'm going that-a-way."

He nodded. "I'm glad you're okay. Goodnight." He began to move off.

"Good night."

Selecting a flavour of ice cream in the convenience store, Merry's breath caught when she saw the reflection in the freezer's glass. The woman the man had flirted with was not who she remembered herself to be.

CHAPTER 12

Drover's rental property which had suffered the fire was a five-storey building on the corner of Redberry Road and A Street. The front entrance was locked and secured by an electronic passcode system. Merry could have called Drover for the access code but instead, liking a challenge, she rounded the apartment complex to the rear of the building. Back doors, especially in older buildings like this one, were notorious for being much less secure than front doors.

It took Merry less than ten seconds to break in. Yes, it was fun, but according to her professional code of ethics (the one she knew she should write down one day), she never committed a break and enter without good reason. Today she did it in the name of investigative research. She wanted to prove to herself (and maybe Detective Sergeant Veronica Greyeyes) that the fire could have been set by someone other than a tenant or Drover, as any outsider, like herself, could easily access the building.

Merry started in the basement, where the fire started. She was in luck. The door to the unoccupied unit where the blaze originated was open. Poking her head inside, she saw workmen busily painting walls and installing floorboards. There was no sign of fire or smell of smoke. The unit would likely be available for rent very soon. It looked good. So good, in fact, Merry wondered if she could afford it.

"Can I help you?" a voice from behind her.

Merry pulled back into the hallway. Standing outside a neighbouring door was a tall, lean guy with a bad complexion and worse barber. He was maybe twenty. He wore a parka, so Merry knew he was either on his way in or out.

"Oh, hi. I'm looking for Gerald Drover. He was supposed to meet me here about maybe renting this apartment."

"How did you get into the building?"

Smart ass. "One of your neighbours let me in. It's cold out, I guess they took pity on me."

"Oh." He didn't look entirely convinced.

"Hey, do you have a minute to chat?" The plan was to start knocking on doors, but a chance encounter was much better. "My name is Merry."

"I guess. I'm Douglas."

"You don't happen to be the neighbour who discovered the fire, are you?" Could she be so lucky?

"Nah. That was Paul. He lives over there." He pointed to a door further down the hallway.

Merry whistled under her breath "That must have been scary, having a fire happen so close to where you live."

"More of a pain in the ass. Everybody down here and I think some people from the main floor had to move out for a few days so they could do whatever they do to get the smoke smell out of our stuff."

"That would be a pain. You don't have any idea who started the fire do you?"

The question startled the man. "Who started it? I thought it was an accident?"

Merry used her eyebrows to communicate doubt. "In an empty apartment? How does that happen?"

"I don't know. I'm not a fire investigator. They would have told us, or it would have been in the news if it was something intentional, right?"

"Maybe. Do you ever worry about living here, you know, in a Gerald Drover building? His reputation isn't the best, from what I hear. Especially when it comes to fires and other safety hazards.

Now that there's been a fire…"

Douglas frowned. "I don't know what you're talking about. Gerald is cool."

Gerald Drover is cool? Merry swallowed, not sure what to make of the unexpected assessment.

The man started to inch away. Merry knew she was about to lose him. "How well do you know your landlord?"

"You know what, I gotta go. You should talk to Mrs. Wu. She lives on the top floor. She's been here forever. She's always home. She knows everything about everyone."

"Thanks for your help. Douglas, can I ask you one more question?"

"Shoot."

"How much do you pay for rent?"

His answer dashed Merry's hopes of getting out of having to move into the Junk House.

For the next twenty minutes Merry trolled the upper floors for tenants to talk to about the fire. Had they seen anything unusual the night of or in the days immediately prior to or after the fire? Did they have any suspicions about how the fire started? Even though it was the middle of the day, Merry managed to speak to at least one person on each floor. The stories were remarkably similar. Everyone liked living in the building. They knew very little about the fire. And, most surprisingly of all, no one had anything bad to say about Gerald Drover beyond what she considered typical landlord complaints. *It took him a week to get my leaky faucet fixed. He's done nothing about my noisy neighbour.* He wasn't beloved, but he wasn't hated either. By the time she got to the top floor, Merry was intent on locating Mrs. Wu who "knows everything about everyone", a P.I.'s favourite kind of person.

On her third try knocking on fifth floor doors, Merry was rewarded. Mrs. Wu was a short, Asian woman who could have been anywhere between sixty and eighty. After asking Merry several pointed questions about her intentions, Mrs. Wu must have concluded she was harmless and invited her inside. Merry was unprepared for what she saw.

CHAPTER 13

Stepping inside Mrs. Wu's corner apartment, Merry's mouth gaped open. As was the norm at the time the building was constructed, the windows were small, but there were a lot of them, each offering a landscape artist's dream. To the south, the multitudinous views took in the South Saskatchewan River, half shellacked with ice, as it meandered lazily through the city on its way northeast in search of its twin tributary where together they would find and empty into Lake Winnipeg. North-facing windows showcased an entirely different picture. They gazed out upon the ultra-modern urban vista that lay beyond the rail lines which separated downtown from Alphabet City as decisively as a machete. Sparkling skyscrapers, none over 30 storeys, perched proud like glass-and-steel peacocks congregating along the riverbank, many of them new constructions part of a nascent redevelopment project.

"You sit."

Before Merry could respond, the woman was gone.

Mrs. Wu disappeared down a dim, narrow hallway that Merry guessed led to a kitchen, bathroom, and one or more bedrooms. She found a free spot on an overstuffed sofa upholstered with rich burgundy velvet and surveyed her surroundings. Coming nowhere near to matching the opulence and grandness of its views, the apartment's interior more closely approximated what Merry had expected given the building's aged exterior: out-of-date, lived-in, worn out. The many windows let in plenty of light from various angles and led one to believe the space was large and airy, but upon closer inspection, Merry could see the front room was actually quite small.

In addition to the sofa, there was a mishmash collection of bureaus, desks, small tables, several upholstered chairs, all likely purchased in the seventies. A small corner of the room was dedicated to a sewing machine and several Walmart quality shelves loaded under with bolts of fabric and sewing notions. Designs by Brenda would shudder at the poorly curated arrangement.

Mrs. Wu returned carrying a tea service on a tray. Setting it on a low table next to Merry, neither her hands nor delicate ceramic cups shook. The elderly woman lowered herself onto the same sofa, their knees almost touching. Merry didn't know if she'd mistakenly taken the woman's spot and should move elsewhere or if her host simply didn't judge the extra closeness between two people who'd just met as uncomfortable. She fixed a smile on her face as Mrs. Wu served the tea, feeling like a giant next to the petite figure. Unlike The Hole, the Louboutins most certainly did not fit in here.

Merry was not a regular tea drinker, but the steaming liquid was flavourful and welcome on such a cold day. She told the woman so.

Mrs. Wu nodded her appreciation for the compliment. "It's nice to have a visitor."

After a bit of chitchat about sewing (Mrs. Wu used to do it as an at-home business, but now only for friends) Merry dived in. "Douglas, your neighbour downstairs, told me to come see you."

"Nice boy. He helped bring up my groceries one day."

"He told me you've lived here for a long time. He said you would know all about Gerald Drover."

"Over twenty years I've lived here." She sipped her tea.

Not helpful. It seemed the woman would need a bit of a nudge to start talking, unlike some other little old ladies Merry knew. "I've read some interesting things about your landlord."

Wu nodded, as slowly as she sipped, adding nothing to the conversation.

"These articles I read make me worry about moving into this building."

"Worrying will give you wrinkles."

Merry sucked in her cheeks as she thought about what to say next. Mrs. Wu might know everything about everybody, according to Douglas, but she certainly wasn't one to give any of it up easily. Deciding it was time to pour a little gasoline on the sputtering fire, Merry recited a precis of the damning Gerald Drover article she'd found online.

When she was done, Mrs. Wu refilled their teacups, spilling not a single drop, then said, "That must have been a very old newspaper you were reading."

Newspaper? Doing another quick scan of the apartment, Merry saw nary a computer, iPhone, or anything resembling technology from the last several decades. "Oh? Why do you say that?"

"That story, it wasn't about Gerald Drover Junior, it was a story about his father, Gerald Drover Senior. It is the father who was— how did you say it?—a slum landlord. It was the father who owned those buildings when they catch fire. It was the father who was responsible for the poor people who died."

Staring at the old lady, agog with disbelief (mostly at her own stupidity), Merry soundly chastised herself. She'd made a foolish mistake. She knew better than to believe internet information without confirming it. Her error, however, was not entirely irrational. Within the invisible but very real boundaries of Alphabet City, where Merry was soon to take up residence, it was widely known that the poor, the underprivileged, the disenfranchised, were routinely taken advantage of. Merry herself had just begun to experience the bitter taste of that same sour candy. Unable to afford reasonable living quarters, subsisting on cheap wine and day-old doughnuts, unsure where her next dollar was coming from, it was a tough life, all at the mercy of a not-so-underground economy that exploited those who lived it. Gerald Drover, upon discovering her anemic financial circumstances, had found a way to scrape her last dollars into his own grimy pockets by convincing her to move into a condemned shack in the middle of a garbage heap. Despite what she'd just learned from Mrs. Wu, it wasn't unreasonable to believe that a rotten apple hadn't fallen far from a father's tainted tree.

Mrs. Wu patted Merry's hand, "If you wish to move here, no need to worry, no need to put wrinkles on such a pretty face. Everything will be good."

Suddenly, it felt inexplicably natural to Merry to be sitting so close to the other woman. Mrs. Wu took a final sip of tea and sat back in a way that told Merry she was ready to tell a story of her own. Merry settled in and listened.

"My husband and I moved to this building when the old Drover was landlord. Things were not so good then, for many years. Then the fire happened, the one you read about. The fire was not here, but in another building not far from here. People were angry. The police could not ignore what was happening. Things turned very bad for the old man and he was sent to jail. Young Drover, Gerald, took over everything; the father's company, all the houses, all the apartments. He knew things must change. It took a long while, but he made these changes. He worked with people from the City who told him what he must do to fix the buildings that could be fixed. He tore down the ones that could not be. And now, it's better than it was."

This new vision of Gerald Drover, slowly sinking into Merry's brain, was not mixing easily with the old one. It was like pouring coffee into porridge. Could it be that Gerald Drover, the younger one, was not who he appeared to be? Was that why he balked when she'd called him Mr. Drover? To him, and probably many others who lived in Livingsky, Mr. Drover was his father, the real slumlord. If what Mrs. Wu said was true, Gerald was doing his best to distance himself from the reign of his father and the mistakes he'd made, intentional and otherwise, as a rental property owner.

"If you move in," the woman said a few minutes later as Merry prepared to leave, "you must come back to see me. We will have more tea."

Merry wondered if the invitation would still hold if she told the woman the truth about why she was really there. "I will." Changing the subject, she said, "I had no idea this building had such spectacular views. I'd love to see them again. You're very lucky to live here."

"Yes," Mrs. Wu replied with a small smile. "And even more lucky to have a long lease with low rent."

Merry's ears perked up. "You have a lease? You don't pay monthly rent?"

"No. All thanks to my husband. He's dead now, but he was a very smart businessman. He made a very good deal with old Drover long time ago. New people who come after me pay very much more. And no lease. Like you say, I am lucky. Born that way, my mother told me. Imagine how much money somebody would pay for such an apartment today."

Or, Merry thought, her mind abuzz with suspicion, *for such a building*. The stupendous river and city views would be available from more than just Mrs. Wu's apartment. Merry needed to check a map of the city, but she was sure there was nothing else quite like it in Livingsky. Even though Drover's building was technically on the "wrong side of the tracks", in many ways it was perfectly located; next to the new Riverside Plaza development, downtown, and the river, and tall enough to take advantage of the views. She thought about something she'd heard on one of those real estate reality shows based in New York City: if you want the best view, you don't live in Manhattan, you live somewhere that looks at it.

The more she thought about it, the bigger surprise would be if some smart developer hadn't already offered Drover a sky-high price to buy the Redberry Road property. And if so, were tenants like Mrs. Wu, with iron clad long-term leases, standing in his way of making a profitable sale? A more worrisome question popped into her head: what would happen to those leases if the building burned down?

Merry began to feel seasick on solid ground. She'd only just come to see her client in a potentially positive light, but now, with a sudden jarring shift of perspective, that light was flickering like crazy and dimming with each passing second. Maybe everything Mrs. Wu believed about Drover was nothing but a smokescreen, hiding who he truly was, more like his father than he let on. Maybe Detective Greyeyes was right, maybe her client *was* guilty of setting his own fire. But if that was true, why hire her? Was he so certain there was no proof to be found of his wrongdoing? Or, Merry wondered indignantly, did Gerald Drover see her as such an incompetent lightweight neophyte, he was confident she'd never find anything to compromise his declared innocence? But to what end? Answering these questions became her new number one priority.

CHAPTER 14

Returning to her office after visiting Mrs. Wu, now knowing she was dealing with two Drovers instead of one, Merry did a deep dive to find out what the internet had to say about Gerald Drover, Junior *and* Senior. Turned out, most of what Wu told her checked out. By all accounts, Senior was the king of all slum landlords. He routinely bought dilapidated properties for cheap, put paint on the pig, then rented them out to people who had no other choice for a variety of reasons—poverty, bad credit rating, naïveté, the need to hide. Merry could relate. Drover Senior spent his days in endless fights with City Hall, the Rentalsman, the Ombudsman, the Better Business Bureau, the fire department, the police service, oftentimes all at once. He appeared unfazed by unflattering media attention, threats of incarceration, vilification, or being socially and publicly ostracized. He thrived on being known as a bad man. The more he could get away with, the more he seemed to like it. Every time he found himself in hot water with one authority or another, he was first in line to talk with the media. He loved nothing better than to publicly air his grievances, portraying himself as the "little guy" being persecuted by "big business".

Whereas Merry found plenty of dirt on the elder Drover, on the flip side, she found next to nothing about Gerald Drover Junior. She was able to confirm most of what Mrs. Wu intimated, that Senior had signed over the family business, such as it was, to his son when he was in his late seventies (and about to head to jail). Over time, Gerald Junior paid off every fine and order of restitution, and quietly either sold, demolished, or repaired the Drover rental properties. Whatever was left weren't pretty, fancy or stylish, but they were safe.

It seemed Gerald Junior had some good in him after all. But in her years as an investigator, Merry had come to learn that not all bad guys are all bad, and not all good guys are all good.

When Drover texted Merry to say the junkyard was ready for occupancy, she was surprised when he suggested she pick up the keys at his home. It was the last thing she wanted to do but feeling guilty about the time she'd been spending investigating him instead of the fire, she agreed.

Gerald Drover lived in Alphabet City, where most of his rental holdings were. The house was nothing like what Merry expected. She'd imagined one of two very different options: a swanky highrise apartment, paid for by the tears of his less fortunate tenants, or the ragged backseat of his ridiculous car. Either would suit the kind of guy she suspected him to be. What stood before her, however, was neither. For the third time that day, Merry found herself questioning her client's character and struggling to figure out one thing: exactly who is Gerald Drover?

The modest home sat on a small lot encircled by a neat picket fence painted white. A cement walkway leading from street to front door was cracked in places and crumbling in others but had been freshly cleared of snow.

Climbing two steps onto a small porch, Merry paused for a deep breath. She chewed off a bit of lipstick then rapped lightly on the door, half hoping he wouldn't hear it and she could leave. It opened, just enough to reveal half of the tall, lanky figure of Gerald Drover. He wore his usual costume of Heavy Metal t-shirt and skinny jeans, but the cowboy boots were missing, replaced by two impossibly long, narrow, white-as-snow, bare feet. Who went barefoot in the middle of winter? The ginger mullet was in perfect, jaunty condition. A strange look crossed his face when he saw her.

"Hello, Merry," he greeted politely. "Would you like to come in?"

Merry. He called her Merry. Not Sweet Lips or Applesauce or any of the other completely inappropriate nicknames he typically used when he saw her. She frowned. Why did that irritate her? Did she actually like it when he called her Sweet Lips?

Merry nodded. Drover stepped aside. She entered. As he took her coat, gloves, and scarf, he gave her another funny look and asked: "Who are you supposed to be?"

Swear words exploded in Merry's head. How did this guy know exactly what to say to piss her off? She'd worked hard to look good for h...to look professional for this meeting. The grey slacks and matching blazer, despite coming off the rack at Value Village, fit her pretty well. Her makeup and hair were toned down like Brenda instructed. Yet this bozo was making fun of her, like she was wearing some sort of Hallowe'en costume! Instead of delivering a sound thwack up the side of his head, she admirably chose restraint. Drover was her client and about to become her landlord. For now anyway.

"What do you mean by that remark?" she asked through tight lips.

"Oh, it's nothing," he shrugged. "I liked how you looked the other day."

Just like that, he was on her good side again. She was glad she'd decided against the thwack, but that could easily change. Until that moment she hadn't considered how the new Merry might be viewed by people who were used to the old Merry. Now it made sense why he'd looked surprised when he opened the door. He didn't immediately recognize her. Was that why he stopped with the nicknames? Did she really look that different? Merry wasn't quite sure how she felt about that, but now wasn't the time to dwell on it.

Drover's eyes went buggy as he watched with concern the pendulum of looks flitting across Merry's face. "This looks good too," he quickly added.

"Maybe we should get to business," Merry suggested, moving out of the entryway into the living room.

If Merry thought the exterior of the house was unexpected, the inside was an even bigger surprise. The space was dominated by two overstuffed couches born in the fifties, with delicate crocheted doilies gracing the chubby arms and backs. A coffee table and several vintage étagère units lining the walls were being used to display delicate ceramic cats and an impressive collection of Royal Doulton china figurines, mostly elegant ladies wearing lacey gowns and fine bonnets. A curio cabinet in one corner exhibited Barbara Furstenhofer Fairy Tale Decorative Plates and a vitrine in another corner displayed a full set of dinnerware appliqued in the distinctive black and red pattern favoured by Ukrainian babas everywhere. The room was carpeted in deep, brown shag, but this was apparently not enough to prevent wear and tear as several area rugs in varying hues of beige had been strategically placed throughout.

Dumbfounded, Merry blurted out the first thing that popped into her mind. "Do you live with your grandmother?"

Gerald appeared unruffled by the implication. "I just moved in…well, I suppose it's been a year or so now. Have a seat if you want."

Merry chose a spot on a couch where she was least likely to disturb a doily.

"Do you want something to drink or eat? I have water and cold Pil and maybe some orange juice that might be out of date."

"No, thank you."

"Okay then," he responded with a quick flash of the gap in his front teeth which Merry decided was a smile. "So," he said, looking down at her, "you're here for your keys and to pay the damage deposit?"

"Actually," she responded, "I'm here to ask you to pay the damage deposit *and* first month's rent."

"Huh?"

"You owe LSI six hundred dollars for time and expenses. Aren't you going to sit down?" He was standing over her like some kind of bird of prey, vulture probably, and it was making her nervous.

"Six hundred dollars? For what? You haven't done anything

yet. Has the fire investigation been closed? I don't think so. Have they found the real culprit? I don't see anyone in jail. Far as I know, you've been sitting around polishing your fancy La-Boot-ens."

"Better than dusting lady dolls and pussy cat statues," she shot back and was immediately sorry. Everyone had their thing. Collecting stamps, sky diving, reading. It's just that never in a trillion years would she have pegged Gerald Drover as a figurine accumulator.

He countered with a baleful glare.

She stared back, not liking this new attitude one bit. It was so different, less…flirty, definitely much less fun. Was it because of her new look?

"They're not mine," he clarified, "the lady dolls and pussy cat statues. They were left behind by the former tenant. I haven't had time to figure out what to do with them. Or maybe I'll keep 'em. Who knows? They kinda grow on you."

"I've actually been doing quite a lot," Merry informed him, still irritated. "Getting my bearings, doing background work. I met with someone who quite possibly set the fire and I performed a stakeout hoping to identify the person who quite possibly hired them. I inspected your building—which you should know is embarrassingly easy to break into—and I interviewed several character witnesses." She hated having to explain herself and defend her activities to this pelican.

"You know who set the fire?" Drover sputtered a bit. "Character witnesses? Whose character are we talking about here?"

"I'll report when I'm ready to report."

"Which will be when exactly?"

"When I have facts, not supposition. My point, Mr. Dr…Gerald, is that you can't expect results overnight. Six hundred dollars is what we call an interim billing." It was also, Merry knew, an act of desperation. She didn't have enough money to pay the man and as grotesque as it was, she didn't want to risk losing the Junk House. *Why the hell is he just standing there*? "Are we sitting or standing?"

"I don't remember discussing any interim billing type situation."

Merry frowned. At Drover. At herself. As much as she hated to

admit it, Drover was right. She'd been lax in the paperwork department. All new clients should sign a contract, one that clearly spelled
out the details of their arrangement with LSI, including interim
billing protocols and maybe something about not having to explain
her every move. She made a mental note to ask Nathan if he had a
boiler plate version she could crib. Further, LSI was also going to
need an invoicing system, assuming someone other than her landlord actually hired her. Merry was coming to the sober realization
that running your own business is not a straightforward thing. But,
until she had things figured out, there was only one thing to do.
Merry reached into her purse, pulled out a pen, and wrote $600 on
her palm. If Drover wasn't going to sit, then she was going to stand.
Once on her feet she shoved the palm in his face.

"Here it is. Your interim bill."

He laughed. "You call that a bill? How am I supposed to report
that to CRA at tax time?"

She scoffed. "The same way you plan to report the rent I pay on
the junkyard."

"It's a scrap metal yard, not a junkyard."

"Do you think I'm stupid?" Given her growing suspicions about
Drover and why he may have hired her, she wasn't sure she wanted
him to answer that. "I know why you want the rent paid in cash. The
same reason you agreed to offset it against whatever I earn investigating your case." If she had any spare money to bet with, she'd put
it all on zero percent of her rent showing up on any tax form. She
had him. He knew it. She knew it.

Despite neither having moved much, both were breathing heavy,
staring at each other like two bulls in a china shop, waiting to see
which would be the first to move aside. Maybe neither would, and
they'd just break a bunch of Royal Doulton shit.

"The interim billing and collecting my key aren't the only reasons I'm here," Merry said, deciding a new subject was a good idea.

Drover dropped into one of the couches and perched his feet
on the coffee table, perfectly placing them between a mischie-
vous-looking Siamese cat and a figurine gleefully swinging a picnic

basket whilst her royal blue gown rippled in a non-existent wind. "Ooo," he said with a gap-tooth whistle, "this is gonna be good."

"Now we're sitting?"

"As long as you're comfortable hanging out with someone with my *bad reputation*."

Oh crap. Merry lowered herself into her original spot. "You talked to Douglas."

"Let's just say I had an interesting telephone call from a concerned tenant."

"As I mentioned, I met with several of your tenants," she began, adding with a pointed glare: "in the course of my interim-bill-earning investigation." She waited for an eyeroll which she took as grudging recognition that she'd been working on his behalf. "Douglas was one of those tenants." Merry said the words as slowly as she dared without Drover thinking she was having some kind of stroke. She needed time to figure out how to get out of this new mess she'd landed herself in. "From those conversations, I learned that I may have...misjudged you."

Gerald listened calmly, the pious look gracing his gopher face irritating Merry even further.

"I may have read some articles online which, as it turns out, were about your father, not you. It was an easy mistake to make." She waited for some kind of response but got none, just more pronounced piousness. Apparently, the man required a bit more grovelling. "I know it was your father who was the slum landlord, not you. I know he owned the buildings when the fires happened that killed those people, not you. I know that since you took over the company you've repaired properties that weren't safe to live in. I... admire that." She decided to stop there. There was no reason she had to lick his hideous cowboy boots just because she'd misinterpreted some information. "Your places are still crap, most of them, but they're not dangerous."

Gerald stared at Merry for a slow count of ten before saying, "I rent cheap places to cheap people. It's what they call a market niche. *You* are in that niche, Sweet Lips. You have no money. You need a place to live. I fulfill your need, right?"

She nodded. He called her Sweet Lips again. She let it go.

"I know what I do is not the most glamourous career, or the most respectable," Drover admitted, "but this city is full of poor people, new immigrants, people who can't get a job because they don't speak the language or don't have the education, people off the reserve or fresh from the farm looking to build a life in the city. They all need the same thing; a place to live until they get their shit together. Just like you. Hopefully they move on to something better one day. Some do. And when they do, there is always someone waiting in line to take their place. If there wasn't, I'd be out of business.

"The way my dad did things was wrong; no doubt about that. I'm trying to fix that and make it better, but I still gotta make a living, y'know? Some people say I take advantage of poor people, but they take advantage of me too. Without me, they'd be homeless. They'd be living in tents, like those people you see down by the river."

Merry blanched. Little did he know she had been perilously close to becoming one of *those people*.

"I made some incorrect assumptions about you. I shouldn't have mentioned them to your tenant. I apologize for that. I thought some bad stuff about you, I know most of it isn't true."

"*Most of it?*" Drover barked with laughter. "Meaning you think some of it is?"

She shot back with: "You are about to hand me keys to a rundown shack in the middle of a junkyard."

"Scrap metal yard."

"Fine. A rundown shack in the middle of a scrap metal yard. Do I have your word it won't burn down?"

"It might smoke a little," he teased.

Merry couldn't help herself. She laughed. In that moment they were two people who might just like each other. Merry kept the ludicrous possibility to herself.

Drover did not. "I think you're smoking too. I like you, Toots. A lot."

Eyes wide, Merry was stricken speechless.

Gerald pulled his narrow, pale feet off the coffee table and sat forward. Hunched low over his knees he inspected his long fingers. "You don't have to like me back," he mumbled, "that's okay. I'm used to it."

Merry stared at the ginger-hued Chia pet, quivering mullet spikes betraying the man's nervousness. He'd taken her silence as rejection. Was he right to do so? Is that what she wanted? To reject him? Of course it was. This was Gerald Drover. He wore a wallet chain and crusty cowboy boots. His hair was all sorts of crazy. He looked like the offspring of Gainer the Gopher and Wile E. Coyote.

She liked Gainer the Gopher and Wile E. Coyote.

Drover jumped up and began to move away. "I've got to go. Tenants to look after. I'll walk out with you."

Flustered, Merry followed Drover to the door. He suddenly seemed in a rush. They donned their outerwear and stepped outside.

"Gerald…"

But Drover was gone, taking extra-long strides as he covered the ground between the house and where Judi Dench was parked on the street.

Merry caught up with him just as he was getting inside the car.

"Gerald!"

He looked up, dizzying blue orbs bashfully peeking out from between those exceptionally thick eyelashes. "Yeah?"

"I'm a trans woman."

This is what she'd meant to tell him before the whole Douglas thing came up. Now that he was more than just a one-time client, she wanted there to be no awkwardness or confusion between them. His unexpected declaration of *like* was just another layer of complexity.

Without hesitation he responded with: "That's one of those letters in that LBQ-something-something, yeah?"

"Uh huh."

"That's cool. Does it mean you don't like dudes?"

"No, it does not."

"So, no problem then, right?"

Merry finally knew what it meant to feel discombobulated. There were so many conflicting emotions bubbling up inside her it was impossible to pin down a single one. The one thing she knew for certain was that Gerald Drover, with the breadth and depth of his unusualness, never failed to surprise her. She had no idea where she wanted this…relationship?…to go. At a minimum she thought it best to give the guy time to google the "T" in LGBTQ.

Merry cleared her throat and lied, "LSI has a strict policy against fraternization between its investigators and clients."

Gerald Drover pursed his lips, scrunched his gopher cheeks, and thought about this. Finally, he came up with: "I don't usually do fraternization stuff until the third date anyway. So, how about this weekend?"

Merry laughed. "Gerald, I have no time for dating. Besides, my weekend is full. I have another stakeout at The Hole on Friday night, and I'm moving into the junkyard on Saturday."

"Scrap metal yard," he corrected before driving off.

It was dark by the time Gerald Drover and Judi Dench left to deal with tenant issues. Merry returned to the front steps of his house to make use of the porch light while she secured an Uber. Her head was so full of cotton batting confusion over their interaction, she almost missed the unusual noise coming from Drover's backyard. Merry knew it was probably nothing more than cats rooting around garbage bins in the back alley, but she'd be a lousy P.I. if she didn't investigate. She also welcomed the distraction from having to think about Drover's asking her out on a date. That's what that was, right?

The path leading around the side of the house was more snow-trampled trail. Inching along the narrow route between the house and fence that separated Gerald's yard from the neighbour's, Merry made note to suggest to Drover that he invest in outdoor security lighting.

Reaching the backyard, she pulled out her phone and engaged the flashlight app. She jumped back with a start when the abrupt illumination caused something (or someone?) to scuttle off at high speed. *What the hell?*

Stepping further into the yard she spotted a small shed at the far end.

The door was hanging open.

"Hello? Is someone there?" she called out, her breath hanging in the frigid air.

No answer.

Step by step she slowly worked her way toward the shed. She wasn't sure if she was shivering from cold or fear.

With the flashlight leading the way, Merry cautiously breached the entrance of the shed.

"Hello?"

Still no response.

"We're coming in," she warned, using the plural intentionally. "So, if you're in there, you better say so."

No answer.

She stepped inside.

She felt around for a light switch but found none. Like a lighthouse beacon, she slowly swung the phone's light across the small space, left to right, right to left, top to bottom. By all appearances, this was a typical shed, used as storage for gardening and other miscellaneous outdoor equipment. Having never been in the shed before, she had no way of knowing whether anything was amiss or missing. Engaging the camera's flash, she snapped a few photos. She'd forward them to Drover later.

Stepping outside, Merry secured the door behind her and took one last look around the dark yard. She spotted nothing of interest, not even the set of eyes watching her every move.

CHAPTER 15

It was late Friday afternoon when Merry heard a light rap on her office door. She looked up to see Alvin Smallinsky standing there holding a heavy stock, off-white envelope like a trophy. *Oh god*, she thought, *was it really his birthday?*

She'd had little to do with her landlord since moving in (in more ways than one), other than brief greetings in the building's foyer and idle chit chat in the shared coffee room waiting for the Nespresso machine (the tortoise of all coffee makers) to do its thing. It wasn't that she didn't want to get to know the man, but until she was no longer a squatter in his building, it just didn't feel right.

"Alvin!" she greeted a little too loudly. "Hello."

Smallinsky was the type of man who people might be inclined to miss in a crowd. He wasn't tall or short, handsome or ugly, he didn't dress poorly or sharply, there was nothing immediately obvious or distinct about him. None of that fooled Merry. She believed everyone had at least one distinctive characteristic. It might be good distinctive, or bad distinctive, but once discovered it would provide the key to knowing that person. She shunned easy labels. For instance, she didn't buy Smallinsky as the stereotypical bland, nerdy accountant. To the contrary, she suspected something quite different lurked beneath the CPA's carefully curated vanilla exterior, she just hadn't had enough time with him to figure it out.

"Hello, Merry," he said, a quizzical look crossing his face as he registered his renter's new look. "Sorry to barge in like this." He barged in anyway.

ANTHONY BIDULKA 125

"No problem. I need a break anyway."

That seemed to interest him. "Oh? Working on a difficult case?"

Was he drilling her for juicy details? People liked to do that with detectives and police officers and doctors, professions with ripe potential for stories that were grisly, gory or titillating. "Something like that."

A professional himself, Smallinsky knew enough to move on. "Merry, I need to talk to you about something."

A crooked smile froze on Merry's face. *Crap.* Did Design's by Brenda turn her in after all? Did her willingness to act as a human birthday present and indulge in girl time bonding over a makeup mirror mean nothing? And then, as if she were Beetlejuice summoned by hearing her name (though Merry was quite certain she hadn't said it out loud), the designer appeared at the door.

"Hello, co-workers!" Brenda chirped in an octave higher than her regular speaking voice.

Technically, Merry thought to herself, they were not co-workers, they were people who happened to work in the same building.

Brenda tickled the door with perfectly manicured, double-bubble-pink nails in lieu of a knock and stepped inside. "May I come in?"

Merry debated a return chirp of: "No, but thanks for dropping by."

Bestowing a perfect smile onto Smallinsky, Brenda explained her intrusion: "I saw you coming into Merry's office, Alvin, and thought maybe you were thinking the exact same thing I was!"

"Oh?" he said, looking doubtful. "What might that be?"

"That we should welcome Merry to the building with a Friday afternoon drinks thingy. You know, like the suggestion I put in the suggestion box about welcoming new tenants."

Merry had an innate dislike for anything referred to as "a thingy" but said nothing.

"Weren't you the one who set up the suggestion box in the first place?" he asked.

"Mmmhmm."

Smallinsky looked worried. "Am I the one who's supposed to read the suggestions?"

Brenda's brow furrowed but she quickly hid her disappointment and moved on. "I've got a bottle of Sauvignon blanc in my office," she exclaimed, "I could just scoot over there and get it."

"Actually, I'm glad you're here, Brenda," Smallinsky said, bypassing the offer.

Merry felt a hive of wasps invade her insides. *Here we go.* Smallinsky was going to confront her with Brenda's accusations in front of the snitch herself. Having an open, in-person discussion was the best way to get to the bottom of any she-said/she-said debate, and Merry might do the same thing if she were in Smallinsky's unremarkable shoes, but that didn't mean she was going to make it easy for either of them.

Smallinsky waved the envelope in the air. "Does anyone know what this is?

Did Brenda actually record her accusation in a letter?

Brenda stepped closer, narrowing her eyes to get a better look. "It looks like an invitation."

Smallinsky appeared crestfallen that she'd guessed correctly. "Well, yes, it is an invitation. But an invitation to what?"

"I don't know," the designer, hand at chest, responded breathlessly.

Merry wished the two would just leave her office.

"Of course you don't, because we've never gotten one of these before." With a flourish that was very non-accountant-like—*was that his distinctive characteristic?*—Smallinsky pulled a 5x7 card from the envelope. "This invitation is for next week's Mayor's Gala!" he cried.

"What's that?" Merry asked. She knew what a gala was, not that she'd ever been to one, but what did it have to do with the mayor?

Brenda squealed with delight before answering the question. "The Mayor's Gala is arguably the most important social event of the year. Attendance is by invitation only. For months Livingsky business owners cross their fingers in the hopes of receiving one of those envelopes. *Officially* it's known as an appreciation event for individuals and organizations who've contributed to the betterment of Livingsky over the past twelve months."

"And unofficially?"

Brenda grinned naughtily. "It means you're in the mayor's good books! An invitation almost guarantees a bump in business. They publish a list of attendees in the Tribune. That exposure alone is worth more than any advertising campaign." She stopped there, a worried look suddenly paining her face. She turned to address Smallinsky. "Alvin, is this an invitation for your accounting practice, or...?"

Alvin, despite being a bit miffed that Brenda hijacked his news, brightened. "As you can see," he hoisted the envelope into the sky like it was Simba in *The Lion King* and he was *Mufasa*, "it's addressed to 'All the Tenants of 222 Craving Lane'. They followed up with a telephone call this afternoon. I confirmed it, we're all invited."

Merry's head tilted to one side. "Really? They called you?" She didn't know anything about galas, but that seemed a little desperate.

"Apparently they became concerned when they didn't receive our RSVP. They were concerned the invitation had gotten waylaid in the mail, which it must have, because this one just arrived by courier and the gala is only a couple of days away. The caller clearly stated that I, along with all of my tenants, were included, and," he nodded in Merry's direction, "he specifically requested I encourage newer tenants to attend."

Brenda frowned prettily. "Why would they say that? The gala celebrates people and businesses who've contributed to Livingsky's well-being over the past year. Certainly, Smallinsky Accounting qualifies, as does Designs by Brenda, but, no offence," she said with a quick glance at Merry, "she just got here."

More than anything else in the world, Merry's business needed exposure. If Alvin and Brenda were right about the gala, attending the event could change everything. LSI needed a boost. Badly. Her entire client roster consisted of one person: Gerald Drover. If he turned out to be shady (which was still open for debate), their association was the sort of thing that could ruin a reputation. Not to mention the niggling fact that she'd been identified by the Livingsky Police Service as being connected to a Vancouver murder investigation (a fact she kept stashed as far back in her mind as possible). If either of those unfortunate realities got out, she and LSI could easily find themselves painted with the same grimy brush. On the other hand, if she insisted on attending the event, would it piss off the woman holding damning information over her head, which could get her kicked out of 222 Craving Lane? People who ran their business out of a knapsack were probably not the desired demographic for the Mayor's Gala.

The timing sucked. The gala was Monday night, she was moving into the junkyard on Saturday, but as of right now, her undies and hair scrunchies were still in residence in the filing cabinets only a short distance from where Smallinsky and Brenda now stood. "I don't have to go," Merry offered rather weakly. Inside her head she was chanting: *I have to go, I have to go, I have to go.*

Smallinsky immediately countered Merry's objection. "You do have to go," he said, almost forcefully. "I want a strong showing from 222 Craving Lane. I want the mayor to know, without doubt, that this invitation did not go to waste. I want to prove that her confidence in me, and the tenants of this building, was not misplaced."

Brenda gamely recovered. "Of course. You're right." She turned a set of liquid cow eyes onto Merry as if it were Merry who'd questioned her own attendance and not her. "Merry, you have to come, you just have to. We're in this together. Say you will?"

"Sure. I can do that."

"Outstanding," Smallinsky declared. "I'll send the details by email." With that, he left the office, leaving Brenda and Merry to stare at one another.

"Thank you," Merry said, relieved the meeting hadn't turned into a battle over her squatting rights as she was worried it might. "I know you think I haven't been around long enough to deserve the invitation, and you're probably right about that, but I am grateful to be included. Thank you for supporting that."

"Of course you should go," Brenda replied, making as if to leave. She stopped at the door, turned around, and said, "Oh, I almost forgot," she smiled benignly as if the silly thought had just occurred to her. "I wonder if you could do me a wee itty-bitty favour?"

It was just before eleven at night when Roger Brown pulled up in front of 222 Craving Lane in a sleek, silver Cadillac Escalade. Apparently, Merry mused as she eyed up the fancy wheels, the Browns were the kind of couple who were incapable of keeping secrets from one another. Roger had come clean to Brenda about what happened at the end of his birthday night, when he slipped Merry a note which had in fact helped to progress her investigation. He also communicated his hopefulness in continuing in his role as a self-appointed informal assistant to LSI's lead investigator, Merry Bell.

The last thing Merry wanted was a wannabe detective hanging around who thought he knew something about real world crime investigations just because he talked about it on air, but her hands were tied. Although Brenda never came right out and said it, the message was clear: indulge my husband or I'll spill the beans about your living situation and get your invitation to the Mayor's Gala revoked. Unspoken threat aside, Roger had done Merry a favour, and it seemed petty not to give him something in return. Besides, she needed the ride.

"Thanks for coming." Merry said as she slipped into the passenger seat and fastened her seatbelt. "I know it's late and you probably have clients first thing in the morning."

"This is totally worth it," he responded with the brilliant smile of someone who was very excited about what they were about to do. "My first appointment is a simple hot tub hook up. I can do those in my sleep. Not that I ever would," he quickly added in case Merry didn't know he was joking.

Merry nodded her understanding. "Let's do this," she said, wishing Roger drove a less noticeable vehicle. A brand-new Escalade, so clean it sparkled in the moonlight, was not the best option for surveillance work, especially at a place like The Hole, but beggars couldn't be choosers.

"Am I dressed alright? This was so last minute I didn't have time to find my black turtleneck."

Merry gave the man a once over. In a way, Roger Brown, with his friendly, everyman vibe, was perfect for this kind of work no matter what he wore. "You're fine."

They drove in silence for a few minutes; out of downtown, across the railway tracks, into the depths of Alphabet City.

"Roger, I have a question for you."

Excitedly anticipating a discussion about crime solving techniques or perhaps Livingsky felony statistics, he turned to give his car mate as much attention as he could without getting them into an accident. "Super, what is it?"

"I've tried several times to find your podcast, but I must be doing something wrong. I've searched using all the parameters I can think of for a Livingsky true crime podcast. I even tried searching under your first name and last name, but I come up with nothing. Well, not nothing. There is one podcast that always pops up, but it's hosted by someone named Stella. Have you heard of her?"

Immediately returning his full attention to the road ahead, he mumbled an answer under his breath. "I have."

"Well, you better watch out. I don't know a lot about podcasts, but I'd say you have some strong competition there. I listened to a couple of episodes and I have to admit, she's smart and seems to know what she's talking about. Who would have thought a place like Livingsky would have even a single podcast dedicated to talking about crime, never mind two?"

When Roger didn't say anything after thirty seconds, Merry wondered if she'd put her foot in it. "I'm sorry, do you not like talking about other podcasts? Are you and Stella mortal enemies or something?" she asked with a light chuckle meant to lighten the mood.

"Hardly," Roger finally said. "And thank you for the compliment.

It means a lot coming from a professional crime investigator like you."

Merry frowned. *Compliment? Am I missing something here?*

Turns out, she was. Something big.

"You're right. There is only one true crime podcast in Livingsky," Roger told Merry.

"You mean, like, only one that counts?"

"*The Darkside of Livingsky*, the one you listened to, is my podcast."

Merry peered through the dim lighting hoping to catch something on Roger Brown's face that would help her understand, but all she found was a firm and determined profile, eyes fiercely focused on the road ahead as if glued there.

"Uh, okay."

"I am the host. I'm Stella."

Merry didn't know what to say, so she went with nothing.

"Would it be okay if I pulled over for a minute?"

"Yeah, sure, of course."

The Escalade slid smoothly into an empty spot on a street populated with small homes, most of them dark or with the telltale flicker of a TV screen strobing in a window. Outside was icy and cold, but the luxury vehicle's highly efficient heater kept the cab cozy and warm, without so much as a hiss of sound.

Merry began. "I take it there's something I don't know that maybe I should? Or maybe I shouldn't, I don't know. You tell me." Merry stopped there, realizing she was spouting nonsense and that this was one of those times when it was best to keep quiet and listen.

"Merry, I'm a crossdresser. I am Stella. Stella is me when I'm crossdressing."

Merry nodded slowly as she took in the information. "Okay."

"This isn't something I tell people, so I'm not even sure I know how to. Are you alright talking about this?"

"Are you telling me this because I'm transgender? Because if you are, I don't think they're the same thing, I don't know if I can help you."

"I'm not asking for help. I've been a crossdresser for many years. I know how to do it." He looked at her and tried a grin. "Pretty well, I think. Especially with Brenda's expertise. You know how good she is at makeup and stuff."

"Brenda knows?"

"Yes, of course. But to answer your question, I'm not telling you this because you're transgender. I'm telling you this because, as you can probably tell, my podcast is very important to me. Delving into crimes and how they happen and how they're solved is something I really enjoy. To have this time with you, doing what we're doing tonight, is...well, it's a wonderful thing for me. Because Stella and the podcast are intertwined, I feel it's only right that I be honest with you. If I expect you to be straight up with me, I should be willing to do the same, right?"

Merry gulped. How had doing a favour for her passive aggressive office neighbour turned into this? "Right."

"Obviously being a crossdresser is not a mainstream kind of thing."

"I have some experience with that," Merry said.

"I've struggled and continue to struggle with how to make it part of my life, part of my marriage, part of my family, without having any of those things blow up in my face."

"Can I ask what is probably a stupid question—and please don't say there's no such thing as a stupid question, because I know there is—I'm just not sure if this is one."

"Go for it."

"It's a simple question, but maybe not so simple to answer. You talk about making crossdressing part of your life, part of your marriage, but why? Why do it if it has the potential to blow them up?"

"Not a stupid question by the way. The best way I can put it is that I have to do it. It's part of who I am. Always has been. I know that because of how it makes me feel, how I feel when I'm Stella."

"It makes you feel feminine?"

"No. It makes me feel calm. I'm calm when I'm Stella."

Merry quickly sucked in and expelled a breath. She did not expect that answer.

"Before I started the podcast, the times when I could safely be Stella were few and far between. I was anxious all of the time. My moods were unpredictable, I worried about things I didn't need to worry about, my work suffered, so did my relationship with Brenda and the kids. But whenever I found an opportunity to dress, it was weird, it literally felt like relief was pouring into me. When Stella emerged, I felt calm, at peace. I felt like me.

"It took time to put two and two together. At first I thought, *Well, I guess I'm just an anxious kind of guy who happens to be a crossdresser.* Turns out, they weren't mutually exclusive.

"I'd already started a podcast about crime, nothing as big as what I'm doing now, but I really loved doing it. It was actually Brenda who came up with the idea. She thought if I had a regular 'appointment' to be Stella and tied it to the podcast which I also wanted to do regularly, maybe I could kill two birds with one stone. It worked. I shut down my old podcast (which wasn't too big of a deal because I had less than ten regular subscribers), and a few weeks later I started *The Darkside of Livingsky* with Stella as the host. The great thing about radio is that the only thing my subscribers really know about Stella is her voice and her ability to host a crime podcast. Fortunately, she's really good at it. Better than I ever was.

"It's perfect. At least once a week, sometimes more, I go to my private studio in the basement, become Stella, and host my show. The kids know it's my private time and that they shouldn't disturb me. I get to do two things that make me very happy every week. How many people can say that? My marriage is better, my work is better, my whole life is better because of Stella and the podcast."

"Wow, Roger...do I call you Roger?"

He smiled. "Yes, of course."

"It's a lot to take in. I don't know what to say other than how impressed I am. You've not only found a way to make your own life better, but the lives of the people around you, your wife, your kids, your business partner, clients. It's truly remarkable. You don't know me very well, but I want you to know I don't say this lightly. I'm not someone who is easily impressed."

Roger let out a sigh he wasn't aware he'd been holding in. "Thank you." He shifted into Drive indicating the conversation was over. "Now let's go catch a bad guy."

✛

Seeing a beehive of activity swarming the area as the Escalade idled past the front entrance of The Hole, Roger let out a low whistle. "Looks like we're late to the party."

Two police cruisers, one in the parking lot, the other on a side street, were lighting up the neighbourhood like a Christmas tree, blue and red lights leaping from building to building, snow bank to snow bank. Sirens in the distance told them more of the same was on the way.

From the passenger seat, Merry stared at the ruckus with a mixture of curiosity and frustration. After their previous failure, Nicky Sokolov had suggested a weekend night might provide a better opportunity to spot the man who'd paid to set the Drover fire. Merry knew there was an even chance the pawnshop owner was simply hoping for another night of free drinks, but for right now, he was her best lead. This mess, whatever it was, threatened to derail the plan.

"What is going on here?" she wondered, trying to see beyond the crowd that had gathered around the place.

A driver behind them honked their horn. A policeman's flashlight encouraged traffic to keep moving. Rubberneckers were not welcome. "I don't know, but I have to keep going."

"Take the first parking spot you see."

A few minutes later, having left the SUV parked a block-and-a-half away, Merry and Roger joined the throng in the alley behind the bar. Merry knew that at most they only had a few minutes before more cops arrived and secured the scene. They'd already managed to set up barriers between the gawkers and whatever it was everyone was gawking at.

"Are we meeting Nicky inside or out?" Roger asked.

"Inside," Merry told him. "Depending on what this fuss is all about, the cops might close down the bar."

"That's not good for us," Roger pointed out.

Merry grimaced. "Nope."

"Let's get in there then," Roger suggested, turning away from the crowd and heading toward the bar's front door.

"Hold on."

Merry dived into the melee, asking whoever would listen: "What's going on? Do you know what's happening?"

"Some guy got beat up," a middle-aged farmer type with a significant beer belly protruding out the front of an unzipped parka spoke up. "Pretty bad by the looks of it. Lots of blood."

"Just one guy?" Merry asked. "Where's the other one?"

He shrugged. "Must have run off. Jeez, it's cold as a witch's tit out here." He eyed up Merry and winked. "Can I buy you a beer inside?"

"Merry!" Roger called out, having somehow managed to get near the front of the crowd.

"Maybe another time," Merry responded, moving toward Roger, stepping on a few toes along the way.

"You've got to see this," he said when she got there.

Merry pulled abreast of her de facto assistant and took in the grim sight, ready for anything but what she saw.

There was something familiar about the battered body on the ground.

It was someone she knew.

Nicky Sokolov.

With warning shouts and a show of brute force, a phalanx of newly arrived uniformed officers pushed back the crowd. Most went willingly, having already seen enough and anxious to warm up inside with some hard liquor. A few complained about their right to stand where they wanted to. Some were mad because they hadn't gotten their turn to get close enough for a decent selfie featuring them and the gore. Officers calmly but firmly explained the error of their ways.

Not interested in being told twice, Merry and Roger slowly backed away, stunned.

"Come on." Merry led Roger back to the SUV, neither saying a word.

"What now?" Roger asked once they were inside the vehicle with its heater cranked to high.

"Good question," Merry muttered.

Staring out of the passenger side window, Merry's mind raced as she considered the possible implications of what they'd just seen. Suddenly, from the corner of her eye, she spotted a dark figure dashing across the street. It was a man, speeding away from The Hole. She leaned close to the window, the warmth of her breath clouding the glass. Hastily wiping the glass clear, she studied the figure.

"No way," she whispered.

CHAPTER 16

It was not the best day to be moving. Right after lunch the sky had erupted like a giant bag of shredded coconut torn open by a hungry gorilla. By late afternoon the city was coated in several inches of snow with more to come. Merry had spent much of the day dissecting recent events, mapping out every possible alternate reality they foretold, and how they impacted her case. It was a dizzying and exasperating exercise.

Merry's interviews with the tenants of the Drover building on Redberry Road where the fire occurred, especially the one with Mrs. Wu, presented contradictory information. While some of what she learned made it seem possible that Gerald Drover was a good guy who quite conceivably could be the hapless victim of arson, other niggling revelations led her to wonder if the opposite could just as well be true. She'd spent hours digging up whatever she could about Drover's properties, previous fires, fines levied, bylaw violations, insurance coverage and subsequent claims, both before and after Drover Junior took over from Drover Senior. Maddeningly, she discovered nothing to convince her with any certainty which of the two possible faces of Gerald Drover Junior was the real one.

Adding weight to her concerns was the previous night's beating of Nicky Sokolov outside of The Hole. A meagerly worded media release from the LPS revealed little other than that "the victim" had survived the beating and was taken to hospital with "serious injuries". Working the phones, Merry tried her best to squeeze out more information, but police and hospital personnel were commendably

(but frustratingly) tight-lipped. Was the attack purely coinciden-
tal, a random act of violence? Or was Nicky specifically targeted?
Even if he was, it might have absolutely nothing to do with Merry's case. Pawnshop owners were notorious for making enemies.
It wasn't inconceivable to think there might be a long list of people
who thought they'd been cheated by Nicky and decided to get back
at him by way of fist sandwich. Not to mention, Nicky Sokolov was
a bit of a dick. Dicks get their faces punched all of the time.

On the other hand, what if Nicky's beating *was* related to the
case? Could it have been a message meant for Merry? This was
a particularly disturbing line of thinking, but one she needed to
consider. If it was true, that meant Nicky had blabbed about her to
someone. But who? The man who'd hired him to set the fire (because no one believed it was a "friend" of Nicky's who'd done the
deed)? Was it possible he went to the cops? Was he a snitch? But
the police wouldn't beat up a source. Would they? Dirty cops on the
Livingsky Police Service was an alarming thought.

There was one more option.

Had Nicky Sokolov talked to Drover?

Contemplating the unsettling notion that her client might actually be her adversary was like having to swallow cough medicine;
you know it's going to taste like crap, you don't want to do it, but
you know you should.

Was Drover worried she was getting too close to the truth? A
truth he'd felt was so well hidden she'd never uncover it or was too
incompetent to? Or had he actually hired her for another purpose
altogether? Why would someone guilty of a crime hire a detective
to prove their innocence? Was it so she could do exactly what she
did: talk to his tenants and collect glowing reviews that painted
Drover as a saintly landlord? Doug, Mrs. Wu—were they plants?
Would Drover call her in a few days and, all innocent-sounding,
say something like, *Oh, by the way, would you mind sharing your
findings with the police? Media? Insurance company?* Was he flirting
with her to keep her on his good side, blind her to who he really
was? Was she, kickass private detective Merry Bell, being played?

The prospect triggered an unruly horde of insecurities and was beginning to make her feel physically ill.

Little did she know, the worst was yet to come.

Thanks to the brewing storm outside, the room had fallen into a depressing shade of blah when Merry heard a sharp rap on her outer door. Most Craving Lane tenants were Monday-to-Friday nine-to-fivers, and this was Saturday, so she couldn't begin to guess who might be seeking her out. She hoped it wasn't Designs by Brenda come to inspect her office for signs of illicit residency.

Instead of calling out for whoever was out there to enter, she jumped up to greet the unexpected guest at the door, where she would have more control over the length of interaction. Once a visitor was inside, especially someone like Brenda, it was harder to get rid of them. As luck, all bad, would have it, the person she found on the other side of the door was indeed someone she really didn't want to see.

"Detective Greyeyes," Merry greeted the cop, "This is a surprise."

The woman's face, all sharp angles and intensity, was unreadable as she nodded and responded with: "I took a chance you might be at work on Saturday." Giving the waiting room a thorough once over, she added meaningfully, "Seeing as I still don't have a home address for you and it seems the phone number you gave me was incorrect."

Merry had forgotten about intentionally transposing the last two numbers. "Sorry about that. I'm borderline dyslexic." A handy lie she'd used before.

Studying the cop's face closer, Merry found something unexpected. Confusion. And then it hit her. Greyeyes was seeing a very different Merry Bell from the one she first met. Gone were the too-tight, too-bright clothes, big hair, and aggressive makeup. This Merry Bell looked more like a serious professional (on a budget). Was this damn makeover going to screw her over? Greyeyes would have every reason to question the change and perhaps wonder if she was purposefully attempting to disguise herself—something a criminal would do.

"May I come in?"

Unable to think of a good reason to say no, Merry stepped aside and invited the cop into her office, indicating the chair in front of the desk while she returned to hers behind it.

"The front door is locked on Saturdays. How did you get in?" Merry asked when they were both settled.

"Sorry about that. I should have buzzed, but another tenant was leaving when I arrived and let me in."

Not good. "How can I help you today?"

"Consider this a follow up visit to our meeting the other day."

"Oh. I didn't realize there was anything to follow up on," Merry said, her voice dripping with courteousness. "Is there something more you'd like to tell me about the fire at Redberry Road?"

Just as she had in the vestibule, Greyeyes made no effort to hide her examination of her surroundings. Dark, interrogating eyes methodically roamed every surface before finally landing back on Merry. "You're a private investigator?"

"Yes."

"I don't remember you mentioning that fact when we first met."

"I don't remember you asking about my work." Feeling the conversation leaning dangerously close to the edge of civility, Merry smiled and quickly added, "Of course I wouldn't have expected you to. What I do for a living had no bearing on our discussion."

"Have you been practicing long?"

"Several years. Mostly in British Columbia."

Greyeyes tilted her chin up then down in slow order, as if using the time to process the information. "*Do* you have a current home address?"

Merry's chin rose, as if in defiance, hardly noticeable except to someone like Detective Sergeant Veronica Greyeyes.

"I don't." Technically not a lie. She wasn't formally moving into the Junk House until this evening. Merry decided, perhaps a tad churlishly, to keep that bit of information to herself for now. Greyeyes needed no help from her. The cop had already discovered where she worked, her status as a private investigator and, by extension, that she was something more than she'd portrayed herself to be in their first interaction. That was more than enough for now.

"Where do you sleep?"

Before she realized what she was doing, Merry's eyes reflexively moved to the floor. She quickly recovered, moving her focus to her hands, hoping Greyeyes didn't catch the slip. She loved her new hands. The fingers were long and slim, and her nails had grown in beautifully, not claw-like or ultra long like some girls liked to keep them.

Greyeyes noticed. "Do you need help?"

Merry looked up, taken off guard by the question and genuine compassion on the other woman's face. Greyeyes was tough as nails and just as capable of scratching if necessary, but she'd just revealed a gentler, compassionate side, something she undoubtedly did her best to keep hidden. Good to know. "Thank you, no."

"I understand."

Determined to steer the conversation away from herself and her living situation, Merry said, "I believe I told you last time we met that I probably wouldn't be moving into the Redberry building. But if there's something more you'd like to tell me about the property, I'd be happy to hear it." In her business, information was the most valuable commodity of all. If there was more the police officer wanted to share, who was she to turn it down?

"No. Nothing about Redberry."

Merry felt the tiny hairs on the back of her neck stand up, one by one, like a row of tiny prisoners about to face a firing squad. She knew what was coming next.

"I thought we could talk a little more about Elliott Vanstone."

Shit. "Oh?"

"I believe I owe you an apology," Greyeyes declared. "When we last met, you indicated Dr. Vanstone's death was a surprise to you. I realized later that, with your having experienced a shock, it may not have been the most opportune time for us to talk." Greyeyes' gaze never left Merry's face. "Now that you've had time to process the information, I wonder if there's anything you'd like to amend about your statement, perhaps about your relationship with the victim?"

Merry felt like gagging but didn't dare in front of Greyeyes. Not only had Merry omitted the truth, she'd outright lied when Greyeyes first asked about Vanstone. Did the cop know that or was she merely fishing to see what she might catch?

"He was my doctor," Merry repeated what she'd already told the officer.

Greyeyes pulled out her phone, tapped a few buttons, then studied the tiny screen. She said, "My understanding is that Dr. Vanstone was a specialist in gender affirming surgeries, specifically—please excuse me if I'm using incorrect or inappropriate terminology here—what people refer to as bottom surgeries."

Merry refused to blink. "That's correct." It was becoming glaringly obvious that Detective Sergeant Veronica Greyeyes knew a great deal more about her than when they'd first met. But how much more?

The police officer proceeded in a way that said she knew she was on fragile ground. "For clarity then, Dr. Vanstone was your surgeon?"

"That's correct."

"I know this is deeply personal information and I appreciate your agreeing to speak with me today."

Did I agree? I don't think so. Crafty girl.

Looking down at her phone again, avoiding eye contact, Greyeyes said: "The Vancouver Police have learned, from more than one of Dr. Vanstone's patients, that he habitually initiated sexual relationships with them, post recovery, in lieu of final payment for their surgical procedures. Were you aware of this?"

Merry swallowed hard. *Fuck.* "I was not."

Lifting her gaze from the phone, Greyeyes asked softly, "How would you describe your post surgical relationship with Dr. Elliott Vanstone?"

Merry grew lightheaded. The serious-looking official in front of her was beginning to sway right to left. Shit! What was happening?

Was she about to pass out? She needed to get control of herself. Quickly. What to say? *What to say?*

"Merry, are you alright?" Greyeyes asked, concern in her voice.

When asked the question a couple of days ago, Merry had indicated that her relationship with Vanstone did not go beyond doctor-patient. The Vancouver police might suspect that was not the case, but there was no way they could know for sure. *Was there?* Was Greyeyes pretending she'd never asked the question in the first place to give her a second chance at telling the truth without the guilt of being revealed as someone who lied to the police?

"How many?" Merry responded, her voice exposing the tension she felt.

"Excuse me?"

"How many girls was he having sex with?"

Greyeyes gazed at Merry unflinchingly. "I'm not at liberty to share that information with you."

Merry knew that's what she'd say, but she needed the time to decide what to do. From what the detective had said earlier, it seemed likely there was more than one girl having sex with Vanstone. But how did the cops know? Did the girls confess? Or was there something more? Was it possible Vanstone was stupid enough to keep some sort of record or, god forbid, taken clandestine pictures or videos? If that was true… *Fuck!*

"Yes."

Greyeyes stiffened. "Yes what?"

Merry looked away and bit the inside of her lip. Hard. What was she doing? She'd never admitted, out loud, any of this to anyone before. So why now? Why to this woman? Was it because Veronica Greyeyes had the power to throw her in jail and toss away the key if she didn't fess up? Was it simply because no one had ever asked before? Was it because she was being backed into a corner and this might be her only way out? Or was it something more?

Merry shifted in her seat, straightened her back, and looked the detective straight in the eyes, chin held high. "Yes, that is how I'd describe my post-surgical relationship with Dr. Vanstone."

The police officer pocketed her phone and gave Merry her full attention. "To be clear, you were having sex with Vanstone?"

"Yes."

"In exchange for a reduction of your surgical bill?"

Merry smirked without evidence of humour in her face. "What you really want to ask is if I had sex with him for money."

"That is not what I asked."

Merry firmed her jaw and stared at the other woman. "Let me put it to you this way, Detective Sergeant, it was a mutually beneficial relationship."

For the first time, Greyeyes face betrayed her, revealing the look of a top seeded tennis player who'd suddenly forgotten how to play the sport and found herself face to face with a powerful opponent she wasn't certain she could beat. "Can you tell me what you mean by that?" she asked carefully.

"Of course. Yes, he got sex, and yes, I didn't have to pay the rest of a bill I couldn't afford to pay. But I also got something else, something I really wanted."

"What was that?"

"Experience."

"I don't understand."

Now it was Merry's turn to lean in, fastening her eyes onto the other woman's. "Imagine, if you can, waking up one day to find that the sexual organs you'd always hoped for, the ones you should have been born with, are suddenly right where they were always supposed to be. It's like having a brand new toy you have no idea how to play with, and there's no one around to show you.

"The sexual life of a transgender person after surgery is not this sudden free for all. Finding partners is not an easy thing, especially partners who know and care about what you're going through. Are you married, Detective Greyeyes?"

"I am."

"Think about all the guys you dated before you settled on Mr. Right. How many of them do you think, upon getting someone like me in the back seat of their car or in their bedroom, would like it when I pointed to my vagina and said: *it's brand new and I'm not sure if it's going to work but let's give it a go*?" Merry said this last bit with a small smile. The atmosphere in the office was heavy and in desperate need of even a small shot of levity. "That's not quite what happens, but can you understand what I'm getting at?"

Greyeyes nodded but said nothing.

"When Elliott," she used the doctor's first name intentionally, "first suggested a sexual relationship, frankly, I was grateful. He built the thing after all. Who better to show me how to use it, help me work out any kinks and learn how to enjoy sex again—no, wait, not again, how to enjoy sex, really enjoy it, for the first time. Of course, I felt a little icky about the money thing, but I really needed it and decided to see it as a side benefit of an already good deal. Judge me if you want."

"I am not in the business of judging anyone," Greyeyes murmured.

"The only reason I moved back to Livingsky was because I was too broke to stay in Vancouver. I'm still poor as hell, but without Vanstone discounting my bill, I wouldn't have been able to get myself this far. In truth, without him, I don't know where I'd be right now."

Veronica Greyeyes fell silent. As did Merry.

Reading the other woman's strong-featured face, Merry saw the bitter truth revealed there. She'd been tricked. Veronica Greyeyes didn't know about her involvement with Vanstone until now. Merry had made a judgement call by telling the truth about their relationship and it turned out to be a mistake. If she'd simply been revealed as a liar, who knew what the consequences might have been, but now she'd revealed herself as something much more dangerous: a very likely suspect. The only hope was that some of the other women who'd admitted to sexual relationships with Dr. Douchebag had less-glowing reports, placing them nearer the top of the suspect list.

Merry startled to attention when Greyeyes asked the only question left to ask. "Merry, did you kill Elliott Vanstone?"

CHAPTER 17

Sergeant Greyeyes left Craving Lane at quarter past five. The timing was good. If anyone was working on a Saturday, Merry hoped they'd have called it a day by then. Her luggage was packed and she was ready to make her move. She'd hoped to have clear sailing out of the building, but a quick inspection of the hallway revealed that Ms. Designs by Brenda next door, the person she least wanted catching sight of her hauling suitcases down the staircase, was working overtime.

By five thirty she couldn't stand it any longer. Pretending she was walking by, Merry stuck her nose through the open doorway. Brenda was sitting at her desk, scrolling through her phone, looking unhappy. "Working weekends?" Merry said in a too bright tone, hoping to water down the irritation she really felt. "The designer biz must be hopping."

Looking up, Brenda plastered on her best pageant smile. "It sure is," she responded. "Like running on a treadmill all day."

"Yeah, me too. I'm heading home soon." Merry made a point of emphasizing the word soon. "You too?"

"Or," Brenda's face lit up, "is it Sauvignon blanc time?"

What is it with this chick and Sauvignon blanc? "Thanks, but I'm hoping to get out of here soon. You too?" Merry wondered if the second "You too?" was too much.

"Yeah," Brenda replied, several bubbles in her champagne voice popping with disappointment. "I guess."

"Great. Have a good rest of the weekend."

Quickly stepping back into the hallway before the woman force-fed her wine through a plastic tube, Merry returned to her office to wait. Leaning against the wall behind her half-closed door, Merry strained to hear something, anything that would indicate whether her neighbour was truly going home or if she was going to be stuck here for the rest of eternity while Brenda polished off her bottle. She was anxious to get on with the move into the junkyard before she lost daylight and the snowstorm got much worse.

After too many slow ticks of a lethargic clock and nary a tell-tale movement from next door, Merry slid to the floor, wrapped her arms around her knees and laid her head upon them to rest. Letting her mind wander, she realized it was the second time she'd caught Brenda looking less than her usual super cheery self when she thought no one was watching. Now having a little more insight into Brenda's personal life, she wondered if her mood swings were because of Roger? To hear him tell it, Brenda was not only under-standing but actively supportive of his crossdressing. Was that the truth? Any good detective will tell you there are always two sides to every story, and rarely did they match.

Several minutes later, Merry was beginning to reconsider the Sauvignon blanc offer when, finally, she heard the sweet sounds of her neighbour locking her door, followed by the delicate clip-clop of high heels down the stairs. She waited ten minutes more for good measure before booking an Uber and dragging her luggage out of 222 Craving Lane.

After battling snow-clogged streets, dodging bad winter drivers, and a quick stop at the grocery store for essentials, Merry's friendly Uber driver, Kamaljit, pulled up at the gate outside the former scrap metal yard.

Surveying the hoary street which, quite obviously, was very low on the city's priority list of streets to clear, Kamaljit commented: "I thought I lived in a poor neighbourhood."

Merry ignored the observation as she fiddled with her key ring, which now included the ones she'd gotten from Drover.

"You're sure this is the right address, Miss?"

"Uh huh."

"I don't understand. Where is the house?"

"Hold on. I have to find the right key to unlock the gate."

"Unlock the gate?" The driver moved his nose as close to the windshield as he could, peering through heavy darkness dotted by falling snow. With his headlights on full beam he could just make out the padlocked entrance. "Your house is behind this gate?"

"Uh huh. When I open it, just drive through. Park in front of the…well, it kind of looks like a shack. I'll meet you there."

Kamaljit did as instructed then turned his attention to the rear-view mirror. He spotted his fare, now transformed into a Yeti, struggling to close the gate against a raging wind and blusters of snow intent on keeping her from succeeding. About to jump out to help, he saw the gate lurch into place and the young woman trudge toward the car through dunes of snow growing at an alarming rate.

Merry had promised Drover she'd lock the gate every time she entered or left the compound. He claimed it was necessary to protect the property's valuable goods. Merry's agreement was more about securing her own physical being than Drover's precious trove of twisted metal and rusted car parts.

Pulling on a toque and gloves, Kamaljit stepped out of the vehicle and, raising his voice to be heard over the howling weather, offered to help Merry move her things into the building. Fighting the deteriorating conditions, they unloaded the luggage and grocery bags from the back seat and trunk and, like ants ferrying breadcrumbs twice their size, dragged the loot to the front (and only) door of the hobbit-house structure. Kamaljit waited patiently, shivering, as Merry battled to insert the key into an unfamiliar lock with mittened hands.

When it finally slid in, Merry turned to Kamaljit, smiled at the look of apprehension on the man's face, and said, "Please excuse the mess inside, it smells funny, and there might be a critter or two running around, but other than that," she added with what she hoped was a reassuring grin, "it's perfect."

The driver nodded, his mouth smiling but the rest of his face registering concern.

Merry swung open the door and reached for the light switch she'd spotted on her first visit. As the bulbs engaged, the duo rushed inside, lugging their goods with them, quickly slamming the door in the face of Old Man winter.

Holding his breath, Kamaljit squinted his eyes as if to protect them from the promised unsightly interior. When he was done taking it all in, he gave Merry a quizzical look.

Merry's mouth hung open, a strange gurgling noise coming from her throat.

What happened here?

The discoloured, ripped, moldy wallpaper had been removed. The banged-up walls and smashed-in plaster had been repaired and painted an unoffensive pale beige. The floors were spotless, the worst bits hidden beneath area rugs so new they curled up at the edges. The lighting was still nothing but bare bulbs hanging from the ceiling, but now all four of them worked. The area pretending to be a kitchen/dining room had been vastly improved. A cheery tablecloth successfully concealed the chipped Formica tabletop. A shiny toaster oven and serious-looking slow cooker joined the existing microwave. A brand-new shelving unit boasted matching sets of dishes, coffee cups, and bowls, six water glasses, a stack of kitchen linens, and a fully stocked utensil tray.

The massive picture window overlooking the scrap metal yard was invisible behind curtains that matched the tablecloth. The desk beneath the window remained where it was but now sported a table lamp and collection of office supplies. In the living room, the rickety TV trays had been replaced by a glass-topped coffee table and two smaller end tables. The television had been updated to a flatscreen that promised more than three stations. The couch was the same but two new armchairs kept it company.

The Uber driver was the first to speak, "I must admit to you, Miss, I was worried for you. I believed this house would be very terrible inside. I was planning to invite you to come home with me, where you would be safe and warm and my wife would fix you a very good meal. But this place, it's not so bad, what my wife would call cozy."

Merry, having regained her ability to move, looked up at the tall man and gave him a sickly smile. "I can't believe it."

Kamaljit glanced at the strange woman, confused by her comment. "Oh, why is that, Miss?"

Merry shook her head as if coming out of a daze. "Long story. Thank you for helping me tonight, especially with the weather being so crazy. I couldn't have done it without you." She pulled out her phone and punched some buttons. "I'm adding a bigger tip and five stars. I wish I could give you more."

"Thank you very much, more is not necessary." He moved to the door, then looked back. "You will be safe here?"

"I think so, yes."

"Good luck in your new home."

"Thank you. I'll walk out with you."

The Uber fishtailed wildly but made it safely out of the junkyard. Merry waved and locked the gate behind him, then ran back to the house.

After removing her boots and depositing her coat on the sofa, Merry warily approached the refrigerator. She winced as she pulled on the door. Instead of the expected frozen horror, sitting in the freshly defrosted freezer compartment was a litre of ice cream.

Ice cream.

Mutely she walked down the hallway to see what other surprises awaited her.

The first stop was the bathroom. "Jeez," she muttered under her breath. The tiny space had been scoured clean and a new shower curtain did its best to brighten up the once-grungy bath and shower stall.

At the end of the hall, across from two small storage rooms (one which Merry immediately decided she'd repurpose as a closet... once she could afford more clothing) was the larger storage room which Drover had attempted to convince her was a bedroom. Merry flicked the light switch.

Her breath caught. "Holy shit."

The walls had been painted pale pink, almost the exact same shade as the blouse Merry had been wearing the day she and Drover met at the Livingsky Plaza food court. New bedding adorned the cot, including a brightly patterned duvet that looked as if someone had sprinkled it with flower petals, and no fewer than half a dozen throw-pillows in complimentary hues. The rug next to the bed was a fluffy pink sheepdog laid down for a nap. A rolling clothes rack was a useful addition, along with a small chest of drawers. A series of framed photographs adorned one wall; crisp, clean black-and-whites that appeared to be scenes from around Alphabet City. Merry marvelled at the skill of the photographer who'd somehow managed to portray the impoverished neighbourhood as stark, moody, but hauntingly beautiful. Leaning in closer, she inspected the bottom right-hand corner of one of the photographs and the scrawled initials: G.D.

Merry's chest tightened. She whispered, "He did this." She studied the photographs for several more seconds, photographs taken and framed by Gerald Drover.

"He likes me." The unspoken words, hushed, burdened with amazement, reverberated in her head.

Shaking herself back to reality, Merry turned sharply and marched with great determination back to the front room. "I need...I need...I need something...water...something."

Rummaging through one of the grocery bags Kamaljit had deposited near the front door, she pulled out a supersized chocolate bar. She moved into the living room and flopped down onto the centre cushion of the couch.

Tearing open the candy wrapper, she felt justified in disregarding the original plan for the chocolate which was as a reward after she'd cleaned up the place. Only after demolishing half of the bar in astoundingly few bites, chews and swallows, did Merry feel the courage to say the words out loud, "Gerald Drover likes me."

Of course, he likes me. Why shouldn't he? What does that have to do with anything?

When Drover first showed her the junkyard house, the place was an utter and complete hellhole. Now it was considerably less hellhole-y.

So what? Isn't that what landlords are supposed to do?

Of course. That was it. Drover was only doing what any landlord would do. Not because he *liked* her, but because he was a landlord. That's what landlords do. Of course he would clean the place, fix the plumbing. Of course he'd paint the walls. Of course he'd…buy fluffy rugs…and pillows….

Certainty dwindled. Was it normal that he'd painted the bedroom pink? Stocked the freezer with ice cream?

Ice cream. The chocolate bar forgotten, Merry jumped up to retrieve the ice cream she'd spotted earlier and suddenly craved like air. Häagen-Dazs. Not cheap. She found a spoon and returned to her spot on the sofa.

The first taste was heavenly but did little to relieve her fuzzy, confused state. Two spoonful's later she mumbled, "What about those framed photographs?" Putting down the ice cream, she shifted in her seat in order to get a better overall view of the room. Even the light switch plates had been changed out for pink ones; not her taste, but certainly a nice touch, thoughtful even. Would any typical Alphabet City landlord go to such lengths?

Merry slowly repeated the words that refused to leave her mind: "Gerald Drover likes me." He'd told her as much. More than once. She'd doubted him from the start, for good reason. Several possible reasons, in fact. One, he was a slime bucket who probably said those kinds of things to every woman he met. Two, he was trying to soften her up to negotiate a better rate on her detective services. Three, he was using her, hoping to distract her from finding out the truth about the fire and encourage her to sell the sanitized version of Gerald Drover to insurance investigators and the police.

But what if she was wrong? What if he really did like her?

When the vanilla ice cream and chocolate bar were gone, Merry went to work. She unpacked grocery bags and suitcases, rearranged furniture and kitchen items, generally readying the place to call it home. The job was far less daunting than anticipated because the hours she'd set aside for cleaning and pest control were no longer necessary. By 10:00 p.m., she was seated at the kitchen table with its cheery tablecloth enjoying a cook-from-frozen lasagna served with day-old garlic bread and a bottle of cheap red wine. As the bottle emptied, more questions filled her mind. Why was Nicky Sokolov beaten outside The Hole? Was his attacker the same man she'd spotted running away from the scene, the same man she'd met her first night at The Hole; the blond, meet-cute Prince Charming, who'd hauled her butt out of a snow bank while harp music played in the heavens? Why was he there that night? Coincidence? She had her doubts. Was Prince Charming the man who'd hired Nicky (or Nicky's "friend") to set the fire? Was the assault meant to shut him up?

With Sokolov recuperating in the hospital and therefore unavailable to identify the guy who paid to set the fire, Merry had pretty much concluded that going back to The Hole was pointless. But every time she'd been there, so was blondie. Maybe he'd show up again.

Merry grinned as she mulled over her new theory, giving full credit to her able assistants, chocolate, ice cream and wine.

Too tired and tipsy to make the trip to the bedroom, Merry nestled into the remarkably comfortable sofa for her first night in the Junk House. A magnolia scented candle flickering on the coffee table was the room's only source of light. Outside, the frenzied wind having died down, oversized petals of virginal snow fluttered down like winged angels. Bandits of cold snuck their way inside the little house through countless invisible cracks and crevices, but Merry kept toasty warm buried within the doughy softness of a down-filled comforter. She sighed deeply, feeling triumphant. She'd successfully prevailed over Designs by Brenda and a raging Saskatchewan blizzard to move into her new home.

Home.

She had a home.

From her snug spot on the couch, Merry had an unobstructed view of the moon-kissed scene outside the giant picture window at the other end of the room. For a long while she did nothing but watch in quiet wonder as the falling snow magically metamorphosized the scrap yard and its gargantuan towers of misshapen, tortured metal into a winter wonderland complete with fairy tale snow sculptures.

It took some time for Merry to identify the unfamiliar feeling arising from somewhere deep inside her, but finally she knew what it was.

Contentment.

She was safe. She was warm. She had a place to call home. It felt good.

With a puff of breath she blew out the candle.

As darkness crowded around her, contentment's mortal enemy, worry, found its wicked way into her head. She tried to ignore the thought, wishing it away, not wanting it to ruin her perfect evening. But it refused to go, pushing and shoving its way into her consciousness, unwilling to be denied. Two searing words burned her brain like a red hot brand: *Greyeyes knows.*

CHAPTER 18

Gazing at the assembled tenants of 222 Craving Lane, Alvin Smallinsky was disappointed. The lot of them were standing in a tight circle in a dark corner of the ballroom, like a sad clique of unpopular high schoolers. Why weren't they circulating amongst the other guests, engaging in scintillating conversation, telling everyone about 222 Craving Lane? And look at how they're dressed! Aside from Brenda Brown and himself he was pretty sure they'd come straight to the gala from work, wearing their tired, everyday work clothes. This was the Mayor's Gala, for goodness sakes! They were in the Truemont Hotel's Grand Ballroom, Livingsky's crown jewel perched majestically on the banks of the mighty Saskatchewan River. He knew that because that's what the hotel's website said.

Built for the Canadian National Railway at the end of the Great Depression as one of Canada's grand railway hotels, the Truemont was the presumptive host for the Mayor's Gala since the late 1970's. With its châteauesque ten storeys lording over the riverbank at the south end of Livingsky's downtown, no skyline photograph or picture postcard of the city was complete without it. More recently, because of its location directly adjacent to the city's proposed Riverside Plaza, the Truemont was considered a key anchor for the massive redevelopment project. And because Riverside Plaza was known to be a favoured pet project of the current mayor, Alvin knew there had never been a more meaningful time in its history to be invited to the Mayor's Gala at the Truemont Hotel than now. And still, Monty Churchill from the second floor was wearing a

badly wrinkled short sleeve shirt—*short sleeve!*—and no tie—*no tie!*
If he didn't need the rental income, Alvin would be tempted to evict
the slob. When they were invited back next year, because they sure-
ly would be, he would certainly remember to institute a dress code.

Brenda Brown, dressed for success, was the standout savior of
222 Craving Lane's sartorial reputation. She'd obviously gotten her
hair and makeup done for the event and purchased a new dress. She
looked shiny and new compared to the rest of them. The newbie,
Merry Bell, at least looked like she'd tried. He frowned and tilted his
head to the side as he more fully assessed her appearance. She was
attractive in an untouchable European movie star sort of way, he
supposed, but there was something about her that made him think
she was wearing someone else's clothes. On the bright side, today's
getup was a vast improvement on when she'd first arrived at Craving
Lane, looking like a cross between Barbie and Tammy Faye Baker.

Tired of staring daggers at his slovenly tenants—didn't do any
good anyway—Alvin scanned the room for the mayor. No sight-
ing yet. He'd been chatting up guests who'd attended prior galas
(which seemed to be pretty much everyone except him and his
motley crew), and everyone agreed that the cocktail hour was *the*
most crucial portion of the evening. The rest of the night was eating
rubber chicken and Saskatoon Berry cheesecake, inane chatter with
whoever you were seated next to, keeping awake during rambling
speeches, and enduring a live auction in support of the Mayor's Be-
nevolent Fund (whose benefactors no one seemed able to identify).
It was during the cocktail hour when guests schmoozed, made connections, sealed deals. It was during the cocktail hour when everyone took note of who was in the room and, more importantly, who
wasn't, having somehow fallen off the invitation list in disgrace.
Most crucial of all, it was during the cocktail hour when the mayor
and her entourage circulated throughout the room and visited with
some, but not all, the assembled guests. If she stopped to talk to you,
your evening was made, if she didn't, you needed to start worrying
about next year.

Carol Durabont was nearing the end of her first four-year term as mayor of Livingsky. She'd handily beat out a three-term incumbent on the strength of her campaign slogan: *A New City for a New Millennium*, promulgating the idea that outdated practices by city administrators, going back to the turn of the century, had kept Livingsky from living up to its potential. She promised a growing base of change-minded young voters that she would "slash and burn" Livingsky's reputation as a sleepy prairie town and pledged growth and renaissance through increased immigration, more tourism, and an aggressive revitalization of downtown. At forty-three she was the city's youngest mayor and the first woman to hold the post. In the past four years she'd proven she wasn't afraid of making tough decisions, even if it meant her own considerable popularity taking a temporary hit.

Alvin felt a chill tingle the length of his spine when he finally spotted Durabont in the room. And she was close. His time was coming. His time was now. As usual, Durabont was not alone. Moving alongside her like a mighty cruise ship's stolid pilot boat, was Mackenzie (everyone called him Mac) Blister, her right-hand man. You rarely saw one without the other. Even at press conferences, Blister could always be spotted in the background, his stern face revealing nothing but tacit support. Tonight, as they made their way around the ballroom, Alvin noticed that as soon as the mayor moved on from one conversation, Blister was in her ear, no doubt preparing her for the next encounter. Alvin wondered who truly steered the ship around this room, Durabont or Blister? He also wondered what Blister would whisper in the mayor's ear about him. He hoped it was something about his success and longevity as a businessman, the fine building he'd renovated on Craving Lane, and maybe, to establish his community-mindedness and status as a man of the people, something about the time he volunteered at the Fringe Festival's beer tent a few years ago.

Signalling Brenda to come stand next to him, he positioned the two of them at the front edge of the tenant's circle, where Mayor Durabont could easily access them for a chat (and be spared having to look at Churchill's shameful, tie-less, short-sleeve shirt).

There were telltale signs the mayor was about to finish her visit with the group next to theirs, a collection of slick lawyers in tailored suits glued to gym-toned bodies. Alvin could smell their combined cloud of cologne and perfume from here. He specifically noticed how the men's pants were intentionally shortened to reveal no socks and athletic shoes. Tsk. He adjusted his and Brenda's position slightly so Durabont could not possibly miss them.

"That's it," he furiously whispered in Brenda's ear, "they're done. We're next. Let's pretend we're talking."

On cue, Brenda, always a willing team player, let out a delightful tinkle of laughter as if Alvin had said something irresistibly humorous.

"Here they come," he uttered under his breath, growing more excited.

There it was, Blister whispering in the mayor's ear. The mayor stopped to listen.

"Why are they stopping?" Alvin was worried. "They don't stop."

"Don't worry," Brenda assured him. "I saw them looking over here earlier. They're totally going to talk to you."

"Really? Are you sure? When were they looking at me? How did I not notice that?"

"See, here they come."

Mayor Durabont and Mackenzie Blister were indeed heading in the direction of the 222 Craving Lane group. Alvin felt himself blush with pride and winced at the sound of his stomach gurgling a little too loudly.

That was when the unthinkable happened. As quickly as the blush had arrived, it faded into deathly pallor as he watched Durabont stop just short of his position, and begin chatting with… Merry Frigging Bell!

⌗

"Mac tells me you've recently moved to Livingsky," Carol Durabont said to Merry in a way that sounded like she was sincerely interested and had all night to listen to a detailed answer.

At 5'10" plus whatever her heels added, Merry was frequently the tallest woman in any room, so she was pleased to see the mayor meeting her eye to eye. Tall women, she'd come to learn, often developed an immediate, unspoken bond, born of a common social experience that was either depressingly unpleasant or gratifyingly powerful. Standing face to face like this, dressed up, in a beautifully decorated ballroom, shoulders back, wearing I-don't-care-how-tall-I-am heels, was definitely the latter.

Before Merry could reply, Durabont added, "Have you met Mac Blister? He's my Chief of Staff but everyone knows he's really the Assistant Mayor." The two exchanged an easy glance and practiced laugh.

Merry shook the older man's hand. "We haven't met." She was surprised by Blister. Unlike Durabont who exuded youth, grace, style, and an irrefutable sexiness, Blister, a couple of inches shorter than his boss, was in his sixties, with steel grey hair and a jowled but severe jaw line. As a saving grace, when he shook her hand his smallish dark blue eyes set deep behind clear, rimless glasses, sparkled like wet marbles when he smiled. "Actually," she said, "I didn't just move to Livingsky, I moved back. I grew up here."

"Isn't that interesting. I love hearing stories of people coming back to Livingsky. No matter the real reason, I like to pretend it's because of my administration's progressive policies," she joked with a lovely self-deprecating laugh. "Makes me feel good about myself."

Merry laughed too. "I'm sure it's often true."

"That's very nice of you to say. What sort of work do you do, Merry?"

"I'm a private investigator."

Durabont exchanged a look with her assistant. "Really? Isn't that funny. Just last week Mac and I were discussing whether the city needed someone to do exactly that, you know, third-party external due diligence on various projects, that sort of thing." Latching tighter onto Merry's gaze, she asked pointedly, "Do you do that sort of thing, Merry?"

Merry was not at all clear what the woman meant by "that sort of thing" but making connections and promoting her business was exactly why she was here, so she quickly agreed that she did do "that sort of thing."

"Excellent. Do you have a business card, Merry?" Mackenzie Blister asked.

"Oh, Mac," his boss chided, "don't be such a luddite. I'm sure Merry would rather airdrop her contact info to you."

"As far as I'm concerned, an airdrop is something that happens with a parachute. Do you happen to have one of those on you, young lady?"

The three of them laughed.

"No, but will one of these do?" Merry said, digging a card from her purse and handing it to Blister.

He studied the card for three seconds longer than she expected, then looked up with another sparkly-eyed smile. "Thank you. I'll be in touch."

After a quick good-bye the politician and her aide were off to another conversation.

Sensing an alarming waft of heat emanating from her left, Merry turned to see Alvin Smallinsky and Brenda Brown glaring at her. The mayor had passed them by without so much as a head nod. Alvin looked like a teapot about to blow its lid. *There*, Merry thought to herself, *there is the real Alvin Smallinsky*. Brenda, on the other hand, looked like she was about to suggest another Sauvignon blanc talk. Merry didn't wait around to find out. The bar was at the opposite end of the ballroom. Despite an overhead announcement warning guests they had only two minutes to claim their seats for dinner, she headed straight for it.

With most of the lineup from earlier in the evening cleared away, Merry fell against the bar's counter and begged the attendant: "May I please have a gin and tonic, light on the tonic."

"Coke, please," a man who'd come up next to her ordered at the same time.

"You know they have grownup drinks here too," she blurted out without thinking or even looking at the guy. It was meant as a joke, but maybe the guy was a recovering alcoholic or abstaining for other reasons. Not cool. "Sorry," she quickly added, giving the bartender a "help me" smile. "Stupid stuff comes out of my mouth all of the time."

When the man didn't immediately respond, she turned to look at him. Maybe she really had offended him. "Oh!" she yipped in surprise. "It's you."

The blond man with the killer dimples who'd helped her when she slipped on the ice outside The Hole was standing next to her. The same blond man she saw days later dashing away—guiltily?—from where Nicky Sokolov lay beaten nearly to death, also outside The Hole.

The man looked equally surprised. "Oh. Hi. It's you. What are you doing here?"

Definitely not as flirty as the first time they met. "Oh, you know, I heard they were giving out free drinks, so…" She quickly glanced at the bartender who was holding out her gin and tonic. "Just kidding. I'm a real guest. I paid for a ticket…well, Alvin paid…" *Wait, does Alvin expect me to reimburse him for the ticket*? If he did, she was in big trouble. Another thing to worry about.

"Who are you here with?" McDimples asked.

Merry responded much too quickly with: "No one. I'm single."

The man smiled. Dimple heaven.

"I meant which company are you here with?"

Merry felt her cheeks explode. "Oh, of course. I'm with 222 Craving Lane. It's a bunch of different businesses working out of one building. For instance, I specialize in making a fool out of myself."

He laughed. "You didn't do that."

Merry nodded, grateful for the assessment but doubting its accuracy. She saw the man's eyes move quickly away then back to her.

He probably had someone waiting for him.

Looking like he was making a hasty decision on the spot, he said, "Sorry, I don't have my phone with me, but do you have a card?"

For the second time that night, Merry pulled a business card out of her purse. Best investment she ever made. Well, at least better than that damn website which seemed to be doing her no good at all. She told herself the only reason she was giving this man her contact information was because he was a person of interest to her case, not to her personally.

He took the card, glanced at it quickly, then buried it in an inside pocket of his suit jacket. "Good to meet you, Merry Bell. Enjoy your evening." With that, blondie walked away, taking his dimples with him.

Merry sipped her drink dreamily, savouring the sound of her name on his lips until...*damnit!* Merry Bell, P.I. extraordinaire, had completely neglected to get her suspect's name. She was thinking about going after him when her phone rang. It was a call she couldn't miss.

"Julia," Merry answered the phone as she ducked behind a ballroom pillar for a bit of privacy. "Thanks for returning my call. I've been trying to reach you all day."

"Sorry about that. I was working a split shift that turned into one long, shitty shift."

"I hate to cut to the chase, but I can't talk long. What's happening out there with Vanstone?"

There was a short hesitation on the line, then, "He's dead, that's what's happening."

There was something strange in her friend's voice. Was she pissed off that Merry hadn't kept in touch since leaving Vancouver? She had a right to be. Although Merry hadn't consciously planned it, she'd pretty much severed communication with everyone. It hurt too much. The city, the people, Nathan Sharpe, Julia Turner, all of it only served as reminders of her failure.

Merry's relationship with Julia was a friendship, of sorts, one built on convenience. They first met in a support group for transgender women. Freshly post-op at the time, it was Julia who'd referred Merry to Vanstone. They'd kept in touch and, much later when Merry was unable to work and desperately struggling with finances, Julia offered her a place to stay, an arrangement that lasted months until Merry returned to Livingsky.

"Do you know what happened?" Merry asked.

Another pause, followed by: "You probably know more than I do."

That was an odd thing to say. "Are you angry with me?"

"Merry, I'm sorry, I've had a long, tough day. I'm tired and I'm not being my best self. Maybe we should talk another time."

"Did you know Vanstone was sleeping with some of his patients?"

"I do now," the words came out sounding like crumbled pieces of rock tumbling over one another.

"Oh Julia," Merry's heart lurched, "you were one of them."

"Yes."

"Me too."

For a beat, nothing was said as both women processed what the other had admitted.

"You should have told me," Julia bleated.

"Why didn't we tell each other?" Merry glanced around the room to make sure no one was witnessing her mini meltdown. "We had so much goddamned shame over having sex as women that we couldn't confide in one another. Why? It was just sex!"

"With an asshole."

"A huge fucking asshole!"

They laughed.

After a moment to recentre themselves, Merry asked: "Julia, did you tell the police about having sex with Vanstone?"

"I did. And I know a few other girls did too. I called around."

"And now the police think one of us did it, one of us killed him."

"Can you blame them?"

She had a point. "Maybe this will turn out like that Agatha Christie story, the one where all the suspects were the killer."

"Agatha who?"

CHAPTER 19

Merry arrived at 222 Craving Lane on Tuesday morning just as Brenda Brown was pulling into the parking lot in her pearl grey BMX 3 Series. Merry wondered why the woman bothered to come in so early. Despite her many not-so-subtle references to the wild success of her business, not once since Merry moved in had she seen an actual client coming in or out of Designs by Brenda.

"Good morning!" Brenda called out merrily, simultaneously juggling a grande mocha latte Merry would kill for, an expensive looking valise, and a bouquet of flowers wrapped in protective winter wear, all while somehow managing to gracefully exit her vehicle.

Civility dictated Merry wait for her neighbour to catch up so they could walk in together. Brenda covered the distance between them on tippy-toe, as if the snow was hot coals and she didn't want to risk burning the soles of her designer boots. Not Louboutins, Merry noted, but nice enough.

When Brenda arrived at her side, Merry noticed the woman giving her a once over, paying special attention to hair and makeup. She wondered how she ranked in maintaining the new look. It was probably best not to ask.

"You disappeared so quickly after the gala dinner last night I didn't get a chance to hear about your tête-à-tête with the mayor," Brenda said as they headed toward the building lockstep.

Merry was pleasantly surprised by the woman's chatty demeanour. She was convinced Brenda and Smallinsky were upset with her for stealing their thunder and time with the mayor. "It was more of a quick chit chat than a tête-à-tête."

"That's not what it looked like. Tell me everything. What did she say? What did you say? She always looks like someone who smells really good? Did she smell good?"

They were now inside and scaling the steps to the third floor. Merry picked up the pace but Brenda easily kept up.

"She smelled fine."

"And? What did you talk about?"

"Nothing really. She asked about my moving back to Livingsky and…"

"I'd like to know more about that too. You see, Merry, that's exactly why I keep pushing Alvin to coordinate some sort of regular social activity for all of us here at 222. He doesn't seem to think it's necessary."

On that one thing at least, Merry agreed with Smallinsky.

"I think you and I should plan something anyway. What do you say, Merry? You in?"

Merry cringed at the thought. "I'm so busy right now, with the move, new business, new house."

Brenda looked disappointed. "I understand."

One more flight to go.

"I saw you exchange business cards with Mackenzie Blister. What was that about?"

Merry shot the other woman a sideways glance. Brenda Brown missed nothing, that much was obvious; first with her not-so-delicate communique about Merry's living situation, how she'd used Merry's profession to please her husband, and now this. Merry couldn't figure the woman out. The note slipped under the door was borderline passive aggressive, foisting Roger upon her was manipulative, yet at the same time she'd done her a true favour by giving her a makeover. She seemed genuinely sincere— albeit irrationally intent—about spending time together drinking Sauvignon blanc. Merry would definitely have to keep an eye on this one.

"It was no big deal. The mayor mentioned something about the city possibly needing an investigator, so he took my card. They were probably just being nice."

Brenda crumpled her pretty kitty-cat face into a perplexed frown. "The city of Livingsky wants to hire a private investigator? That's odd, don't you think?"

Merry had to agree. "I suppose. But like I said, it was probably just something they said to make a first-time guest feel welcome."

They'd reached the third-floor landing. Merry was about to make a run for her end of the hallway when she heard a gasp and felt Brenda's hand pulling her back.

What the fig is wrong with you, lady? She turned to ask the question out loud but stopped when she saw Brenda's perfectly manicured finger pointing at the wide-open door of LSI.

When Alvin Smallinsky spotted the mayor's Chief of Staff, Mackenzie Blister, step into the foyer of 222 Craving Lane that morning, he could not believe his eyes. For a brief moment he swore he could hear songbirds twittering about his head like in one of those Disney Princess movies.

Could it be? Had last night's snub actually been nothing more than an oversight? He could picture it, Mayor Durabont in her office, sipping scotch at the end of the evening, reviewing the gala with her second-in-command, when suddenly it strikes her: I didn't talk with Alvin Smallinsky of 222 Craving Lane! "*Mac,*" she would have exclaimed, "*you have to get over there first thing tomorrow morning and deliver my apology in person.*" Perhaps there'd be a lunch to make up for it, just him and Carol.

"Mr. Blister!" Alvin enthused as he quick-stepped out of his office, holding out his hand. "Welcome to 222 Craving Lane."

Blister smiled and took the hand. "I can't say I've been in this building before."

"It used to be a private home. I had it renovated," Alvin replied without being asked, "at quite some expense. Now there are seven businesses operating from this location. It was a risk, as I'm sure you can appreciate, but one which has paid off. All of my tenants, including my own CPA firm, Smallinsky & Co., are very successful."

Blister nodded. "You're Alvin Smallinsky, the owner of the building."

Alvin's smile faded slightly. *Why did he say that as if he wasn't quite sure?* Never mind. "Why don't you step into my office? I'll rustle up some coffee and we can…"

"That's exceedingly kind of you, but I'm afraid I won't have time for coffee this morning. I was hoping to speak with one of your tenants. Merry Bell? Do you know if she's in this morning?"

Alvin felt his cheek twitch. He knew if he wasn't careful, the involuntary tic would move to his nostrils and top lip. But who could blame it? The nightmare was real. Once again, the mayor's representative was more interested in his latest tenant than himself. "I'm not sure," he said tightly. "Why don't you follow me upstairs and we can find out."

Smallinsky led the way to the third floor. It was early, but he thought it quite possible that Bell was in. Ever since she'd rented the office, he was often surprised to arrive at work only to find her already there. Hard workers scored points with him.

He tried the door to LSI. It was locked. He pulled out the master key that opened every door in the building and slipped it into the lock.

"Oh, that isn't necessary," Blister said. "I don't actually have an appointment. I was passing by and…"

Smallinsky opened the door and ushered the man into the tiny reception area. The door to Merry's inner office was also closed, probably locked. He debated using his key again, but quickly decided that might be crossing a line. "I'm sure Merry will be here any minute. Why don't I get us that coffee and we can chat about last night's gala? Very successful evening from what I could tell."

Just at that moment, two faces appeared at the door, Merry Bell and Brenda Brown.

What are those two doing together, Smallinsky wondered. "Merry! Brenda!" he greeted them with forced cheer. "I believe you both know our guest, Mackenzie Blister, the mayor's Chief of Staff?"

The women and Blister shook hands and exchanged pleasantries.

Smallinsky sidled up alongside the older man, just short of throwing a companionable arm around his shoulders. "Mac and I were just reminiscing about last night's gala. I was telling him how thrilled we were to be there."

"We certainly were," Brenda agreed. "A very professional event. The room looked beautiful. As you probably know, I'm a design expert, owner of Designs by Brenda, right next door, and I've done more events like that than I can count, so I would know. It was really, really well done, really, really nice, mostly, hardly anything I would change."

Merry smirked at Brenda's shameless self-promotion.

"Thank you, Ms. Brown. I appreciate the compliment. Especially from someone with your expertise. I'll certainly pass it on to the team. We always strive to make the gala an event our constituents and community members will enjoy in every way."

Brenda beamed.

"Merry," Smallinsky spoke as if he was chairing a meeting. "Mac would like to have a few words with you. Would that be possible right now?"

Blister jumped in. "I must apologize, Ms. Bell…"

"Merry is fine."

"Merry then. I'm sorry for showing up unexpected. I was on my way to the office, noticed this was your building and took a chance. I'm happy to make an appointment for another time if now isn't convenient."

Merry hesitated then said, "Now is good. Let's go into my office."

The foursome rearranged positions in the small antechamber. Smallinsky looked like he wouldn't say no to being invited to join them. Merry unlocked the door and Blister preceded her inside, then she slowly turned, smiled sweetly at Smallinsky, and closed the door in his hopeful face.

After settling themselves on the appropriate sides of Merry's desk, Blister repeated his apology and Merry waved it off.

"Mr. Blister…"

"Call me Mac. Everyone does."

"How can I help you, Mac?"

"Do you recall last night when Carol mentioned that we'd been discussing the possibility of using a third-party investigator?"

"I do. I thought you were just being polite."

Mac smiled his face-saving smile. "We're always polite."

Merry smiled back. "Of course."

"But that's not why we said what we did. Meeting you last night was rather serendipitous. You see, we've been dealing with an issue recently which has begun to feel like it might benefit from outside perspective."

"Outside of city management?"

"Yes."

"That sounds unusual to me," she said, mimicking Brenda's opinion.

"That's very perceptive of you, Merry. This *is* an unusual situation. One that requires delicate handling. You see, we feel this situation would greatly benefit from a pair of fresh eyes, eyes belonging to someone who—how shall I put this?—does not have quite as many constraints on their activities as do our civic and municipal authorities. Now, this isn't to say, Merry, that we do not have faith in our people. Quite the contrary. We simply want to assist them in any way we can. I'm hoping you might agree to help us do that."

Merry heard bells ringing. What she didn't know yet was whether they were alarm bells, warning bells, or just everyday town-crier kind of bells announcing breaking news.

"I expect everything we say within these four walls will remain confidential?"

"Of course," she quickly agreed. Blister was certainly taking a chance trusting her when he'd just met her. "I hope I can help. What do you have in mind?"

"Several weeks ago, probably before you moved back to Livingsky, there was a fire in Alphabet City."

Uh-oh. Warning bells. Definitely.

"The building in question is an apartment complex owned by a local property management company with a…shall we say, less than sterling reputation. You should know, Merry, this is a building where children live, elderly people too, many of whom were temporarily displaced because of the fire. As you can imagine, the fire and its cause are of great interest to the mayor's office."

"I understand, but don't you have fire and police department investigators for this sort of thing?" She knew the answer.

"Of course. And they have done a superb job, unquestionably so."

That, Merry thought to herself, *was a fine bit of cover-your-ass bullshit.*

"Regrettably, their investigations have stalled. They keep coming up short when it comes to uncovering irrefutable evidence about what caused the fire." Blister held up both hands in a defensive gesture. "Now, believe me, Merry, despite the reputation of the building's owners, nothing would make me happier than to know this fire was nothing more than an accident, a tragic twist of fate. But, you understand, I must know for sure. That's where you come in."

Alarm bells.

"Merry, I'd like you to undertake a private investigation of the matter, maybe spend some time digging around in corners where our people can't."

"Mac, I need to stop you there."

Blister did as requested, staring at Merry expectantly.

"As much as I would like to help you, I can't. I believe I may have a conflict of interest."

Blister let a few seconds pass, analyzing Merry's face the entire time. "Is that so? I must say you've surprised me."

Merry studied Blister's face in return. The man was as hard to read as a closed book. The jowls were stern, the bushy eyebrows lowered, all intense and not a little intimidating, and yet his bright blue eyes continued to twinkle as if he was goddamned Santa Claus.

"Would you mind telling me in what way you feel you are in conflict?"

Merry thought hard about what she could say without exposing her professional relationship with Drover. "If I'm wrong about this, then we have no problem, but, Mac, are you referring to the fire at 101 Redberry Road?"

His mouth tightened. "I am."

The air in the little room sparked with intensity, as if an invisible bare wire had suddenly gone live.

Merry chose her words carefully. "LSI has been engaged to investigate that fire."

Blister took in the information and appeared to think on it for a few seconds before continuing. "I see. Merry, may I ask who engaged you?"

The two exchanged knowing looks. Merry added a "you know I can't tell you" shrug.

Blister licked his lips and readjusted himself in his seat. "Merry, as you know, I've shared with you the very real concerns that I, and Mayor Durabont, have about this fire. Concerns that are far beyond specious. Our main concern is for the wellbeing and safety of the residents of our great city. I would never ask you to breach client confidentiality, but I have to ask: is there anything you *can* share with me regarding what you've found out in the course of your investigation thus far?"

Merry nearly gagged. Was the mayor's Chief of Staff attempting to make her feel guilty for not doing exactly what he said he wouldn't ask her to do: breach client confidentiality? What to do? She couldn't afford to make an enemy of the people who ran the city where she hoped to build a successful new business, but she couldn't in good consciousness betray Gerald Drover, no matter how despicable he may or may not be (she was still a far cry from making a final call about that).

"I wish there was," she began slowly, "but, like your own investigators, I've found nothing concrete so far." It was the best she could do to keep both sides happy. Hopefully.

With a sudden move, Blister was on his feet. Merry followed suit.

"I want to apologize one last time for intruding on your time like this. I also regret we weren't able to do business today." Friendly, but the eyes weren't shining quite so brightly anymore.

"Same." The bells continued to ring.

Blister stepped toward the door, opened it as if to leave, then turned to face Merry, a fatherly look on his granite face. "I know you lived in Livingsky once before, but as someone returning to the city after being away for several years, I hope you'll accept a bit of advice from an old man."

"Of course." The ringing became clanging.

"Be careful, Merry. Be careful about the people you do business with. Livingsky is a wonderful city, a beautiful city, but it also has an ugliness. I'd hate to see you get swallowed up in all of that." His eyes shone cool steel. "Good-bye for now," he said cheerfully. "I'm sure we'll see each other again." Then he was gone.

Merry swallowed the dry lump of clay that had lodged in her throat.

The phone rang. She picked it up and got the second big surprise of her day.

There would be three.

CHAPTER 20

"It's Peter Wells calling."

From the caller's tone of voice it sounded as if they knew one another, but Merry did not recognize the name. "Yes, Mr. Wells, how can I help you?"

After a slight hesitation: "That's a cooler reception than I expected."

There was something about the voice, but she couldn't quite place it. "I'm sorry, but you have me at a disadvantage. Should I know you?"

"It's Peter. Wells. From last night."

"McDimples!" Merry blurted out the nickname before she knew what she was saying. *Damnit.* There was something about this guy that threw her off. Even as a high schooler who thought he was gay, she'd never been the kind to swoon over a cute boy, but now she understood the feeling. "I'm sorry. I shouldn't have said that. But in my defense, until this very second I didn't know your name. I had to call you something, right?"

"You didn't know my name?" He sounded doubtful.

"No. I gave you my card, but you didn't give me yours."

"You really don't kn…" He stopped there. A beat later he asked, "Why were you at the gala last night?"

Merry felt herself growing miffed by the change in the man's tone and inappropriate line of questioning. What business was it of his? "I told you. I was a guest, a local businessperson like everyone else. It said so on my card if you'd bothered to read it."

"I did," he said quietly.

"Why were *you* there?" she shot back.

Her question was greeted by a series of garbled sounds. Someone must have walked into the room and Wells covered the receiver to converse with them. After a second, he was back. "Merry, I'm sorry, I have to go. Can we meet for coffee? Tomorrow morning?"

If this was only about flirtation, she'd have told the guy he could take a long walk on a short pier, but this was something more. She needed to know why McDimp...Wells was at The Hole the night of Nicky Sokolov's attack. He was either somehow involved in this whole thing, or nothing more than a blond-headed red herring. She was hoping for the latter.

After agreeing to meet and making arrangements on location and time, Merry hung up, only to have the phone immediately light up with another incoming call, surprise number three.

"LSI, Merry Bell speaking."

"Merry, its Gerald. I need your help. The police got me."

As soon as she hung up from hearing Drover's story, Merry called the Livingsky Police Station. Within minutes she scored a late afternoon appointment with Detective Sergeant Veronica Greyeyes. This made her uneasy. Cops prioritized you in their schedules for one of two reasons: to arrest you, or to squeeze you for information. It had been a couple of days since Greyeyes had blindsided her with an interrogation over her relationship with Elliott Vanstone. At the end of that meeting, Greyeyes had asked Merry if she'd murdered the doctor. Merry's simple response was "no". The detective accepted the answer, but in her wake had left behind an indisputable reek of unresolved suspicion. Merry hadn't taken an easy breath since.

From her minimal interaction with Greyeyes, Merry could tell the cop was the kind of person who was used to knowing what she wanted and exactly how to get it. She had hoped her physical distance from where the crime was committed and its investigation would shield her from further scrutiny, but was another shoe about to drop?

At the station, Merry was directed to wait in a sterile interview room identical to the one where she first met Greyeyes. She didn't have long to wait before the Sergeant stepped into the room carrying a laptop, a folder of papers, and a cup of coffee. Merry stood to shake hands.

The women took their seats and Greyeyes opened and logged into her laptop, ensuring the screen was out of Merry's line of sight.

Greyeyes examined the woman through narrowed eyes (another habit she'd do away with if she knew about it). "I didn't expect to hear from you," she said.

After Greyeyes confirmed with the Vancouver Police Service that she'd made first contact with Bell and had little of substance to report, they responded by telling her the investigation was ongoing and all suspects were still in play. They requested she keep track of Bell's whereabouts and arrange a second interview. Having fewer opportunities than her big city counterparts to keep her detecting skills sharp, Greyeyes was more than willing to comply.

Since submitting the report detailing the follow up meeting, Greyeyes had yet to hear back from VPS. That was bloody poor response time, in her estimation, especially on an active case. According to the briefing she'd had with Vancouver's lead investigator, one of Vanstone's "supremely pissed-off" former patients was the first to voluntarily admit having a sexual relationship with the doctor. Her unapologetic view was that "the bastard deserved to have his dick chopped off". It didn't take long before two other former patients admitted to the same "arrangement". VPS asked Greyeyes to ascertain if Merry Bell fell into the same category. Although the confirmation would certainly place Bell near the top of the suspect list, the police had not yet uncovered any evidence to tie any of the current list of women who'd had sex with Vanstone to the commission of the crime.

When Bell reached out requesting another meeting, Greyeyes immediately placed a direct call to the lead investigator, Detective Graham Carruthers. She was irritated that she was the one having to make the call. It wasn't as if she was asking for an update out of idle curiosity. They'd solicited her help, and as such she considered herself part of the team and believed it to be her professional duty to see the case through to its conclusion. Before she saw Bell again, she needed to know whether she should treat the woman as an on-going suspect or nothing more than an innocent civilian.

Eventually Carruthers admitted that the reason for his negligence in getting back to her was not because he didn't want to share information, but because he had so little to share. It was a sprawling case, and not going particularly well. Despite having multiple possible suspects, Merry Bell included, they'd been unsuccessful in nailing down any solid evidence with which to pin the crime on any of them. He thanked Greyeyes for her work, but for the time being they had no cause to ask her to continue investigating Merry Bell. *A situation*, he portentously noted, *which could change at any time.*

"Thank you for seeing me again," Merry said.

"Mm hmm." Greyeyes raised an eyebrow, ever so slightly, settling a practiced, ambiguous gaze upon the woman.

Taking a deep breath, Merry dove in. "There've been some developments in terms of my involvement with the fire on Redberry Road."

"Oh? Let me see if I have this right. The last time we chatted about 101 Redberry Road, you stated you had safety concerns about moving into the building. Instead of talking to the landlord, however, you came to see me, a detective with the Livingsky Police Force." Greyeyes didn't push any further on how ridiculous that sounded. Did Bell really believe she'd pulled one over on her?

Merry squirmed. Put that way, her actions did seem a little absurd. "Yes, that sounds about right."

"And," the detective marched on, "I believe that on both occasions when we talked, you made it very clear that you had decided not to move into 101 Redberry Road."

"Yup. That's right too."

"I'm glad we're up to date. So, let's talk about these 'developments.'"

"Well, as stated, I did not move into 101 Redberry Road. Since I last saw you, however, I did enter into a professional relationship with the building's owner, Gerald Drover." Merry stopped there, as if awaiting confirmation whether or not this was something Greyeyes already knew. With nothing but a baleful glare facing her, Merry continued. "I assume you gathered, from when you showed up at my office a couple of days ago, that I'm a private investigator. Mr. Drover hired me to look into the Redberry Road fire."

"I see." Greyeyes did not betray the fact that she already had this information. It took a little digging, but eventually she'd found out a great deal more about Merry Bell, private eye, of no fixed address, and possible murder suspect.

"I've just learned that my client is being held in police custody. I understand a search was conducted of his property during which evidence was found allegedly implicating him in the fire. Is that correct?"

Greyeyes nodded, interested to see where Bell was going with this. "Just to be clear," she said, "you didn't also become Gerald Drover's lawyer since we last saw each other, did you?"

Merry pursed her lips as if to keep from blurting out a knee-jerk response. "No, I did not."

"I see. Then I should explain to you that the Livingsky Police Service is not in the habit of discussing ongoing investigations with members of the public."

Pulling in a deep breath, Merry said, "Gerald told me what your officers found in his backyard storage shed."

Greyeyes peered at Merry, wordlessly challenging her to say more.

"A red crowbar and some glass jars."

Continued silence from the police detective.

"I'm guessing the paint chip samples found embedded in the

tampered door of the apartment where the fire originated will match the crowbar. Both red?" She swallowed and kept on. "You told me there was evidence of an accelerant at the scene. Something to do with a specific kind of glass jar perhaps?"

Greyeyes remained perfectly still on the outside, but inside her heart began to beat faster.

"Today's Tuesday, right?" Merry asked.

"Mm hmm."

Greyeyes did not expect what came next.

CHAPTER 21

At 7:00 p.m., when Gerald Drover Junior was released from police custody, Merry was waiting for him. He insisted on taking her out for dinner as a thank you. Pyeongchang Korean Restaurant was at the far end of F Street in a rundown strip mall that was also home to a laundromat, a shuttered pharmacy, and a Reiki practitioner. When they got there, the place was nearly empty and they were seated immediately. The owner, who was also the seating hostess, server, and cook, greeted Drover warmly.

Having never eaten authentic Korean food before and bewildered by the menu, Merry asked Drover to order for both of them. He chose samgyeopsal to start with (sizzling pork strips served with lettuce, perilla leaves, sliced onions, raw garlic kimchi and chili paste), Bibimbap (rice, mixed vegetables and beef prepared with sesame oil and more chili paste and topped with a cooked egg), a kimchee sampler, and soft tofu stew.

"You seem to know your Korean food," Merry commented, impressed.

"Now that you live in Alphabet City," he said with his trademark gap-toothed smile, "you'll need to spend time getting to know it's food scene. It's like a mini New York. So many immigrants live here, you can find almost any kind of restaurant. Most of them are just like this one, holes-in-the-wall no one's heard of, but the food is really good and really cheap." His eyes bulged. "Not to say this is a cheap date."

Merry laughed and shook her head. "Not to say this is a date at all."

"Whatever you say, Sweet Lips."

The owner brought over two Tsingtao beers.

"Is this a Korean beer?" Merry asked.

"Chinese, I think," Drover told her. "We're all friends here." He raised his bottle to clink Merry's. "Here's to you. Thanks for getting me out of the slammer."

"When I told Detective Greyeyes I happened to be in your storage shed on Friday night and saw no sign of a red crowbar or glass jars, she had no choice, especially when I showed her the time-stamped pictures. It's still not proof positive you didn't set the fire, and I suppose you could have moved the crowbar and jars in there after I left, but it raised enough reasonable doubt to convince her to let you go. For now."

"You had to add that 'For now' part, didn't you? Way to ruin my happy buzz."

"Gerald, why did you call me, instead of your lawyer?" It was a question that had distracted her all day.

"The bastard didn't pick up his phone!" he told her with a bark of laughter. "Besides, I knew you'd know how to help me."

Merry was far from confident he was telling the truth. It was time to push him a little. "Did you know I was in your storage shed Friday night?" Was that why he called her first, because he knew what she saw, or rather didn't see, and how it could be used to persuade Greyeyes to question the veracity of her newly obtained evidence? Talk about crafty. If it was true, Drover was definitely proving himself to be much smarter than he looked.

"Do you want the truth?" The man's usually puckish face had grown serious.

Merry's blood ran cold. Were her suspicions correct? Was Drover manipulating her and the entire situation? "Yes. I do."

"The truth is…I trust you, Merry Bell."

Merry stared at Drover. He stared back.

The samgyeopsal arrived with a clatter, the pork still hissing with spice-infused heat. Drover took the opportunity to drive a wedge into the strange mood that had suddenly clouded the space between them to tell Merry about what they were eating. "In Korea there are restaurants that serve nothing but samgyeopsal. It's like a big party, where all you do is drink soju shots and keep ordering more samgyeopsal to soak up the alcohol."

"Sounds like fun," she said with little enthusiasm.

"It is." He tossed a tidbit of pork into his mouth and immediately began fanning away the burn. "You visited Redberry Road, right?"

"I did."

"I grew up there."

"What? Really?"

"Yup. I lived there with my mom until she died, when I was sixteen."

"I'm sorry. That must have been hard on you and your dad."

"My father couldn't have cared less. He and Mom were divorced longer ago than I can remember. He paid for everything though. He was good that way. And he let us stay in the apartment for free."

Drover had Merry's attention. With the mulleted gopher flash and sass turned down low, she felt she might actually be catching a glimpse of the real Gerald Drover. "Is that why the building, and the fire, and finding out what really happened is so important to you?"

He chewed thoughtfully, then answered, "I guess so."

"It's a nice building. And talk about prime location, right on the river, Alphabet City on one side, downtown on the other, and those views, at least the ones I saw from Mrs. Wu's apartment, are spectacular."

"I know. You wouldn't believe the developers who've tried to buy it off of me. I like money as much as the next guy, but you're right, that place is special. I can't sell it. Even though everybody knows it wasn't my father's strong suit, he always took good care of that building, so it's stayed in pretty good shape. That's why I was surprised a few years ago when someone reported the building to the city, saying it was a rat trap and should be condemned. None of that was true. The city found that out soon enough, but it still stung. In more ways than one. But hey, it's a tough business I'm in. If it's not one thing, it's another."

Listening to Drover, the hairs on Merry's forearms began to quiver. As a woman, she hated those hairs, but as a detective, they came in handy. "What do you mean?"

Drover reached into a pocket, pulled out a crumpled letter, and handed it across the table for her to see.

"What is this?"

"Another offer to buy. Showed up yesterday. That's why I have it. I had it on me when the cops came for me."

Merry inspected the document and its envelope. The timing seemed more than a little suspicious, arriving on the same day he was arrested. "There's no stamp or postage mark."

"Someone dropped it in the mailbox at my front door. That's happened before."

"070719 Ltd?" she read the letterhead. "Do you know who that is?"

"I don't. A lot of developers use numbered companies. Don't know why. The same company made another offer a while back, a much lower offer." Gerald slumped over his plate, gazing discontentedly at the food he'd lost appetite for. "I dunno, maybe they're right. Maybe I should give it all up and sell. It's a crap load of money."

Merry agreed. It was a lot of money. If it was her building, she'd sell in a heartbeat and buy some decent clothes and a car, move back to Vancouver, get a house, maybe a dog. But something other than competitive commerce was going on here, she could smell it. Or was it the samgyeopsal?

The next morning Merry put in a call to Nathan Sharpe, her first since leaving Vancouver. Like her telephone conversation with Julia Turner, the vibe felt off. Even though Nathan sounded pleased to hear from her, she could sense her former boss was holding something back. On top of that, at the sound of Nathan's familiar, growly but friendly voice, she was taken aback by her immediate, visceral response. She quickly identified it as pangs of homesickness. And doubt. Had she made a huge mistake by giving up her life in Vancouver? It took her less than a minute to settle on an answer: a resounding no. That big, beautiful city had been siphoning cash at such an alarming rate she'd barely gotten out of there before having to hawk her beloved Louboutins for lunch money.

It did Merry's heart good to hear pride in Nathan's voice when she told him about landing her first big case for the Livingsky satellite office of Sharpe Investigations. She didn't tell him she was billing in rent money. Or that her client might actually be using her for his own nefarious purposes.

After giving Nathan a brief rundown of her case, Merry moved on to the real purpose for her call. Sharpe had significantly more resources and deeper contacts at his disposal and she hoped he would be willing to use them to dig up information on 070719 Ltd, the numbered company making offers on Drover's building. He agreed without hesitation.

When that was done, the conversation again fell into an uncomfortable rhythm. Even though they hadn't spoken in a long time, this was unusual for them and Merry couldn't hang up before finding out why. Over the years, Nathan Sharpe always had her back, no more so than when she revealed her transition plan to him. Having no experience with trans people, it took him a beat to understand what was about to happen, but he immediately shifted into a support role, fumbling along the way but doing better than most.

The plan had never been for Merry to be off work for as long as she was. Not only couldn't she afford it, but according to her doctors, there was no medical reason for her not to return to her regular life. After recovering from the final major surgery, she'd intended, with Nathan's backing, to return to her job, with the only change being that she was now a female detective instead of male. No big deal. As it turned out, it wasn't the work or its physical demands that presented a challenge, it was Merry's mental state. She'd grossly underestimated the time she needed to acclimate to her new body. Being a successful P.I. required a great deal of concentration, commitment, and mental stamina. So did transitioning from male to female. For Merry, one of the two had to give.

"How's everything at the office?" she asked. "Have you found two or three people to do half my job?" she quipped.

"It will take four at least," he shot back. "You are missed."

"Anything else going on I should know about?" It was a question she would regret asking.

Nathan wished it was later in the day so he could reach for the bottle in the bottom drawer of his desk. He also wished he'd had warning that Merry was going to call today so he could have had time to plan out what he wanted to say to her. He'd been an idiot not to have thought it through already. He wasn't sure which would be worse, telling her he thought she was a murderer, or telling her what he'd done when he found out she was a murderer. To complicate things even further, as a man of his word, he fully intended to keep his promise to Julia Turner not to reveal to anyone, least of all Merry, what she'd shared with him the night she visited his apartment.

"It's this thing with Vanstone," he finally uttered, a pitiful opening salvo.

"I was surprised to hear about that."

If Merry was upset he was bringing up Vanstone, he couldn't hear it over the phone. Maybe she expected it. The murder of a prominent local doctor renown for reassignment surgeries was exactly the kind of titillating news that made headlines in Vancouver papers. He knew Vanstone was the surgeon in charge of Merry's transition, so it made sense he'd want to discuss it with her. Didn't it?

Nathan bit his lip. What now? He knew the two of them could never move forward in any meaningful way if they didn't deal with this head on. But maybe they weren't meant to? Maybe this was it for them? She did what she did, he did what he did, both were atrocious acts, maybe the inescapable penalty was the death of their friendship.

Screw that. He made a decision. "Were you?"

"Was I what?"

"Surprised to hear about the murder?"

Three seconds dragged by before she spoke. "Of course I was. What do you mean by that?"

Sharpe's jaw tightened. It was time to dive into the deep end, where the water was murky and cold as a shark's heart. "Merry, I can't tell you how I know this…well, I, you…" he stumbled for a bit then recovered. "I know someone who knows stuff about this case, insider stuff."

"Uh huh, so?"

"There's evidence, strong evidence, that points to you."

"What are you talking about? What sort of evidence? How does it point to me?"

Now she sounded a bit freaked out. Nathan scrambled to figure out what was going through his former employee's head. Was she an innocent crying out at being unjustly accused? Or was she a guilty party feigning ignorance to protect herself? If she was guilty, Sharpe mused, was her crime any worse than his own, what he'd done to protect her?

"I can't tell you that."

Sounding disoriented, Merry asked, "This evidence, have you taken it to the police?"

In his mind, Nathan recounted his final minutes with Julia Turner:

"Mr. Sharpe," she said slowly, eyes wide. "Merry killed him."

Nathan watched in horror as the woman pulled a clouded plastic bag from her purse. She handed it to him for inspection. Inside was a hammer, covered in age-darkened blood.

"That night, the night Elliott was killed, Merry came home really late. She was wasted, high on something, blathering on about something I couldn't understand." Julia's chin pointed at the bag. "She had that with her. In her coat pocket. When I saw it had blood and…other

stuff on it, I put it in this plastic bag, mostly to keep it from making a mess. I never saw Merry like that before. At first nothing coming out of her mouth made sense. After a while I got that she was talking about Vanstone, he was my doctor too, but she never said anything about killing him."

Sharpe laid the gruesome package on the coffee table. *"Then why do you think she did?"*

Julia looked pointedly at the hammer in the Ziplock bag.

Putting on his detective hat, Nathan said, *"You said Vanstone was killed in his apartment in Yaletown. Is your apartment near there?"*

"God no. Only rich assholes like him can afford to live there."

"So, if you're right and Merry killed him, that means she somehow made her way all the way from Yaletown, with this bloody hammer in her pocket, all the way to wherever you live?"

"Yup. Like I said, she was out of it. I don't know how she managed it."

Nathan frowned. He knew Merry liked a drink now and then, but he never knew her to abuse alcohol, or anything else. It was a side of her he'd never seen before, nor, apparently, had her friend. *"What happened then?"*

"She kept talking, she cried for a while, talked some more, then all of a sudden she jumped up like a jack rabbit and said she had to go to bed. Before I knew it, she was passed out on the couch."

Nathan indicated the hammer, sitting between them like an unexploded bomb. *"Why bring this to me, Julia?"*

"I know how much you care about Merry. At least she told me you do. I hope that's true?"

"It is. I want what's best for her."

"That's good. I do too. And," she added with a half-lidded gaze, *"I want ten thousand dollars."*

Everything happened so fast. Before he knew what he was doing, Nathan had agreed to pay Julia Turner ten thousand dollars in exchange for her silence and possession of the damning hammer. He spent the rest of that night and the next day tortured by what he'd done, by what Merry had done, and what he should do next. Then Merry called and they had their meeting where she told him she was leaving Vancouver. Within a week she was gone. He was left holding a murder weapon. He did it to protect his friend, an act that made him as much a criminal as she.

"No, I did not go to the police."

"Why not?" Nathan couldn't tell if she sounded relieved or incredulous.

"Why do you think?"

"Do you really believe I killed Elliott Vanstone?"

With great care, Nathan tread into his reply on verbal tiptoes. "From everything I've learned about the man, I believe you—and the others—would have had good reason to."

"What happens now?" she asked in a voice that sounded defeated, and very sad.

"That's up to you."

"Nathan, I want you to know, whatever proof whoever it is thinks they have on me, it's not true." She took a deep breath. "If you don't believe that, you should turn me in. But if you do, I need you to prove it."

Merry wasn't a crier, but following her phone call with Nathan Sharpe, she wished she was. Instead, she found herself staring at a wall, unsuccessfully attempting to comprehend the implications of what her former boss had just told her. On the one hand she was grateful to have someone like Nathan Sharpe on her side, so willing to support her he was ready to risk his own reputation and freedom to protect her. On the other hand, what did it say that he could so easily accept that she'd murdered someone, even someone as reprehensible as Elliott Vanstone? Why did she have to proclaim her innocence and ask him to prove it instead of him immediately assuming it in the first place? What had she unthinkingly done in the past to convince him she could be a killer?

CHAPTER 22

"You can say this about our guy, he's consistent," Roger Brown commented as he parked across the street from Cuppa Joe.

"What do you mean?" Merry asked, checking her face in the car's sunshade mirror, wishing she could remember what Brenda had told her about dealing with puffy eyes. She touched up her lipstick, patted down her hair, and hated herself for doing it. What did how she looked matter if all she was doing was having coffee with a suspect?

"This place is in the middle of nowhere."

"This isn't the middle of nowhere."

"It kind of is, just like The Hole. He definitely likes hanging out in off-the-beaten-track kind of places."

Merry had to admit Roger had a point. Other than the Mayor's Gala, the only other places she'd seen Peter Wells were the kind frequented by people who didn't want to be seen. What's that about? "Thanks for driving me." The electrician had made her promise to call if she ever needed a ride and if he wasn't working he'd happily oblige. She handed him a ten-dollar bill. "Down-payment for gas."

Roger waved away the cash. "It's no problem. My morning job got cancelled at the last minute. Besides," he added with a wink, "what are interns for?"

Merry chuckled. The man hadn't even stepped foot in the LSI office but had already upgraded himself from chauffeur to intern.

"You don't have to stay," she said, slipping on gloves. "I can call an Uber when I'm done."

"If you don't mind, I think I'll wait. I don't like the idea of leaving you alone in this part of town."

Merry shot the man a sceptical look.

"Okay, okay. I really do have concerns about your safety, and Brenda would never forgive me if I let anything happen to you…but I have to admit I'm dying to get a look at our suspect." He pulled out his phone. "Besides, I won't just be sitting here. I can work on job quotes while you're inside."

Merry stepped out of the car. Before closing the door, she leaned in and said, "To be clear, I'm not in the market for an intern."

Roger was already tapping away on his phone. "Doesn't mean you don't need one. Now please close the door, it's freezing out there."

Pulling up her collar against a nasty wind, Merry skittered across the street, once again swearing at the uselessness of her beloved Louboutins. There was little traffic to worry about; none actually. The city's North Industrial area was the part of town where metal fabrication shops and seed cleaning operations went to live. No one ever came here unless they worked here. Was that why Peter asked to meet here? He didn't strike her as an industrial type, then again, she'd learned long ago that a person's outsides didn't necessarily match their insides.

Cuppa Joe most definitely had an inside and outside that matched. Both were bland and a little grimy around the edges. What you saw is what you got. Merry immediately spotted Peter sitting in one of three booths. The others were empty. Four small tables were also empty. The only other customers were an older couple at the counter, nursing cold coffees in silence, having long ago run out of things to say to one another.

Peter slipped out of the booth and greeted her with a strange half-smile that still managed to fully bring out his dimples. "Thanks for coming. I wasn't sure you would."

"Oh, I come here all the time."

"Really?"

Was he really that gullible? She'd have to remember that. "No, not really."

He laughed. She liked the sound of it.

"Sorry," he said, "I'm just a little...off today. Do you want to hang up your coat?"

Merry pulled off her jacket and gloves, threw them in the booth and slipped in after them. "Nope."

Peter sat across from her.

For several seconds they stared at one another.

"I kind of wish we could stay like this," he said tenderly.

Merry wasn't sure what he meant. "You mean, not talking?" Like the couple at the counter.

"Yes."

"Why?"

He sighed. "I'm afraid that as soon as we start talking, all of this will be ruined."

Merry caught her breath at the words. Suddenly she knew exactly what he meant.

"Coffee or what?" an uninterested waitress in her mid-seventies groused at them upon approach, holding aloft a glass carafe of dark brown liquid that smelled like a forest fire.

"Sure," Merry said.

The woman poured two coffees and disappeared.

Merry took a sip and wished she hadn't.

"After we first met..." Peter began.

"In a snow drift, another hot spot I frequent."

He grinned. "Yes, in a snowdrift. After that I felt...something weird happened to me that night. Ever since then I can't stop thinking about you. That hasn't happened to me since, well, since high school. Which was okay at first, it was a fun, innocent distraction that didn't really mean anything because I'd never see you again."

"And then you did."

He nodded. "At the gala. You probably noticed I was a little shaken to see you."

"I may have noticed that."

"For me it was like seeing...I don't know...like seeing a polar bear in a desert."

"You think of me as a bear then? Is it the hair?"

"There you go, always making me laugh. I like that."

"Laughing?"

"Yeah. I miss it."

"You miss laughing?"

"I miss being with someone who makes me laugh." His look drew her heated chocolate eyes into his icy blues; if they touched there'd be a molten explosion. "And someone who looks at me the way you do."

Merry followed a deep breath with an instantly regretted sip of gag-worthy coffee. This was not going as expected. She was here to grill him, not bask in his compliments and blush like a bird watcher on a nude beach.

"When I saw you at the gala, I was worried. I thought…"

"You thought I was stalking you?"

"No…yes. Then I realized how impossible that was, how stupid I was to think that, but then I knew…oh, god, Merry, you confuse me."

"I don't understand. You like me, maybe I like you, who knows, what's the big deal? Maybe it's confusing, but it's still fun and innocent, isn't it?"

The dimples disappeared. "The big deal is that this can't happen. That's why I asked you to meet me here. I don't know what's going on with me, or why I'm feeling the way I am. I certainly don't know what's going on with you, but before anything more happens or we happen to see each other again, I needed to tell you that. Merry, this cannot happen."

"Peter," Merry tried for a calm, soothing voice, hoping to disguise her disappointment and allay a bitter spike of self-loathing for being disappointed, "nothing has happened. You pulled me out of a snow drift, we ran into each other at a gala, and now we're having coffee at a very swanky coffee shop. That's it. My god, I only learned your name yesterday."

"I guess so."

Merry watched as the man's face changed. *Is he sad? As disappointed as I am? Relieved?* Merry's heart lurched at the thought. In the end, it didn't matter. The fantasy, as all fantasies must, had come to an end. He was shutting it down. Done was done. But all was not lost. If this wasn't going to be about pleasure, it could still be about business.

"Peter, there's one more thing."

"What is it?"

She hated herself for how hopeful he looked. "There was one other time I saw you. You didn't see me."

"Oh?"

"At The Hole. It was a couple of nights after the first time we met. There was an altercation in the back alley. A man was badly hurt. I saw you there." She was about to add that it looked like he was running away but decided against it. She did, however, check his knuckles for bruises.

A chill descended upon the table, so real Merry shivered. In stark silence Peter slipped out of the booth and pulled on his coat. He stood over the table, laid a ten-dollar bill between their coffee cups, and turned to Merry. He said, "I don't know what or who you thought you saw, but it has nothing to do with me. Good-bye, Merry."

Grateful that Roger had waited for her as promised, Merry slumped into the shiny SUV's passenger seat and glumly said, "Let's get out of here."

When the vehicle didn't move, Merry turned to find Roger fully rotated in his seat, facing her head on, eyes the size of saucers. "Merry, what is going on here?"

"What are you talking about?"

"That man. That man who just came out of the coffee shop, the one in the long, brown coat, was that the suspect?"

"Yes. That was Peter."

"That was Peter Wells."

Merry frowned. She knew she hadn't told him the man's name. She was getting to know Roger better, but not yet enough to be assured she could trust him not to blurt out the name on his podcast. "How did you know that? Do you know him?"

"Everyone in Livingsky knows him."

Oh shit. This wasn't going to be good.

"Do you really not know who Peter Wells is?"

"I don't."

"Then you better hold on to something while I clue you in."

"I'm not going to like this, am I?"

Roger shook his head like a lion with fleas in its ears. "First, if you've got a crush on Peter Wells, which I think you do, no matter how well you think you're hiding it, you should know that man is married."

If the top of Merry's head could have exploded, it would have. Why the hell hadn't she thought of that? Meetings in out of the way places, uneasiness when they ran into each other in public—how stupid was she? Of course he was married.

"That's not all," Roger cautioned.

"Of course it isn't." Merry braced herself.

"You know his wife."

CHAPTER 23

"Peter Wells' wife is the mayor of Livingsky."

"Hell no." Merry was truly flabbergasted. For several seconds she made sounds that no one should make in front of other people. "Are you sure?"

"Like I already told you, I know this city, I know its people... well, some of its people. If I recognized the face of an Alphabet City pawnbroker, you can bet I know the face of the mayor's husband. Merry, one of these days you'll have to start believing in me. I can be very useful to you."

She decided to withhold judgement on that. "His last name is Wells, the mayor's last name is Durabont." She knew that much.

"You might not know this," Roger stated with a twinkle in his eye, "since your experience with being a woman is relatively short, but nowadays women are allowed to keep their own last names."

If the term wasn't so outdated, she'd have responded with: "Ooooo, snap!" Instead, she shot Roger a look, half sour and half grudging respect for the clever comeback. This podcasting electrician was a little bit spicier than he let on, or had she just witnessed a hint of Stella peeking out from behind a Roger facade?

"I guess that explains why he was at the gala," Merry said, still shell-shocked by the news.

"And why he hangs out in backwoods bars and out-of-the-way coffee shops when he wants to pick up women."

Merry scowled. Was that true? Could it be true? Nothing about the man had set off alarm bells that even hinted he was that kind of guy. And would *that kind of guy* be so insistent that nothing could happen between them?

Until now, Peter Wells was just some guy she saw running away from the scene of a crime (a fact which he denied). But now she knew that guy was also the husband of the most powerful woman in Livingsky. Coincidence? Merry's extremities began to tingle.

A "ding" told her she had a text. She looked down at her phone. Nathan. She hadn't expected to hear back from him so soon, or maybe ever.

"Who's that?" Roger asked in a nosey intern-y way.

"My old boss."

"Is everything okay? You look a little pale."

Merry stared at the screen, replaying the worst of their recent call. She'd challenged him to prove she was innocent or else turn her in. Had that been a colossal mistake?

"Is something wrong?" Roger tried again.

"No. Nothing."

"Then why are you sitting there looking like there is?"

Interns were irritating. Merry opened the text, read, and breathed a sigh of relief. *Good old Nathan.*

"Actually, it's good news. I asked him to look into the numbered company that's been making offers to buy Gerald Drover's building on Redberry Road."

"He found something?"

"No names, but we have an address for its head office, and guess what?"

"Tell me."

"070719 Ltd. is right here in Livingsky."

"Let's go!" Roger shifted the car into Drive and attempted the electrician/intern version of burning rubber.

⊞

Several minutes later, parked in a very different part of town, the Escalade idling like a purring kitten, Merry and Roger eyed up a substantial estate built to impress, and succeeding. Gerald Drover's apartment building was located on Redberry Road on what some considered the "wrong side of the tracks," but there was also a *right* side to Redberry Road. The street, one of the longest in the city, ran alongside the Saskatchewan River as it sliced through Livingsky, east to west. The dividing line between the right and wrong sides was an actual railroad track that separated downtown Livingsky from Alphabet City. Everything on the Alphabet City side, beginning with Drover's property, was considered Redberry West (the wrong side of the tracks), everything on the downtown side was Redberry East (the right side of the tracks).

The first several blocks of Redberry East belonged to the proposed Riverside Plaza site and the Truemont Hotel, fronted by a long, narrow expanse of public park grounds, where people enjoyed leisurely strolls alongside the river during the day and, at night, other people cruised for sex and drugs. Further along, downtown eventually petered out giving way to high-end homes with sizeable lots and coveted views of the South Saskatchewan. According to Nathan Sharpe's research, 070719 Ltd. was headquartered in one of the grandest.

"I know it might sound silly to you," Roger commented as he scribbled in a notepad, "but I love being on a stakeout."

Merry delivered a droll look. The only other stakeout he'd been on was a goodie, a man was nearly beaten to death and they'd spotted a potential suspect sneaking away. "You've been lucky. I hate to tell you this, but most stakeouts are about as exciting as tofu."

Roger thought about this for a moment, then said, "I know that's probably true, and you probably think I believe being a detective is exactly how it appears on TV and in movies, but for me it's more about the whole experience, the atmosphere, the chance that something exciting might happen, even if it usually doesn't. I'm an electrician. My days are pretty predictable. This, what you do every day, is exciting and fun, even if it's just sitting in a car for hours waiting for something to happen. I just wish…" He let the sentence die off.

"What? What do you wish?" Merry was surprised to admit she

was actually interested in the answer.

After a brief hesitation, he said, "I wish Stella could be here."

Merry nodded. It made sense. Roger indulged his passion for crime fighting during his podcast, which he hosted while indulging his other passion, being Stella. The two were unpredictably but intricately linked.

"Well, I can't help you with that, but I can pretty much promise you that when it comes to stakeouts, I think you're going to get another lucky break with this one." After the morning she'd had, Merry was in the mood for action.

Roger grinned with anticipation. "What are we going to do, boss?"

"*We* are doing nothing. *You* are staying here." She nodded toward the big house. "I'm going to find out who's in there."

"How does that not make this a boring stakeout for me?" Roger countered.

"It's called passive observation."

Roger looked glum. "Okay, I understand."

"Maybe next time," Merry promised as she exited the car. *Next time?*

Hoping she'd come up with a plan during the long walk from the street to the mansion's front door, Merry didn't rush. By the time she reached her destination, the best she could come up with had something to do with taking a census poll.

She rapped the door with gloved knuckles.

No answer.

She tried the doorbell.

That did it. She heard footsteps approaching from inside.

The door was opened by the last person she expected to see.

Nathan eyed the unsatisfactory text response from Merry: "Thank you."

The text he'd sent her was about the research she'd asked him to do, but he'd hoped she'd respond with something about how they'd left things the last time they talked.

Setting aside his phone, he reached for the bottle of scotch in his bottom desk drawer and, forgoing a glass, took a healthy swig. Wiping his lips with the back of his hand, he replaced the bottle where he found it in the hopes it didn't call out to him again until a more appropriate time of day.

Merry's ultimatum had left him in an impossible situation. During their conversation he'd made reference to having knowledge of evidence pointing to her guilt in Elliott Vanstone's murder. She'd countered by saying he should either prove the evidence wrong or turn her in. What she didn't know was that he'd already tried. In the P.I. business, success was built on irrefutable proof. Merry's former roommate, Julia Turner, was a woman he barely knew. No detective worth his salt would accept the word of a stranger, or anyone really, without corroboration. Certainly, the bloody hammer she'd presented him, purportedly the missing murder weapon, went a long way in making her account of what happened undeniably convincing. Convincing enough that he'd agreed to pay her off instead of risking the chance she'd take it to the police. But that wasn't enough.

The fact that Julia Turner was willing to profit from her friend's felonious activity and use the threat of turning her in to do so, put into question exactly what kind of person he was dealing with. Nathan knew more than most that desperate people sometimes did desperate things. It didn't take a lot of digging to reveal that Turner was someone who lived on the fringe of mainstream society. Following her gender alignment surgery, she'd fallen into a spiralling financial black hole she couldn't crawl out of. Until now.

Julia Turner saw her shot at making some much-needed cash and took it. The question was, had she fabricated the opportunity, or was it for real? Nathan didn't know her well enough to know whether she would go to the extreme of faking a bloody murder weapon and, judging him to be a prime patsy (who knew what Merry told her about him?), use his paternal affection for Merry against him. All he knew for sure was that, con or not, he'd fallen for it, or rather, he didn't so much fall as believe he had no choice but to go along with it. He knew murder investigations evolved fast, particularly in the first twenty-four to forty-eight hours. Turner had offered him a way to keep suspicion from falling on Merry during that all-important window of time. He had to do it.

Or did he?

How had he, Nathan Sharpe, a respected, experienced P.I., so easily, so quickly, broken the rule of law he'd dedicated his career to upholding? The answer to that question might very well haunt him for the rest of his life. As a private detective, he saw himself as much a criminal justice professional as any police officer or criminal attorney; yet in agreeing to exchange cash for that bloody hammer he'd taken a giant leap over the line onto the dark side.

What was done, was done, he'd decided. There was no point in worrying about that now. The big question was, had he risked everything for the right reason? He needed to find a way to validate Julia Turner's assertions. There was no way he could think of to test the blood on the hammer for a match to Vanstone's without the entire Vancouver Police force showing up on his front doorstep. But there was something else he could do that was nearly as good.

Over the years Nathan Sharpe had collected a group of *experts* to whom he turned when the official way of doing things was inadvisable. They were the kind of people who operated in that murky place floating just below the radar, where rules were judiciously ignored. One such contact was Fast Fred, a fingerprint expert who, without hesitation, agreed to Nathan's request for assistance. The first thing Fred needed, a set of Merry's fingerprints, was easily lifted off one of the items she'd left behind at her desk. It was considerably less straightforward to do the same with the goo-and-blood covered hammer. Nathan was relieved when Fred unblinkingly agreed to do it for him, with a commensurate increase in fee.

Half a bottle of scotch had disappeared while Nathan waited to hear back. Unlike a typical report sent by a forensics department or latent print examiner, the results of Fast Fred's examination cut right to the chase. Examining all factors associated with latent fingerprint exclusion when comparing the two prints, Fred made a determination: the prints on the bloody hammer belonged to Merry Bell.

Now he knew for sure. He'd protected a murderer.

Re-reading Merry's text for the umpteenth time, one thing ran through Nathan's head: Merry's ultimatum. There was only one thing left for him to do.

Standing in the open front door of his home, Peter Wells' face grew rigid. He was feeling a million things at once. At one end of the spectrum was a rush of pleasure at seeing Merry Bell; that inexplicable, heart-pounding thrill when you're in the presence of someone who makes you feel giddy inside. At the other, was the dawning realization that perhaps his intuition had been right the night of the gala when he found Merry standing next to him at the bar, supposedly by chance. At best, she was an opportunist who knew exactly who he was and was planning to take advantage of his obvious interest in her. At worst—the possibility rearing its ugly head when she'd handed him a business card that read: Private Investigator—she was somehow involved in the mess he currently found himself in. Either way, she was dangerous, to him, his wife, her career, their marriage.

"This isn't what it looks like," Merry uttered, standing in the doorway.

Wells studied her face, frowning. She'd appeared genuinely shocked when he opened the door. Or was he being fooled again by an exceptionally skilled actress portraying a falsehood? He'd never been good at reading people's true intentions, a failing which had cost him dearly in the past. "What does it look like?"

"It looks like I followed you here." She stuttered her reply.

"Yes, it does. If not that, then what is this? Why are you here, Merry?" Could it be she was feeling the same things he was? Had her heart trilled at the sight of him too, immediately followed by distrust over feelings she knew she couldn't have, shouldn't have?

"I can explain. It's a long story. Can we talk?"

"Not here. Not now."

"Peter, it has to be now. It's important."

"No!" The word came out sounding harsher than he'd intended. Aggression, of any kind, toward anyone, was not his thing. But neither were all the other things happening recently. He'd gotten in too deep. It was his fault. He should have left well enough alone. Now it was too late. Now he was…afraid, and fear was making him hostile. He glared at Merry, then softened his gaze when he saw nothing but unthreatening earnestness. Could he trust himself? Or was he being duped by a beautiful stranger? Hearing movement behind him, he made a snap decision he hoped he wouldn't regret. "Tonight. Nine o'clock. By the Holodomor."

"Nine o'clock," she agreed.

He shut the door in her face.

After being dropped off at Craving Lane by Roger, who rushed off to work, Merry prepared an extra-large mug of coffee in the staff room and, careful not to catch the attention of Alvin or Brenda, locked herself in her office. It was time to take a deep dive into the life of Peter Wells.

Positioned in front of her computer like a warrior preparing for battle, Merry began, ready to wield one of her favourite tools in the detective's toolbox: cyber stalking. The first thing Merry took note of was Peter's nearly non-existent social media presence. She surmised this was likely due to his position as the spouse of a high-ranking city official. If you were mayor, you probably didn't want your partner posting inappropriate pics on Instagram, supporting call outs to "Free the Whales" on Facebook, or anything else that could potentially be used against you in the highly combative political arena. From that angle, Peter Wells was clean as a whistle. But Merry was nothing if not persistent. Eventually she hit paydirt.

According to a simple but ample website, Peter Wells was em-

ployed by Well-made Furniture (an uninventive name if ever there
was one), owned-and-operated by the Wells family, manufacturing
high-end hardwood furniture in Livingsky since 1991. Scanning the
"About Us" page was an educational read. Well-made's custom pieces were meticulously crafted using a variety of "joinery techniques,"
which were dependent on a given joint's requirement for strength,
desired visual appeal, discreetness, and practicality. Many of the
techniques listed, Merry thought, sounded unnecessarily personal: the mitred butt joint, the half-lap joint, the tongue and groove.
Furthermore, not just any wood would do for a Well-made offering. Only "real" woods were used in production, including Oak,
Quarter sawn Oak, Maple, Tiger Maple, Birdseye Maple, Birch, Af-
rican Mahogany, Black Walnut, Cherry, Beech, and Sapele. Merry
wouldn't have been able to tell them apart in a fully lit forest.

Peter's specialty was design, working directly with customers
to create the perfect piece based on their personal specifications
and tastes. Well-made's main construction and distribution facility was located in the city's North Industrial Area. That explained
a lot. She'd been (at least partially) wrong about Wells. He hadn't
chosen to meet her at Cuppa Joe because it was an out-of-the-way
hole-in-the-wall where they wouldn't be spotted. He knew the place
because his family's shop was only a few blocks away. Why he frequented The Hole, however, was still a mystery.

Digging deeper, Merry learned that Peter had married Carol
Durabont fourteen years earlier; he was six years her junior. Carol,
married once before, brought two sons into the marriage. At the
time of the marriage the boys were nine and eleven. An archived
newspaper article, published back when Carol was serving her first
term as city councillor, quoted her as saying how fortunate she
was to have a husband who worked mostly from home and could
therefore take on the greater share of looking after "their" children,
allowing her adequate time to meet her responsibilities as both a
lecturer at Livingsky University and a city councillor.

It wasn't until her third hour of online research that Merry
found a connection between Peter Wells and 070719 Ltd. An incor-

porating document (curiously redacted) named Wells as a principal in the entity. The numbered company itself, however, remained shrouded in mystery in terms of its purpose and activities.

Knowing that no exposé is ever complete without investigating a subject's spouse, as soon as Merry was satisfied she'd wrung the internet dry of every drop of information about Peter Wells, she turned her attention onto Mayor Carol Durabont.

As a public figure, a simple search turned up an abundance of source material, much of it retelling what Merry already knew. Prior to taking on the role of mayor, Durabont was a tenured Political Science professor at Livingsky U and a three-term Livingsky city councillor. The woman was definitely a political animal and knew her way around the workings of municipal and provincial governments.

Durabont was currently nearing the end of her first term as mayor, which she handily won on the strength of her campaign slogan: *A New City for a New Millennium.* According to her, it was time to "punt the old and usher in the new," a sentiment which didn't exactly ingratiate her with long-term city staffers and sitting councillors. For the first time in the city's electoral history, more than half of incumbent councillors were ousted by newcomers who were, according to the Livingsky Tribune's political columnist, not-so-covertly firmly in Durabont's camp. Once in power, she couldn't do a lot about duly elected councillors who'd managed to survive the change in leadership, but over time made "adjustments" (as much as union contracts would allow) to the salaried personnel she'd adopted, recruiting an inner circle of people she trusted for high-ranking staff positions.

Following the election, political pundits wasted no time questioning whether the new mayor could follow through on lofty campaign promises without significantly raising taxes. It turned out she couldn't, and her actions suggested she always knew it. With surprising speed, she bulldozed council into significantly increasing taxes (typically an unpopular move) by convincing them they'd eventually blow citizen's away with their wide-reaching platform of positive changes. Short term pain for long term gain.

Balancing opinion pieces by serious journalists, outraged letters to the editor, and conflicting news reports archived by local TV stations, it took significantly more effort for Merry to judiciously piece together what happened next. Mostly, it seemed, Durabont met with success. By the beginning of her third year, net in-migration and sustained population growth indicated confidence in the people who ran the city and their policies; tourism statistics skewed upwards which in turn resulted in exponential positive effects on the local economy. Small businesses thrived, investment in the city was at an all time high, and for the first time in decades, the city's downtown core was dotted with cranes as new commercial and residential high-rise construction boomed.

On the flip side, Durabont's most vital project, the one meant to cement her legacy and make good on her vision for downtown revitalization, faltered. Riverside Plaza, which she was often quoted as referring to as "her baby," continued to meet with one obstacle after another: rezoning issues, developers pulling out of deals, public protests, and, interminably, cash flow problems. The longer it took to get the project underway, the higher the projected cost rose. The higher the cost rose, the more citizens and politicians who represented them began to balk. With at least two strong candidates rumoured to be considering throwing their hat into the ring for the coming election, scuttlebutt was that Durabont would lose if she didn't pull off some kind of win at Riverside Plaza.

With her eyes drying out and mind melting into mush from reading article after article, editorial after editorial, endlessly wordy letters to the editor, either supporting or lambasting the current mayor, Merry found herself developing a headache and vigorous revulsion for anything having to do with politics. Hoping for relief, she switched focus to Durabont's personal life, the kind of research that was typically more fun and, if she was lucky, a bit juicy.

Carol Durabont married her first husband when she was just eighteen years old, the summer following high school graduation. Son Donald was born that fall. The marriage ended four years later, but not before the couple welcomed another son, Charlie. The union's failure seemed to fuel a change in Carol and how she wanted to live life. A single mother of two toddlers with a dead-beat ex-husband and nothing but a high school education, Durabont altered course.

Setting her sights on something better, Durabont enrolled in university, managing full course loads while simultaneously working multiple jobs and taking care of her children. She excelled in her classes and eventually built the foundation for a promising academic career. She was twenty-nine when she met and quickly married Peter Wells, retaining her maiden name which she'd taken back at the end of her first marriage. Today Carol was forty-three, and Peter thirty-seven. First son Don, twenty-five, lived out of province, pursuing a career in ballet. Charlie, twenty-three, currently lived at home with Carol and Peter and attended Livingsky University, with no discernable declared major.

That was it. No obvious skeletons in the closet, no reasons to suspect Carol Durabont and Peter Wells of being anything but a wholesome, young, upwardly mobile, professional couple, soon to be empty nesters.

Merry wasn't convinced. Even the cleanest houses had dirt hidden in dark corners.

Nicky Sokolov was currently a guest of St. Peter's Abbey Hospital, infamous for being the facility of choice for victims of random violence and domestic abuse. Its emergency room was not the kind of place you wanted to spend your Friday night. Founded in 1907 by an order of monks who once lived in an adjacent building, The Abbey, as it's more commonly known, was Livingsky's oldest hospital; one of three, located smack dab in the middle of Alphabet City.

Merry was not entirely surprised when no one stopped her from entering Room 238 where Sokolov was recovering from his injuries. The lack of security was probably due to him convincing police that the assault he suffered behind The Hole was nothing more than a case of wrong-place/wrong-time and likely the work of young hooligans hoping to score a few bucks for beer. That was exactly the kind of narrative that put investigations on slow burn and the shifty pawnshop owner knew it.

Maybe what happened that night *was* simply bad luck. Maybe it had nothing to do with Merry's case and Nicky's promise to identify the man who'd paid to have Drover's property torched.

"Oh, hell no!" Nicky bellowed the instant he saw Merry's face. "You get the hell outta here, lady!"

On second thought, maybe what happened that night had *a lot* to do with her case.

Approaching the bed, Merry reproached herself for suddenly feeling kindlier toward the petty criminal just because he'd called her a lady. *When am I going to get over that?*

"How are you, Nicky?" she asked sweetly.

He didn't need to answer. The man's face and right hand were grotesquely swollen and other parts of his body were covered in bandages. He didn't look good.

"You shouldn't be here," he growled. Warning or threat?

"I won't stay long."

"That's too long as far as I'm concerned."

"Nicky, you need to tell me who did this to you."

"Why I gotta do that?"

"Do you know who did this to you?"

"What do you think?"

"Will you give me a name?"

"I'm not giving you nothing. Because of you, my idiot cousin is running the pawn shop and probably robbing me blind while he's at it."

Merry reached into her purse and pulled out her phone. Placing it squarely in front of his bruised face and one un-bandaged eye, she showed him an image she'd downloaded off the internet. "Is this the man who paid you to set the fire? Is he the man who beat you?"

Sokolov let out a small laugh that sounded more like a grunt, but it made his mouth hurt, which made him swear. When the swearing was done, he asked in an incredulous tone: "Are you kidding me? This some kind of joke? I know who that is."

A quivering sensation she couldn't quite identify took hold of Merry's spine. She swallowed and pushed harder: "Was it him?"

Sokolov raised his good hand, his thumb positioned above a button at the end of a cord. He could have been a suicide bomber wearing a jacket made of explosives, threatening to push the detonator. "If you don't leave," he grumbled darkly, "I'm calling the nurse and telling her to kick your ass out of here."

"Wait!" Merry responded, fiddling with her phone as a last-minute idea popped into her head. She figured she could risk it as she was fairly confident she could convince any nurse who came into the room to side with her. Sokolov was not a charming man, and undoubtedly a miserable patient. Finding what she was looking for, she thrust the phone's screen back in front of the pawnbroker's face. "What about this person? Is this who did it?"

He pushed the button.

CHAPTER 24

Merry had visited the statue once before, shortly after it was erected. Derived from the Ukrainian words for hunger and extermination, Holodomor was the sobering name given to the politically motivated, Stalin-era, man-made famine in Ukraine which lasted from 1932 to 1933, resulting in the deaths of nearly four million Ukrainians. Saskatchewan, home to over one hundred thousand Ukrainians, was the first jurisdiction in North America to recognize the genocide with the passing of The Ukrainian Famine and Genocide (Holodomor) Memorial Day Act in 2008. Shortly thereafter, with the financial assistance of several levels of government and local Ukrainian organizations, the city of Livingsky commissioned a memorial structure. Known simply as Holodomor, the monument was located in Riverside Park, halfway between the Truemont Hotel and proposed Riverside Plaza site, in a sheltered alcove overlooking the river. The memorial consisted of a stunning bronze rotunda, engraved with thousands of stalks of wheat swaying in an invisible breeze below a dome of intricate filigree. At its centre stood a frail young girl, starving amidst the field of life-giving wheat.

As Merry wound her way down the meandering paths that led to Holodomor, two thoughts came to mind. The first was how much she was looking forward to seeing the statue again. She remembered the unbearable sorrow of the little girl, but also how there was something a great deal more in the child's wan, enigmatic face: there was strength, determination, and most surprisingly, gentle reproach. The crucial message was clear: "*Do not allow this to happen again.*"

The second thought, more of a worry, was whether what she was about to do was ridiculously foolhardy: agreeing to meet a man she barely knew, a man who quite possibly could be the bad guy she was after. To be fair, in her line of work, finding the bad guy was exactly what she was paid to do. But did she really have to do it after dark, alone, in the middle of winter, in a spot renowned for its seclusion?

Rounding the final clump of foliage that, even stripped of leaves, did an admirable job of concealing Holodomor, Merry immediately caught sight of Peter Wells. He was standing on the raised platform within the rotunda, hands braced against its railing, silvery moonlight washing over his face as he gazed out at the river. A nearby lanterned light post was the only other source of illumination. Feeling the now familiar cheek-reddening rush that overcame her each time she saw Wells, Merry mutely chastised herself: *Stop it!*

Hearing her approach, Peter turned.

Just as they had in the coffee shop, several silent seconds passed as they stared at one another, both feeling what they shouldn't feel, accepting it, then pushing it away.

"What are you after?" he barked.

She followed suit. "I know you were at The Hole that night."

"Who do you work for? Why are you after me?"

"Why did you hurt Nicky Sokolov?"

His laugh was bitter. "Hurt him? I didn't hurt anyone. If you knew me, you'd know...oh, god, never mind."

"Peter, I saw you there."

"So that's why you supposedly *slipped* and fell in the snow? You were trying to trick me, to get close to me. Why, Merry?"

"That's not true. I would never do that." Not really true. If the situation called for it, of course she would fake a fall. But that's not what happened, so, so...*so how dare he*! "I slipped and I fell. You saw it and helped me. It was a coincidence." As she said the words, she had a flash of hearing them with Peter's ears. Would she believe them? "Never mind that. I'm not talking about the night we met. I'm talking about the night Nicky Sokolov was attacked. You were outside The Hole that night. I saw you."

"Did you see me attack him?"

"No," she acknowledged.

"Have you seen Sokolov, the size of him? I'm a furniture design-er, Merry. I don't think I'm exactly the type of guy who could take him down in a fight."

Merry's jaw tightened. Wells had just screwed up. "So, you know who Nicky Sokolov is."

Wells was caught short. "What if I do? It's a small town."

"Not really. You're a furniture maker, he's a Pawn Shop owner. Not exactly a recipe for good friends."

"That's a snobbish attitude."

She felt a corner of her mouth tic upwards. He was right about that. "Are you telling me you and Sokolov are drinking buddies who regularly meet at The Hole for a guys night out? Is that your story?"

"Why are you asking all the questions and answering none?"

"I'm a detective. That's what I do."

"Who are you really? Why are you following me?"

"I just told you. I'm a detective."

If only that could be enough to encourage him to spill the beans. Unfortunately, experience had taught her that was rarely the case. Unlike the police, or a really good bartender, Merry was power-less to coerce anyone to talk to her. Generally, things worked much better when she resorted to chicanery, but this strange relationship with Wells—part suspect, part flirtation partner—was something she wasn't quite sure how to deal with. When she first met him, the only thing she cared about were his dimples. But now, he was a key person of interest in her case. She'd given up her identity as a detective too soon, and now it was too late to pull the wool over his mesmerizing ice blue eyes. That, however, did not mean she was entirely out of tricks.

"Who hired you?" he asked again, anxiety creasing his forehead. Merry shrugged.

"Did they hire you to follow me? What have you told them?"

This is interesting. Why would he ask that? Did the mayor's husband already suspect someone might have been hired to tail him? Who would do that? Why? Maybe it didn't matter. Merry's main priority had to be her client and solving his problem. Her recent visit with Nicky Sokolov at the hospital had given her direction, now all she needed was Peter Wells to clear the road for her.

"I haven't told them anything yet," she responded in a flat tone. Merry felt herself growing numb, not from cold, but as a shield against the web of deception she was preparing to weave.

Peter stared at her. "Shit," he murmured.

The numbness dropped away, leaving Merry shocked by the tormented look twisting Wells' features. She had done that. She had single-handedly erased his beauty and painted over it with pain.

"What exactly do you know?"

"Peter," she said it in a way that said: "Come on, man, you know I can't tell you that, but assume the worst." She bit down on her lip, hoping the pinch would distract her from the guilt of telling unyielding lies.

Wells turned away, preferring to face the moon than his tormentor. He sucked in deep breaths of deadening cold into his lungs, three in a row.

Merry looked away. This was harder than she would have expected it to be, witnessing what her deception was doing to him, but she had no choice. "I can tell you one thing."

He turned back, his eyes pulling at hers. She hated how he looked at her now. The attraction, the affection, the "what if?" was gone, dead. He looked at her as he might a stranger. And really, she was.

"I know about 070719 Ltd," she said.

Peter moved slightly, shifting away from the shaft of moonlight, leaving himself backlit by its milky brilliance as he glowered at Merry. She was shaken by the look, fed by fear, maybe hatred. What was happening here? This was not what she wanted.

"Merry," his voice cracked when he finally spoke her name, "you have no idea what you've done."

She was wrong. The look in his eyes wasn't fear, or hatred. It was betrayal.

Slowly, Peter began to back away, darkness swallowing him.

She followed his movements but stayed still.

Suddenly he stopped. He was staring at something, something over her shoulder.

She turned to see what it was and gasped.

Rounding the stand of foliage protecting Holodomor were three men, coming at them, fast. She couldn't make out who they were, but she could see one thing very clearly: they were armed.

CHAPTER 25

The men were coming fast. A filtered beam from the light post caught the face of the first one, leading the charge like a commando. Merry turned to Peter, and with a controlled but forceful tone she said: "I'm sorry, Peter. Run."

Peter stumbled backwards, as if physically assaulted by the unexpected words. "Do you know these guys?" he hissed, confused. "I'm not leaving you…"

"I know them." Not exactly true. She knew one of them. "I know what this is." Her voice faltered as she saw the damning admission reflected in Peter's face. "You need to get away from here. I'll be okay, but you won't."

Peter stared at her, looking wounded, deceived.

With a final stonecast glare and saddened shake of his head, Peter Wells turned and disappeared into the thicket of trees.

Fearing he'd waited too long to escape, Merry released a curdling scream meant to distract the attackers' attention, and launched herself into the first man, all six-and-a-half feet of him, headbutting him in the gut with every bit of strength she had.

Gerald Drover groaned in agony as he lurched back, clutching his stomach, willing himself not to cry. "What the hell, Sweet Lips?" he groaned through clenched teeth.

The ploy worked—Gerald was waylaid and the other two marauders stopped in their tracks, not sure if they should check on Gerald, protect him from another headbutting from Merry, or chase after the guy who was getting away—but not for long. Simultaneously deciding the latter course of action was more to their taste, Drover's louts headed for the bushes where Wells had just disappeared.

"No!" Merry shrieked, racing after them. "Stop! Gerald!" she pleaded, "Tell them to stop!"

"I would if you hadn't just knocked all the air out of my lungs," he grouched, still wincing with pain.

The men kept moving, about to dive into the trees.

"Gerald!" her voice ripped through the air like shears through fabric.

"Johnny! Costanzi! Hold on!" he commanded the men.

Looking like two hunting dogs who'd been interrupted just as they were about to sink their chompers into a juicy Canada Goose, they grudgingly skidded to a halt, causing Merry to crash into the one directly in front of her. Scraping herself off of him, she used the opportunity to share a colourful array of words she rarely used.

Figuring it was safer than being near Merry, the thugs skittered back to Gerald's side.

"Who the hell are these goons?" Merry demanded to know, placing herself directly in front of the three stooges. "And why are they carrying bats?"

"Who the hell was *that* goon?" Gerald shot back, using his own bat to point at the spot in the trees where Wells was last seen.

"What are you doing here?"

"What are *you* doing here?"

"Jay-zus! We're not being paid enough to stand here listening to your lover's quarrel," one of the men said. He was nearly as tall as Gerald but sans mullet. "Are we going after that guy or what? He's getting away."

Gerald stared at Merry. She scowled back.

"No. We're done."

"You still gotta pay."

Gerald reached into a pocket, pulled out some bills, dividing them between the two men. Skinny-no-mullet kept his hand outstretched.

"I paid you what I promised, now get outta here," Drover barked, employing an extra dose of bluster.

"No problem, but I ain't going nowhere 'til you give me back my bat."

Gerald handed his bat to the man.

It was a small thing, but Merry was relieved to see Drover didn't have his own bat. She hoped it meant this type of activity was not typical for him.

The men were about to skedaddle when the shorter one stopped in front of the statue. "Who's the little girl?" he asked, entranced by the sculpture's complicated gaze.

"Long story for another day," Drover told him.

He stared at the bronze edifice for another second or two then scarpered to catch up with his partner.

Unsure what to say in the awkward silence that followed, Drover went with: "You changed your hair again."

Merry stepped closer in a menacing way. Gerald recoiled, cradling his recently injured tummy.

"Of all the stupid ass moves!" Merry spit the words in his face. "Why did you do this? How did you even know I was here?" she demanded to know. But before Drover could reply, she took a step back and rolled her eyes. She knew the answer. "It was Roger, wasn't it?"

Drover shook his head. "Nope. It was some crazy lady named Brenda? Apparently she's some kind of famous interior designer? Do you know her?"

As infuriated as she was, Merry stifled a laugh. She could see it all now. Roger, concerned about her meeting Peter Wells alone, late at night, told his wife everything. Brenda, never one to shy away from sticking her nose in someone else's business, agreed with Roger's estimation of the danger Merry might be in and took it upon herself to reach out to Drover. And yet, despite the seriousness of the matter at hand, and even as she was attempting to counteract the potential for harm coming to Merry, she couldn't help but get a plug in for Designs by Brenda.

"Oh yes, I know Brenda."

"I guess she was worried about you. I have no idea how she got my number, or why she called me, but by the looks of that guy, it's a good thing she did. Looks to me like Mr. Barbie Doll was about to bore you to death." He waited for a laugh or at least a smirk from Merry. When neither appeared imminent, he added, "By the way, if there's a way you can get her to lose my number, I'd appreciate it. That lady is bonkers."

Given that she and Brenda weren't exactly best buddies, and even though her actions were a bit over-the-top audacious, she had to admit it had taken someone with chutzpah to track down Drover and demand he help her. Merry couldn't be entirely mad at her.

"Who is that guy anyway?" Drover asked again, his nose flaring. "Did that asshole try to kiss you? Is that what this was? Were you on a date? Is he your boyfriend?"

"What? No!"

"Then who is he?"

"Brenda didn't tell you?"

"No!" he griped. "She spewed some bullshit about detective-client confidentiality. I told her I was the goddamned client, but that didn't seem to make any difference. She told me—no, she ordered me—to get my ass down here."

Merry couldn't help it any longer. She laughed. It felt good, given what a crap evening it had been so far.

"I'm glad you find that funny," he grumbled. "If it wasn't for her, I wouldn't be sitting here with a hernia."

"Oh, come on, I didn't hit you that hard."

"Wanna bet? I'm delicate in certain places. And you've got a freakishly hard head. Besides, you should be thanking me. I interrupted my plans, called up reinforcements, and came all the way down here to protect you."

"First of all, I don't need your protection. Second of all, *what the hell*? You come down here with two oily creeps carrying bats thinking you're going to do what exactly? Beat the shit out of someone?" A terrible thought suddenly occurred to her. Was Nicky Sokolov beaten with a bat? Was this Drover's modus operandi? Just when she'd convinced herself he couldn't possibly be responsible for the attack on the pawnbroker, he goes and does this.

"I don't know what I was thinking!" he crowed. "I didn't know what you'd gotten yourself into. Your famous designer friend was short on detail. I didn't know if there'd be one guy here or ten. I had to come prepared for anything. And I didn't think you'd want me calling the cops."

He was right about that.

Taking a deep breath to calm himself, Drover said, "Listen, here's the deal. You got the police to release me from the clink. You had my back, Merry Bell, so I have yours. Whatever it takes. That's just the way it is. Okay?"

Merry nodded. "Okay," she said in a quiet voice. Except for the boneheaded move of hiring two gangsters with bats, she couldn't exactly bring herself to stay mad at Drover. The guy was like a bad haircut. Just when you think you should cut it all off, you start to like it a little.

"So, are you going to answer my questions? What are you doing here? Who was that guy?"

Merry was glad to learn she wasn't the only doofus in Livingsky who didn't recognize the mayor's husband on sight. She sighed and shook her head. "I'll tell you this: you may have just ruined our only chance at finding out who set your building on fire."

Sitting in the idling car on a dark street, its tremble matching his own, Peter Wells' mind was reeling. The meeting in the park with Merry Bell had turned into a disaster. Then again, what did he think was going to happen? He knew Bell was a detective. He knew she'd latched onto him for some as yet unconfirmed reason, a reason that quite obviously had nothing to do with the spark of mutual attraction he'd mistakenly believed existed between the two of them. When he finally forced himself to disavow that silly notion, he'd naively blundered into his next mistake: believing that her sudden presence in his life was motivated by greed. The woman caught sight of him at The Hole, realized who he was, then tricked him into a flirty interaction, all with the intent of leveraging it into some kind of blackmail scenario. If only the situation was so simple.

It was becoming very clear that Merry Bell was more than some low-level con artist.

She was a spy, hired by someone to catch him.

This was all his fault. If he'd only kept his nose out of where it didn't belong, she'd have nothing to catch him at. Now it was too late.

After years of mounting concerns about his wife's mysterious behind-closed-doors activities, he'd reached his limit. Either he confronted her with his suspicions and demand to know the truth, or he shut up and accepted the fact that, by his inaction, he was a de facto co-conspirator in nefarious goings-on. If what she was doing was illegal and she was caught, the first question people, and the police, would ask would be: "What did the husband know?"

The truth was, he didn't know anything, and that was the cause of his current dilemma. In fact, he knew so little, there was nothing to confront Carol with, even if he wanted to. All he had was gut instinct, vague awareness of late-night phone calls, meetings that didn't appear on her official calendar, and too many conversations that ended with "Oh, you don't need to worry about any of that, sweetheart."

With nearly fifteen years of marriage under their belt, Peter knew his wife very well. She was often the smartest person in any room she entered, and she knew it. She possessed steely determination. She was fiercely independent and liked to be in control. She was driven to succeed, and firmly disregarded the concept of failure. Ironically, these were the traits which had at first drawn him to her, like a man-shaped pile of metal shavings to a magnet.

Before he met Carol, Peter lived a calm, uneventful life within the protective dome of the Wells family unit. His parents, siblings, and their extended families were as close as a family could get without being labelled a cult. Most adult members of the unit, including in-laws, were involved with the family business in one way or another. Some even lived in homes intentionally located within the same secure, serene, comfortable Livingsky neighbourhood. Over the years, other than the occasional death, illness, or temporary downturn in business conditions, nothing bad ever happened to the Wells family. It was, Peter's siblings liked to joke, like living in a Sesame Street world.

But everyone isn't cut out to live on Sesame Street. When Peter met Carol Durabont, single mother, dedicated career woman with political aspirations, and sexy as whipped cream, Peter was hopelessly entranced by her. She was exactly what he was looking for, and he, for reasons he didn't quite understand at the time, was exactly what she was looking for.

The first years of their marriage were thoroughly enjoyable. Almost all of their time and energy went into the care and feeding of Carol's two boys and her two careers. They were a team. Or so Peter thought. Over time, the deeper Carol became enmeshed in the political intricacies of being an elected official involved in running a major Canadian city, the less a part of the process Peter became.

As Carol climbed the ladder, she was smart enough to know she needed a high-functioning team around her, one whose sole job was to support her professional aspirations. They got her elected to whatever post or position she coveted and ultimately steered her into the big chair in the mayor's office. By then, Peter was no longer a member of the inner circle, a fact which, in subtle but firm ways, was made exceedingly clear to him by the people who were.

Being mayor was as vital to who Carol Durabont was as a human being, as the beating heart within her chest. Her swearing-in ceremony was like another wedding, one where Peter was most definitely not the groom. Busy with the boys and his own career, he didn't immediately notice, but once the children were grown and needing him less, Peter realized that somewhere along the way he'd become an outsider within the walls of his own home. It was, after all, known as The Mayor's Residence, not The Mayor and Family's

Residence.

He could have accepted it, lived with it, at least until Carol's tenure was over—after all, no one held onto the mayor's seat forever—but the increasing secrecy, the sense of urgency, blooming like a bouquet of black irises, began tearing him apart. Instead of believing in and unquestioningly supporting his spouse, he began suspecting there was something ugly happening within the bowels of her administration, all of it revolving around one thing: Riverside Plaza.

Late one night, after yet another of her ubiquitous clandestine meetings with Mac Blister in her den, Carol went straight to bed, leaving Peter wandering the halls of the manor unable to sleep. He'd had a bit too much to drink, emboldening him to enter her den, a room which, although she hadn't explicitly forbidden him from visiting, he knew she expected him to consider off limits. At first all he did was circle the large space, sipping his drink, pretending to look at art, books on the shelves, framed photographs of Carol smiling her charming smile alongside a collection of dignitaries with matching smiles of their own. Then, like a light switch turning on, he decided *Screw it* and headed straight for her desk.

The search for something that would help him understand what was going on was over before it started. Right there on the top of the desk, as if Carol couldn't even conceive of the idea that he would dare come into the room and find them, were two files. One was labelled: RP Done, the other: RP To-Do.

It didn't take long for Peter to figure out that RP stood for Riverside Plaza. It was no big surprise that Carol and her right-hand man, Blister, would have been meeting about the proposed development. The plaza site had been a thorn in her side ever since she first identified the ambitious project as a major component of her election campaign platform. If only she'd bothered to consult with him about it, he would have cautioned her. He would have reminded her that she knew better than to put all her eggs into one basket, yet it seemed that was exactly what she'd done. Now the eggs were cracking and the mess was driving her mad.

The RP Done file was the thickest. It contained RFP documents, developer and contractor proposals, final signed contracts, cost estimates and ground surveys. It was the guts of the project, or at least the portion which, for the most part, was public knowledge. Knowing Carol as a staunch proponent of using technology, Peter was surprised to see the information printed off and kept in a paper file instead of left in its digitized form and uploaded to the City of Livingsky server where everyone involved in the project would have access to it. There was only one reason he could come up with why it wouldn't be. And that worried him.

The other file, RP To Do, was much thinner. As he riffled through the first few pages, Peter quickly surmised that it contained details of various problems in need of fixing in order for Riverside Plaza to move ahead. He was surprised the file wasn't bigger. From the little Carol did share with him and what he gleaned from the Livingsky Tribune, he knew there continued to be significant roadblocks plaguing the build.

The first thing he noticed was that every document in the file had a *Post-It* attached to it, colour-coded to match the notation written on it. Were these meant to indicate potential solutions for the problems identified? Included in the small pile was a land titles document for a building at 101 Redberry Road West. Attached to it was a police report on a fire at the same property. Digging deeper he found several more documents referencing the building, its owner and tenants, building and zoning documents, police and fire department reports, none of which seemed particularly damning or of obvious import to the Riverside Plaza project. Curiously, the top page of each Redberry Road document bore a bright orange *Post-It* note with the words "The Hole" written on it.

A google search for "The Hole" produced several cheek-reddening results, after which Peter changed the parameters to "The Hole Livingsky." Although the search did not identify a website or social media page, scrolling down he found a scathing review on TripAdvisor that told him what he needed to know: The Hole was a bar, or maybe a nightclub, where, according to the reviewer, "no one should be caught dead". Whether it was the alcohol in his system, or the nascent growth of a brand-new spine, Peter decided right then and there that he was going to find out what The Hole had to do with his wife and Riverside Plaza.

It was on his second night at The Hole, feeling foolish and rather like a creep for skulking around outside a dive bar, when he saw a beautiful woman slip on the ice and fall into a snow drift.

If only he'd left her there. Instead he decided to offer his assistance.

Slamming the palm of his hand against the steering wheel, Peter swore, something he rarely did. His plan to uncover what his wife was up to had gone horribly awry. But how? Had Carol somehow discovered he'd read the files on her desk? Had she hired Merry to find out what he knew…or thought he knew? Or was something else going on here?

He couldn't go home without finding out.

Looking up, he saw what he was waiting for. Pulling out of the Riverside Park parking lot was a ridiculously oversized two-door coupe. Sitting in the passenger seat was Merry Bell.

CHAPTER 26

Merry had just stepped inside the junkyard house after bidding farewell to Gerald Drover when her phone alerted her to a new text message. She was surprised to see the sender was Peter Wells. After what had just happened at the park—an uncomfortable confrontation followed by a surprise attack by bat-wielding hooligans—she thought the poor guy would take to ground and never speak to her again.

What didn't surprise Merry was Peter Wells' obvious confusion when she'd mentioned 070719 Ltd. Earlier in the day, when she'd visited Nicky Sokolov in the hospital, she'd shown the battered and bedridden pawn shop owner a photograph of Wells. He laughed out loud when she suggested the mayor's husband could be behind his attack and the Drover fire. Sokolov's amusement wasn't conclusive proof, but it was enough to get Merry thinking that Peter Wells might be a dupe in a much larger scheme.

The text read: "*I'm outside.*"

"What the hell?" Merry exclaimed to the empty room. How on earth could Peter know where she lived? She looked at her phone, it was late, almost 10:30. Maybe by "outside" he meant outside 222 Craving Lane? She texted back: "*Where r u?*"

"*Outside a gate. Garbage dump? I saw the guy with the bat drop u off.*"

He was here. At the junkyard. How? Why? Was he a bad guy or a good guy?

At least at The Holodomor, if things went awry, she could have run away. Even in the Louboutins, she was fast. This was different. This was her home. Did she trust Peter Wells? Maybe that didn't matter. Maybe what mattered was how far she was willing to go, what level of potential danger was she prepared to submit herself to, to help her client. One thing she was certain of, dupe or not, Peter Wells knew more than he was letting on.

She typed into the phone: "*BRT.*"

As soon as she typed the response, she wondered if she'd made a mistake. Was she taking an unnecessary risk? Nathan Sharpe once told her that the most dangerous combination of traits a private investigator could have was bravery and stupidity. Merry was brave, but certainly not stupid. Although she'd very recently chided Gerald Drover for his use of a weapon, the current circumstance demanded a different point of view. She never carried a gun (something she might have to re-think), and without a baseball bat on hand, she grabbed the only thing that came to mind: a kitchen knife, long blade, serrated edge, meant to cut bread, but it would do the trick if used correctly.

Still in her coat and boots, she marched outside. A shadowy figure stood on the other side of the gate. Was it really Peter? Was he alone?

On snow-silenced feet she approached the gate, mentally thanking Drover (there's a first time for everything) for insisting she keep it locked. The black silhouette revealed itself. A moonlight tattoo criss-crossed Peter Wells' pale, chilled face, blue eyes frozen into ice. They stared at one another through the chain link, Merry replaying the scene at Cuppa Joe.

"*I kind of wish we could just stay like this,*" he said tenderly.

Merry wasn't sure what he meant. "*You mean, not talking?*"

"*Yes.*"

"*Why?*"

He sighed. "*I'm afraid that as soon as we start talking all of this will be ruined.*"

She grimaced. Turned out he was right.

Having done it once or twice before, the staring thing worked for them, but had gotten them nowhere, and it was too cold to keep up for long. Glancing both ways to confirm Wells was alone, Merry unlocked the gate, and motioned him through.

Wordlessly, he followed her indoors.

"You...live here?" Peter asked when he was inside, giving the peculiar space a careful study.

"I know its not a mansion at the good end of Redberry Road, but I like it." *What? Do I?*

"It's interesting," he said, quickly adding, "Unusual, but in a good way."

She smirked. "You should see the guy who owns it." As she said the words, an uncomfortable thought occurred to her. Could Wells and Drover be in cahoots? A definite possibility. Hanging her coat on the rack, careful to position the knife in an easily accessible pocket, she pointedly did not offer to take his.

Following Merry into the living room, Peter took a seat in an armchair. Merry chose the end of the couch furthest away from him.

"I'm sorry about what happened in the park," Merry warily volleyed the apology into the void between them.

He nodded acceptance and said, "What exactly was that all about?"

She shrugged. "A miscommunication. Friends worrying about me when they didn't need to." Or maybe they did, she wasn't quite sure yet.

"Do all your friends carry baseball bats?"

She winced. "They're very sporty."

He grinned. "I see."

"I was surprised to get your text. You followed me here?"

"Yes."

"Why?"

"We didn't finish what we started in the park. I need to know what you know. I need to know who hired you, and what the connection is with the numbered company you mentioned?"

"070719 Ltd."

"Yes."

"You tell me. You own it."

"What? That's not true. I've never heard of it before."

Merry studied the man. She hadn't known Peter Wells for long, but something about the look on his face told her he was telling the truth. Which meant someone else had signed his name on the incorporation documents. Who was most likely to have done such a thing? And why? Quickly considering the options, Merry decided it was time for some artful manipulation and, as with all successful manipulations, the best way to start was with a whiff of truth.

Clearing her throat, she began. "070719 Ltd. is a numbered shell company. Over the past several months they've made increasingly aggressive offers to purchase a property at 101 Redberry Road. The company's main shareholder is listed as Peter Wells of Livingsky, Saskatchewan."

Wells stared at her, a strange look contorting his face.

"Are you familiar with 101 Redberry Road?"

"I am," he croaked.

"I've given you some of what I know," Merry said. "Now it's your turn. What do you know?"

"Nothing," he replied without hesitation.

Merry narrowed her eyes. "I don't believe you." Although she kind of did.

"It's Carol, isn't it?" he blurted out. "She hired you, didn't she?"

Merry held her breath. There it was: a smoking gun, aimed directly at the mayor of Livingsky by her husband.

Peter kept on. "She's worried that I found something out, isn't she? Thanks to you she knows I've been snooping around The Hole, doesn't she? Does she know I saw the files?" He hesitated as if another, more bothersome thought had just occurred to him. "Did she leave them out on purpose? Did she want me to see them? Does she want to implicate me somehow?"

Files, what files? None of what Peter was saying made sense to Merry. Whenever that happened—Nathan had wisely advised her—it was best to keep your mouth shut and let the other person talk until it did.

As hoped for, a clearly distraught Peter filled the silence with stream-of-consciousness speculation: "If I saw the files, I couldn't truthfully deny knowing what was going on in case things got out. She left enough in the files to pique my interest, to keep me on the hook, but not enough to really know anything. But she never expected I would act on it, that I would go to The Hole to try to figure things out.

"I suppose that's when she hired you," Peter shot Merry an accusing look. "Was the plan for you to report back if I actually found out anything damaging? Was she going to confront me if I did?" When Merry didn't answer, he laughed a mirthless laugh. "She didn't expect this though, did she? She didn't expect I would catch you. So now what? I know she knows. If you tell her about today, she'll know I know she knows."

Not exactly right, Merry thought to herself. Other than the gala, she'd had nothing to do with Carol Durabont. Peter didn't need to know that. Yet. Not until Merry had the whole picture, or at least more than she had now. "Why did you meet with Nicky Sokolov at The Hole?"

"I told you, I had nothing to do with that guy. The only reason I was at The Hole was because the name kept showing up in the files. I thought it might have something to do with…something…I don't know…this is all so frigging confusing. As far as I know, The Hole could be a big hole somewhere on the Riverside Plaza building site, that's how little I really know about what's going on."

Riverside Plaza? A niggling thrill snuck up Merry's spine. Now they were getting somewhere. Were The Hole, Riverside Plaza, 101 Redberry Road and 070719 Ltd. tied together somehow? She hoped Peter was lying about how little he knew or knew more than he thought he did. "Tell me what's happening at Riverside Plaza."

He shrugged. "I know what everyone else knows, what the public reads in the newspaper. My wife doesn't talk details with me."

Merry wasn't about to let him get off so easy. "You admitted you were familiar with the building at 101 Redberry Road. How?"

Peter squeezed his eyes shut and released a massive sigh.

"Peter," Merry said quietly, "you can trust me." She hoped she meant it.

Peter stood, paced around the chair, sat back down.

Merry yearned to reach out and hug the obviously distraught man. This was an impossible situation. He had to trust someone eventually. Who would he choose, she wondered, *His wife? Me?* How could he be certain which one was on his side? Whose side was he on?

"I read about the building in a file I found on Carol's desk, a file about Riverside Plaza," Peter finally said, exasperated. "Are you happy now? You caught me. I admit it. I was snooping around in her den like some half-baked private eye. No offense."

What did he mean by that? She shrugged it off. He had reason not to like her very much at the moment; she'd allow him a dig or two. Besides, whether he meant to or not, right now he was giving more than he was getting. But she needed more, she needed to know what else was in those files. "What do Riverside Plaza and an apartment building on Redberry Road have to do with one another?"

Peter opened his mouth then promptly shut it.

Merry immediately noticed the abrupt change in Peter. Colour drained from his face like water down a drain, his dimples disappeared as if never there, and the vivid sheen in his eyes dimmed to half wattage. If Merry had to guess, she'd say Peter Wells was beginning to question his own level of guilt in what was going on.

"What is it?" she asked, insistent, but also concerned the man was about to pass out.

He looked at her and shook his head.

He knew something. Whether he knew it all along and had been stringing her along or just had a eureka moment, she needed in on it. It was time to come clean.

"Peter, I lied to you."

He gave her a funny look. "Uh, yeah, I know."

"No, not about our meet-cute."

"Our what?"

"Never mind. I didn't actually lie, but I didn't correct an assumption you made."

"Which one? I seem to be making a lot of them lately."

"I don't work for your wife." If Peter believed that whatever he said to her now would get back to his wife, he'd never utter another word. "I work for the owner of 101 Redberry Road. He hired me to find out who set fire to his building."

Peter's jawline tensed at the words.

Merry chewed off some lipstick while she waited. Peter was no doubt beginning to realize it wasn't him she was after, but his wife. He needed time to take this in and, hopefully, decide to trust her. She needed time to think too. The second photograph she'd shown Nicky Sokolov (before he pushed the nurse's call button which led to her being unceremoniously escorted out of his hospital room) was of Mac Blister. Sokolov didn't say anything, but he didn't need to. When she showed him Peter's picture, he laughed, when she showed him Blister's, he scowled, looking like he might spit at the man's likeness. The reaction said it all. Mac Blister, the mayor's Chief of Staff, was not only responsible for putting Sokolov in the hospital, he was also the person behind the fire at 101 Redberry Road. Whether Sokolov would have actually given up Blister if he'd shown up at The Hole or was only leading her on for a free drink or two, Merry would never know, and right now she didn't care. Everything was beginning to point to shady dealings at the mayor's office. Peter Wells might very well be the key to putting it all together.

"Peter," Merry began carefully, hoping she was making the right move. "I know Mac Blister is involved in this."

He looked at her as if wondering how they had ended up here. Instead of an innocent school-boy crush, Merry had become someone capable of blowing up his life into a million pieces. "Involved how?"

"I have reason to believe he was the one who hired Sokolov to start the fire at Redberry Road. I believe..." She stopped there as another thought hit her. *Could it be*? It made sense. "I think Sokolov was playing both sides, trying to squeeze both of us, me and Blister, for whatever he could get. Blister must have found out and decided to take action."

"You think Blister beat him up?"

"Blister is the kind of man who hires that kind of thing out."

"To guys who carry bats?"

Merry gagged. "It wasn't my guys," she insisted. *No. Can't be. No way.* Drover and Blister were on opposite sides of whatever this was, she was sure of it. "Really, Peter, it wasn't them." Besides, Nicky was beaten the old-fashioned way, with fists, not baseball bats. "It was Blister. And I think you know why."

Peter glared at Merry, hard.

"Peter, I have proof that *someone* attempted to frame my client, someone responsible for setting the fire." She waited a beat then added, "You should know, if I can't figure this out to my client's satisfaction, I'll be forced to give everything I have to the police." Merry stopped there. What she said was not exactly true, but it could be. Depending on what happened next.

Peter buried his eyes in wringing hands.

Merry was about to make her next move, then stopped herself. She'd been about to intimate to Peter that Sergeant Veronica Greyeyes of the Livingsky Police Service already suspected a tie between the framing of Drover and 070719 Ltd., which would lead the police to him and, inevitably, his wife. But if Peter believed that to be true, he would be left hopeless. Hopeless people were of no use to her. Hopeless people did stupid things.

"Merry…"

"Yes?" she said, leaning forward, ready for anything.

And then the world exploded.

CHAPTER 27

Flashing blue lights lit up the scrap metal yard's monoliths like magnificent pieces of modern art. Merry and Peter stared at the light show in shock. Knowing what it meant, their eyes met, hers communicating alarm, his depthless betrayal. Again.

"Merry," his voice croaked, "How could you?"

"Peter, I did not do this!" she begged him to believe her.

"You left the gate open on purpose," he said with a dead voice.

"No!" she insisted. "I didn't. I always lock it. I just…I just forgot this time."

"When did you call them?" he asked, making it sound like it didn't really matter anymore, like all was lost. "We've been together the whole time."

"I didn't call them. Peter, you have to believe me."

His face told her he didn't.

Three strong, insistent raps landed on the door.

Peter pulled in a deep breath. Merry reached for his hands. He pulled them away.

Three more raps, this time accompanied by a command. "Open the door. This is the Livingsky Police."

Merry recognized the voice. Greyeyes. In that moment, she knew exactly what was happening. She stepped closer to Peter and whispered furiously: "This isn't about you. It's about me. You need to hide. There's a storage room down the hall to the right."

"Wh-what…?"

"Go. Now!"

"Merr…"

"It's your only chance. If they find you here with me, there'll be questions you won't want to answer."

He gave her a questioning look, but with another round of pounding on the door they both knew there was no time to waste. He mouthed the words "thank you" and disappeared down the hallway.

Merry pulled out her phone and checked her text messages. Only one. From Nathan. It simply read: "I'm sorry."

Without giving herself time to think about it, she marched to the door and threw it open. Sergeant Veronica Greyeyes, flanked by three officers, stood in a blinding corona of blue and white. Merry stepped back to let the officers through and watched dispassionately as they tramped inside, a single, forceful unit.

"Merry Bell?" Greyeyes' voice boomed the official question she was required to ask.

"Yes," Merry replied. She searched Greyeyes' face and was taken aback by what she saw there. The tough-as-nails, unrelentingly professional cop was looking back at her with something Merry could only describe as disappointment mixed with regret.

"Merry Bell, you are under arrest for the murder of Elliott Vanstone."

The hammer was confirmed to be the murder weapon. The blood on the hammer belonged to Elliott Vanstone. The fingerprints were identified—by a Vancouver Police forensics team this time—as belonging to Merry Bell. Investigators were still attempting, with little hope, to track down the person who left the hammer, sealed in a plastic Ziplock bag, in a park's disposal bin. They'd been alerted to its presence there by an anonymous caller who they'd also been unsuccessful in identifying. Whoever did this knew exactly how to avoid being found out.

Although the move surprised her, Merry accepted that Nathan

did the only thing he could do, should do, the very thing she'd asked him to do: if he couldn't prove the evidence against her was false, he should turn her in. She had, however, expected the former and not the latter.

✛

Merry never returned the keys to the small apartment and could have just walked in, but instead decided to knock. The door opened after the second one.

"Merry!" Julia answered with a look bordering on shock quickly replaced by an oversized welcoming smile. "What the hell are you doing here, girl? Are you back from Little House on the Prairie already?"

Merry returned the smile. "Looks that way. May I come in?"

"Of course. Have you moved back to Vancouver?" Julia asked, sounding a little less welcoming as she stepped back to allow her former roommate inside.

Merry ignored the question. "The place looks good." It didn't. No fault of Julia's. There was only so much you could do with a poorly-maintained, never-renovated studio apartment in a 1960's building on the razor's edge of being condemned. *Perfect for Gerald Drover,* Merry thought to herself, knowing Drover would laugh his ass off if he knew what she was thinking at such an inappropriate time.

"Sit down. Let me get some wine."

Merry knew better than to turn down the drink. She took a seat at one end of a ratty sofa draped with a cheap blanket she knew Julia kept there to hide tears and stains. Julia returned with two glasses filled to the brim with room temperature white, and settled at the other end.

"So, what's up?" Julia asked, flinty eyes searching her unexpected guest's face as she took a healthy swig.

For the next few minutes they chit-chatted about their respective lives. Merry talked about Livingsky and how difficult it was starting a new business in a new city. Julia talked about an endless string of dead-end jobs at an endless string of restaurants and nightclubs. The stories were always the same. She started each job with high hopes, then something would happen, usually a fight with another employee or complaints from customers. Julia would blame every-thing on someone else, then quit, but not without giving manage-ment a "piece of my mind."

When the time seemed right, Merry segued into what she really wanted to talk about. "I can't stop thinking about Elliott."

Julia gulped more wine. "Oh gawd, such old news," she declared, waving off the subject. "Tell me, what are your plans now? Are you moving back? I told you so. You're a big city girl, not a prairie bumpkin. Did you at least meet some cute farmers?"

Merry was not about to be so easily diverted, gossip time was over. "I keep thinking about what you said about the investigation after he was killed. Do you remember? You wondered if it would end up like that Agatha Christie book, the one where all the sus-pects turn out to be the murderers? I wouldn't be surprised. Maybe it *was* a patient who killed him, maybe more than one of them."

Julia frowned. "Was it me who said that? I think it was you."

"Makes sense though, doesn't it? He was sleeping with…how many did you say? Six or seven of us? All at the same time."

"I guess so."

"And none of us knew about the others. You didn't know about me. I didn't know about you. It's crazy. He was a monster."

Noticing Merry's glass was still three-quarters full, Julia popped up to refill her own which was three-quarters empty, this time bringing the bottle back with her.

"Obviously it wasn't all of us who killed him," Merry kept on. "But it had to be one of us, don't you think?"

Julia shrugged, having become decidedly less chatty.

Merry drank some wine. It was warm and too sweet for her lik-ing, but she made an appreciative sound before setting down the glass. "They thought it was me who did it. That's why I'm back."

"What?" Julia jerked in her seat, sloshing a bit of wine onto her chest. "How do you know that? Did the police tell you that? What happened?"

"Nothing really. They called me in, asked a few questions, that sort of thing. But, in the end, they had to let me go. I have an airtight alibi for the time Elliott was murdered," she lied.

"You do?"

"Yes. I was right here, watching TV, with Jessica."

"Jessica was here?"

"Well, not here here. I was here, and she was on the phone with me, all night. It was something fun we used to do together. We'd watch reality TV, make snarky comments and live tweet. Thank goodness too. It's an easy alibi for the police to confirm. Just like yours. You were out with a friend that night, right?"

"Yup."

"So, it definitely wasn't one of us who killed him. Who do you think did?"

Another shrug, another sip. "Hadn't really thought about it. Like I said, it's old news. So, you want to hang out tonight, watch a movie, or go out or something?"

"I suppose a guy like Elliott probably had a lot of enemies, not just patients," Merry proposed.

With a wrinkled nose as if she'd smelled something bad, Julia responded with, "I doubt that. Elliott was an okay guy."

There it was, Merry thought, the wee little bit of string that needed pulling.

"An okay guy? Are you kidding me? It was Pygmalion all over again."

"Pig what?"

"Pygmalion. The play? They made a movie out of it. My Fair Lady?"

Julia shrugged and drank more wine.

"Elliott was like Henry Higgins but way worse. He transformed male bodies into female bodies and loved his creations so much he had sex with them, with us. That's not an okay guy."

"It wasn't just sex!" Julia shot back, eyes flashing.

"What do you mean?"

Julia slammed her wineglass on the coffee table, the sound of glass hitting glass spearing the tension-filled room like a jagged shard. "He might have been fooling around with the rest of you, but Elliott and I didn't just have sex, we made love. We'd been together for almost two years."

"You loved him," Merry said quietly, not a question but statement of fact.

"Yes. And he loved me. He said it all the time."

"I'm glad you told me," Merry said, carefully inching out onto a precarious limb.

"What do you mean? Why?"

"It's a relief, that's why. I loved him too. I didn't want to tell anyone, especially after everything that's happened, but now I know I can talk to you. We went through the same thing."

"That's not true," Julia snorted, the timbre of her voice heating up. "I was Elliott's real lover, not you. He didn't care about you. Any of you. You were nothing but his sluts. You used him to get new vaginas, then you used them against him. You ruined everything. You ruined our lives, our relationship. How dare you pretend you were in love with him."

"You knew he was sleeping with other patients the whole time?"

Julia shook her head, oddly becoming calmer. "Do you remember the day you asked me if I'd seen a pearl earring you'd lost?"

"I do." Merry also remembered Julia chiding her for being the only woman under eighty who wore pearl earrings.

"I found it, a few days later, in Elliott's apartment."

So that's where this began, Merry murmured to herself.

"My own roommate, someone I thought was my friend, was sleeping with my boyfriend."

"Julia, I didn't know about you and Elliott. I was just…I was just having fun and getting experience."

"You weren't the only one."

"You found out about other patients he was sleeping with?"

"He gave them up once he and I got serious. All of them. Except for you."

Merry could easily see the pattern Julia refused to. Vanstone was in the business of creating new women, and each time he did, if she turned out pretty enough, sexy enough, he'd sleep with her, until the next one came off the assembly line, and the next and the next. Elliott Vanstone manufactured his own harem. Although Merry didn't know any of that at the time, she always knew she meant nothing to him other than being his latest successful creation. He never cared about her, she didn't care about him, he used her, and she used him right back.

Julia was right about one thing, Merry acknowledged, she *was* different, she did not fit the pattern. Even while he slept with new girls, Vanstone didn't let go of Julia as he had her predecessors. He continued to have an intimate, and in Julia's estimation, loving relationship with her. Was it simply because, amongst his many creations, Julia was uniquely stunning, perhaps the pinnacle of Vanstone's surgical prowess, his trophy woman, the one he could not push aside as he did the others? Or, Merry hoped, perhaps the bastard, in his own twisted way, truly had feelings for her.

"I'm sorry that happened, Julia." She meant it. "And I'm sorry it made you so angry."

"What do you know about my anger?" Julia spit out, downing more alcohol.

Merry's eyes moved slowly to the wall opposite, where a pretty, gilt-edged mirror was mounted above a small bistro table where they'd sometimes share a pot of coffee on the rare mornings Julia woke up before mid-morning. The time had come. "I know about the hammer."

Julia followed Merry's pointed gaze. "I don't know what you're talking about," she said weakly, looking away.

"I remember the day we put up that mirror. You joked about how, now that you were a woman, you were suddenly all thumbs when it came to handling tools. You asked me to do it, to hammer the nail in the wall."

"So what? What does that have to do with anything?"

"That same hammer was used to kill Elliott."

"Are you crazy, Merry? I think living in a snow globe must have frozen your brain cells or something."

"You must have handled it with gloves after I touched it, so the fingerprints would be mine and not yours. Then you used it to kill him."

Julia stared at her, saying nothing.

One more push. "He deserved it," Merry said.

"Yes, he did," she said, her voice flat, eyes dead.

Almost there. "You did it while he was sleeping?"

"Passed out more like it. He only drank on nights when he didn't have surgery or consultations the next day. He was very profession-al that way. But when he drank, he liked to go hard. I made sure he went overboard. He was so drunk he couldn't even get it up. He just closed his eyes and was gone. I put on a rain poncho, gloves, took the hammer out of my purse and really made him gone. It was harder to do than I thought, but after the first couple of hits he couldn't really move around too much. I kept going until I was sure the job was done. You were right, Merry. I was angry, very angry." She stopped there, then added softly, "I feel so much better now."

Merry shivered. "Why didn't you leave the hammer? The cops would have found it, arrested me, you'd get everything you want-ed: him dead, me in jail as punishment for sleeping with your boy-friend."

"That wasn't *everything* I wanted," Julia explained. "I'm not as dumb as people think I am. I didn't just get mad and decide to kill him. That's what a stupid woman would do. I am not stupid."

No, Merry thought to herself, *a more apt descriptor for Julia Turner would be cunning...and bat-shit crazy.*

"Yes, I wanted him dead for screwing you and all those other girls behind my back. Yes, I was pissed at you, but no more than the rest of those bitches. The only difference is that I knew you better. I knew more things about you. I knew about Nathan Sharpe, how he's in love with you and would do anything for you."

Merry sat up abruptly. Nathan Sharpe was not in love with her.

Not in that way. Or…was she as blind about Nathan as Julia had been about Elliott?

"I knew he had money. That's what I wanted…needed. Money. So I made a plan to get some. I knew they'd find my fingerprints in Elliott's apartment, right along with about a million other fingerprints belonging to all the other whores he was screwing. All I needed was a friend willing to lie for me so I had an alibi. That was easy. I know some dumb bitches. Then I killed him like I told you, with a murder weapon that would lead to you. I never did it to put you in jail, Merry, I just really needed cash. You know how expensive this city is, especially for girls like us, with all the expenses we have, how hard it is to find a job that pays more than minimum wage. Your old boss' hard-on for you was my ticket to finally having money in the bank. My only mistake was not asking for more." She narrowed her eyes. "Hmmm, maybe I still will."

Sounding eerily similar to when Veronica Greyeyes pounded on the Junk House door, three loud thumps landed on Julia Turner's apartment door.

"What the hell?" Julia uttered, her words beginning to slur. "It's like Grand Central Station around here this morning." Her unfocused eyes landed on Merry.

After being arrested by Greyeyes and transported to Vancouver for questioning and confinement, Merry found herself in boiling hot water. The police had recently acquired a damning piece of anonymously donated evidence, leading them directly to her, Elliott Vanstone's former patient and most recent sexual conquest. It was a lucky slam dunk for a team of investigators desperate to narrow a broad field of suspects to one person they could put behind bars. But Merry had a little bit of luck going for her too. She knew things the police did not.

A confluence of information, bits of which were provided by Veronica Greyeyes (who, despite their not-exactly friendly relationship, found it difficult to believe Merry was a murderer), Nathan Sharpe, and the Vancouver Police themselves, when put together in the right way, revealed the real murderer. All Merry needed was the opportunity to prove it.

Only Merry knew, once he admitted it to her, that Julia had ex-
torted cash from Nathan in return for handing over the murder
weapon, a fact she could not give up to the police without implicating her old boss. But that knowledge led Merry to piece together the ruse cleverly orchestrated by Julia to get her fingerprints on
what would become a murder weapon. In the end, she had Veronica Greyeyes to thank for somehow convincing her Vancouver colleagues to give Merry a chance to get an outright admission from
Julia, the real murderer. She worried what that would cost her in the
future, but it was worth it.

"I don't think you'll be getting any more money from Nathan,"
Merry calmly told Julia. She thought about revealing the recording
device hidden under her blouse, but realized there was no point.
The jig was up, and Julia knew it. "I'm sorry," she whispered.

CHAPTER 28

It was Roger's idea to meet Drover for an official "signing off on our first case" (the "our" part was Roger's descriptor, not Merry's). Thinking it over, Merry concluded it wasn't the worst idea and one that presented a handy opportunity to deliver a final billing. Maybe, if she was really lucky, Drover would hand over the much-needed cash on the spot. She chose a place called Gus & Gran's as the venue.

An Alphabet City mainstay since long before Merry left Livingsky, Gus & Gran's was a drinking establishment that took up most of the main floor of the Coronet Hotel, known for cheap rooms and the occasional stabbing. Stepping into the busy, dimly lit bar, it didn't take her long to see that neither the crowd nor décor had changed much since the last time she'd darkened the door as a rebellious teen. Gus & Gran's was popular with Alphabet City's fringe crowd— which was pretty much everyone who lived there—low level thugs, street people who managed to score enough coin in their begging basket for a cheap pint, and university students getting their kicks by slumming it in a "scuzz" bar where beer was cheaper than water. There was a pool table, dart boards, a long bar with swivel stools, a handful of stand-up deuces and a few booths usually reserved for canoodling or drug deals or both. Even at lunchtime the music was loud, heavy metal rock, and although smoking in Livingsky restaurants and bars had been banned since 2005, the air was inexplicably thick with a smoky haze that reeked of nicotine and pot.

"You been here before?" Merry asked, slipping into a booth Roger had laid claim to. He looked surprisingly at home.

"No," he admitted, offering to pour Merry a glass of draft from a pitcher on the table. "But I'd heard of it."

Merry chuckled. "You've heard of everything and everyone, haven't you?"

He smiled. "I do my best to stay on top of things that might impact my podcast."

Just as she had on their stakeout, Merry detected a faint twinge of Stella in Roger's voice. As she accepted the offer of beer, she noticed his own glass was filled with water. She had reason to feel celebratory. First, she'd completed her first solo case as a Livingsky P.I. Second, she'd escaped a future as an imprisoned convicted murderer by the hair of her chinny chin chin. After what she'd been through the past few weeks, hell, the past few years, she deserved a drink, and Gus & Gran's was probably the only place in town where she could afford one.

"Roger, can I ask you something personal, before Drover gets here?"

"Of course."

"If, and it's a big if, and I'm not saying it will ever happen, but if I should ever need your assistance again or need someone with a car for a stakeout, would you like to…"

He cut her off with an emphatic: "Yes! I would!"

"You didn't let me finish," she said drolly.

"Oh. I'm sorry. Please, go ahead," he said with a mile-wide smile.

"Would you like to do it as Stella?"

"Yes!" he quickly responded, then immediately followed up with a vehement "No!" followed by another yes, another no, then a look so profoundly confounded, Merry thought he wouldn't know his name if someone asked for it.

"You don't have to answer me right now. Just something to think about."

He nodded mutely.

They were saved from further discussion by the galumphing arrival of Gerald Drover, his ginger mullet particularly springy that day, cowboy boots nastily dirty, wallet chain strumming the side seam of his jeans.

Merry jumped up to sit next to Roger on one side of the booth, leaving Drover and his coat room to slide into the other. He positioned himself directly across from Merry, winking a greeting. "Hey, Sweet Lips." He nodded at Roger. "Not Sweet Lips."

Roger held out his hand. "Hello, I'm Roger Brown. I consulted with Merry on your case."

A waitress approached. "These two were talking about having the fish and chips," she said with a wink for Drover. "You want the same?"

Merry wondered if every restaurant and coffee shop employee in Alphabet City knew Gerald Drover.

"Sounds good, Margaret." He looked at the jug of beer and asked Roger, "Is some of that for me?"

"Of course, Mr. Drover."

Merry immediately saw the telltale shudder of the mullet as Drover responded. "Call me Drover or call me Gerald, never Mr. Drover."

Roger's eyes widened but he took the vehement instruction with the steady calm of an electrician facing an exposed live wire. "Of course, Gerald." He looked up at the waitress who was enjoying the interaction. "Can we get another pint glass for Gerald, please?"

"Sure thing, babes." She moved off.

"I was surprised to hear from you," Drover began, redirecting his blue gaze onto Merry. "I was beginning to think you were ghosting me. You haven't been answering my texts or returning my calls."

Merry cleared her throat. "Oh, yes, well, I'm sorry about that. I was called to Vancouver on some urgent business." Technically not a lie.

"Text messages don't reach you in Vancouver?"

She smiled as sweetly as she could given the colourful rebuttal swarming in her head. She was saved further discussion on the matter when Margaret delivered their lunches, disarmingly quickly, no doubt directly from beneath a heating lamp waiting for a table of suckers to order fish and chips. Merry dug in, hoping for the best but expecting the worst. Hope prevailed. The fish was surprisingly moist and flavourful, the chips nicely spiced and extra crispy, just the way she liked them, and the tartar sauce obviously homemade. While they ate, she changed the subject by recounting her final meeting with Peter Wells after he followed her to the junkyard.

"Jay-sus," Gerald exclaimed when she got to the end of the story. "Ever wonder why that dude keeps running away from you, Honeytart?"

Merry was deciding between giving Drover the finger or a raspberry when he grinned to show he was kidding. "I'll tell you why. Cuz he's got crap taste, that's why."

Merry sighed. Just when she thought her first impression of Drover as a weird and wholly unappealing asshole was right on the money, he said something like this, bordering on sweet. How was she supposed to respond to something like that? Both Drover and Peter, in their own screwed up ways, had made it clear they liked her. Talk about comparing apples with oranges, or rather, a bright shiny apple with a strange smelling durian. One of them knew she was trans and didn't seem to care. One of them made her feel like a princess just by looking at her. She suspected Drover preferred the way she looked when they first met, pre-Designs-by-Brenda-makeover. Peter had been attracted to post-makeover Merry. What to do?

When in doubt, Merry thought, *do nothing*.

She cleared her throat and said, "To be clear, Peter ran away the first time because three demented idiots were coming at him with baseball bats."

Drover had the decency to look sheepish. "Only two of those idiots were demented and, to be clear, I was just doing what needed to be done to look after my…tenant."

Roger expertly stuck his foot in it by saying, "I suppose there's nothing like being chased off by bat-wielding maniacs to put a kink in a budding romance."

"Wait….what?" Drover stuttered, aghast, looking at Merry then Roger then back at Merry. "You actually like that guy? Was I right?

Was that a date?"

Merry cringed. Drover looked hurt. She shot Roger a disapproving glance. He winced, barely aware of what he'd done.

"Not that it's any of your business," Merry responded more as a reflex than knowing what she wanted to say, "but no, it wasn't a date."

Drover looked unconvinced. "You got rules about not dating a client, but no rules about not dating a suspect? Seems unfair."

"Of course that's a rule." There were no rules, but no one needed to know that.

"Good." He sniffed, running a hand through his carrot top to spruce it up a bit. "So, what now? You gotta get him to talk, right? I think I should be there for that, just in case he doesn't know about your rule."

Merry shook her head. "No need." She smiled as she speared the perfect combo of flaky, battered fish chunk and two fries dipped in tangy sauce.

"What do you mean? If my fire is somehow related to whatever is going on at Riverside Plaza, isn't Peter Wells the only one on our side who can prove that?"

"I wouldn't say the mayor's husband is exactly on our side," Roger offered in a whispered tone to keep anyone nearby from overhearing, even though not a single person in the bar was paying them an iota of attention.

"Maybe not, but from what you just told me, he's our only way of finding out what's really going on."

"I know what's going on," Merry said, placing the fish and fries in her mouth, moaning in satisfaction as she savoured the insanely wonderful flavour.

"You do?"

"Mm hmm. Once I understood from Peter…"

Drover scowled. "You call him Peter?"

Merry scowled back. "Stop it already. There's nothing between me and Peter Wells." A piercing pain stabbed her heart hearing the words out loud. Did that mean they were true? Or did it mean she wished they weren't? "Once I realized who he was, thanks to Roger, I did some research on Peter *and* his wife. It's no secret how important the Riverside Plaza development is to the mayor, but I didn't think much of it until I started finding connections to the fire at Redberry Road.

"As soon as Durabont became mayor, the city started putting out calls for RFPs..."

Drover held up a hand to interrupt. "RFP?"

"Request for Proposal," Merry told him. "These RFPs asked developers to submit proposals, including budgets and timelines, for building Riverside Plaza. Apparently, only one developer submitted a proposal."

"That's surprising, isn't it?" Drover remarked. "The plaza's a huge project, probably worth millions. I'd have thought developers from all over the country would be climbing on top of each other for a chance to take it on."

"I thought so too," Merry said. "But it looks like most of the usual players concluded the project was too big for a city the size of Livingsky. There's never been a project like it in the province before. It would be a risky investment of time, money and resources, for both the city and a developer."

"But the mayor has been telling us for years how good this is going to be for the city," Roger chimed in, "how she's building 'A New City for a New Millennium,' how Riverside Plaza will change Livingsky forever."

"Just because a politician says something is going to be successful, doesn't mean it will be."

Gerald grunted in agreement. "Durabont said it so many times since she got elected, we all just started believing it."

"To be fair," Merry said, "she could be right. Maybe Riverside Plaza is exactly what Livingsky needs, maybe it will change everything for the better. But maybe not. That's the thing with risky investments; the potential rewards are huge, but so are the potential losses."

"And this mayor can't afford to lose anything," Roger proclaimed ominously. "Not with an election coming up."

"You said there was at least one proposal submitted, right?" Gerald asked.

"Yup," Merry said. "There was a single developer willing to take on the risk in partnering with the city. They submitted a proposal that included buying the land and developing the property, pretty much exactly as Durabont intended."

"So, everything is good then?"

Merry shook her head. "Not so good. The proposal had a proviso, and if they didn't get what they wanted, the deal was off."

Beginning to connect the dots, Drover nearly popped out of his seat like a jack-in-the-box, his Caribbean blue eyes expanding to twice their normal size. "101 Redberry Road! They want my building!"

Merry smiled and nodded. "According to the document I read, the developer wants the land where your building sits to construct a high density, luxury high-rise apartment complex. The plan is to harmonize the two developments, the high-rise and Riverside Plaza, to take advantage of shared amenities and any commercial and business ventures that arise. It's a great idea, actually. The two developments would compliment each other perfectly. Riverside Plaza tenants would be a massive, ready-made market looking for a place to live, and where better than a nearby, luxury high-rise apartment building with stunning views and easy access to all the restaurants, shops and entertainment provided by the plaza and downtown?"

"Wow," Drover gasped. "I had no idea any of that was going on."

"And imagine how Mayor Durabont would have flipped her lid when she realized that to make it happen she'd be forced to go into business with…" Realizing a little too late what he was about to say out loud, Roger almost swallowed his tongue.

Drover stared dead-eyed at the electrician and growled, "You gonna finish that sentence?"

Merry jumped in. "Get over it, Gerald. I'm sure Roger meant no offence, but we were all thinking the same thing. When the mayor found out it was *your* land they were talking about, she would not have been a happy camper. I know most of the bad reputation is thanks to your father, but no one in public office in their right mind would want anything to do with the Drover name, especially when it comes to real estate. There's no way she'd want you to be part of the biggest deal of her career."

Drover grumbled, "*Most* of the bad reputation is thanks to my father?"

"You know what I mean."

He did not appear to. "So, Carol Durabont wants my building?"

"I don't have direct proof of that, but yes, I'd say she wants your building," Merry concurred, "or, more accurately, she wants the land your building sits on. And she wants you out of the picture."

"Which is why that numbered company was trying to buy it off of me for cheap."

"She couldn't have the city be seen as manipulating the situation or taking advantage of a local businessperson, even if, no offence, it was you. So, she created 070719 Ltd., named her husband the owner—to add another layer of distance and deniability from herself and the city—and tried to get her hands on it that way."

"I kept saying no, they kept upping the offer."

"When they realized throwing money at you wasn't going to work…"

"I'm sure *that* came as a big surprise," Roger noted, once again choking on his words, but not before they came out of his mouth.

Merry eyed up her—whatever Roger Brown was—and wondered: *Why is he being so snarky?*

The answer was obvious.

Stella, when dealing with the city's criminal goings-on on her podcast, was known for smart-alecky remarks and blunt rejoinders. Usually, her existence was limited to a 10x10 room in the family home's basement in front of a microphone, but for some reason Roger's crossdressing persona was leeching into this booth, as if elicited by their criminous conversation.

Drover shot Roger an angry gopher frown. Merry did her own version of the same but kept on. "…they got desperate and arranged the fire."

Drover whistled through his gap. "That's pretty desperate."

"That's the crux of it," Merry explained, her eyes sparkling with the pride-filled zest of getting to the bottom of a complicated case. "The developer made it very clear that without 101 Redberry, Riverside Plaza was too risky and the entire deal would be off. The reliable revenue generating potential of the residential complex was the only thing that made the numbers work. It was all or nothing."

"And without the plaza project, Durabont would probably lose the next election," Roger added in the most un-Stella manner he could muster.

Merry nodded. "She built her entire campaign on a promise that was falling apart. She couldn't let that happen. It was desperate and dangerous, but she, or someone in her camp, decided the only way to keep the Riverside Plaza project alive was to burn down your building. When that happened, the hope was that you'd either decide to cut your losses and sell, or get framed for the fire, land in jail, and they'd buy it out from under you anyway.

"Like it or not, Gerald, if Carol Durabont is at all the kind of woman who might lose sleep over using arson to get what she wants, the fact that the building in question belonged to the Drover family, who have a history of serious shortcomings when it comes to providing safe living spaces for Livingsky residents, probably helped douse any morality-based misgivings she might have had."

Drover's doughy lips grew thin as the egregious actions taken against him and his property began to sink in. "Those sons of bitches! How many times do I have to prove to the world I am not my father!"

Merry reached out and laid a hand over Drover's. She met his eyes and said firmly: "You are not your father. Neither you, nor your property, deserve to be treated this way."

Drover curled his hand around Merry's as if to hold it. He winked at her. She winked back but pulled her hand away.

"But we got 'em, right?" Drover asked. "We can go to the cops now and tell them to arrest the whole lot of 'em!"

"Nope," Merry replied, sounding remarkably cheery. "We can't prove most of what I just told you."

Drover was incensed. "Then what the hell are you looking so happy about, Sweet Lips?"

Merry grinned at her client. "This morning I received a phone call from Sergeant Veronica Greyeyes. We're so chummy now," she joked, "I should probably start calling her Ronnie."

Drover pursed his lips, not amused. Merry knew why. Greyeyes was the cop who had him arrested and thrown in jail. If it wasn't for Merry, she'd likely have been more than happy to throw away the key.

"As of this morning," Merry formally announced, "the fire at 101 Redberry Road has officially been ruled an accident by both the Livingsky Police Service and Livingsky Fire Department. All investigations have been halted. I am pleased to tell you, Gerald Drover, that thanks to the efforts of LSI, you have been cleared of any wrong-doing. It's over."

Before Merry knew what was happening, Gerald reached across the table, grabbed her shoulder gently, and pulled her in for a kiss. On the cheek. It felt soft, sweet, nice.

"I apologize if that was inappropriate," he said when it was done, "especially with all your silly detective/client rules. I don't know how you managed it, Merry, but before you keep on talking, I wanted to do that, to say thank you."

Merry worried the idiotic flush of pleasure blooming on her face was noticeable, but if it was, Drover and Roger wisely decided not to mention it.

"So," Gerald quickly moved on, "how did this happen? You said yourself you have no proof, right?"

Having recently had her own experience of getting to the truth despite a lack of hard evidence, Merry understood Gerald's confusion and desire to know more. Still, she didn't exactly know how to answer his questions. Although she'd done her best to convince Greyeyes to take her into her confidence, even going so far as to invoke a "you owe me one for falsely arresting me for murder" stance, the cop resisted, clearly stating that the arrest was in no ways false given the facts at hand at the moment.

"It's true I have no proof, but the pictures of your shed strongly suggesting someone was trying to frame you for the fire is a good indication."

"The pictures showed that the red crowbar and glass jars implicated in the fire weren't actually in the shed the day before the cops were anonymously tipped off to find them there, right?" Roger asked for clarification.

Merry wondered if he was mentally taking notes as fodder for The Darkside of Livingsky. If they were going to spend more time together—which they probably weren't—they'd need to have a talk about that. "Yes. When I shared them with Greyeyes, it planted a seed of doubt. She told me it was because of my photos that she began looking at the case in a new light. She didn't tell me exactly what she meant by that, but she did tell me, in a very guarded-serious-cop way, that the decision to rule the fire an accident and close the investigation was made '*in close consultation with city administration.*'"

"Meaning the mayor?" Gerald asked, incredulous.

"I can only guess," Merry slyly replied as she slid a piece of paper across the table.

Gerald picked up the paper. "What's this?"

"A copy of a press release scheduled to be issued first thing tomorrow morning."

Gerald read the document, his rodent cheeks growing fuller by the second.

Merry grinned. "The mayor's office is announcing that Mac Blister will immediately be stepping down as Chief of Staff and leaving city hall, due to 'personal reasons.'"

Gerald looked up from the paper. "Wow. It was him."

"Maybe," was all Merry felt right about saying. Knowing how important Riverside Plaza was to his boss' success, and his own continued employment, it was possible Blister was solely responsible for the fire and any other shenanigans he thought necessary to acquire 101 Redberry Road. Merry doubted it but she couldn't be certain. It was also possible that Blister was a convenient scapegoat for Carol Durabont, the mastermind behind the whole thing. The mayor may have instructed her "assistant mayor" to do whatever was needed to obtain ownership of the land at 101 Redberry Road, leaving herself with plausible deniability should the *whatever* come to be questioned in the court of public opinion; or worse, a court of law.

Merry *was* certain of one thing; the positive outcome for her client would not have come to pass without the behind-the-scenes influence of Peter Wells.

On the night he visited her at the junkyard, Merry believed the mayor's husband had come to a huge realization: he needed to pick a side. If he gave up everything he knew, including everything he'd learned from the Riverside Plaza files, at best a police investigation would be opened, quite possibly leading to job losses or jail sentences. At the worst, his wife would be implicated in the wrongdoings and suffer the disgrace of being the first mayor of Livingsky to be removed from office for criminal activity. Alternatively, if he didn't act on what he knew, what did that say about him and the type of man he'd become. Merry did not envy him the task of figuring out what to do. Whichever way he went, she knew, he would carefully consider the repercussions for his children, his marriage, and the legacy of Livingsky's first female mayor.

It didn't take much for Merry to conclude that Wells would have been resolute in wanting to protect his family. But he was also a good man, hopelessly honourable, one who knew that by doing nothing he was showing passive support for what had happened at 101 Redberry Road in pursuit of Riverside Plaza and his wife's promise to the city. Merry's best guess was that he would have confronted his wife with an ultimatum: come clean and ruin everything or stop what you're doing and find a way to make it right. One would cost her everything, the other cost only one thing: her most trusted lieutenant.

The press release, Merry believed, documented her choice.

Although Peter vowed they would never see each other again,

Livingsky was small, maybe one day they would meet again, and Merry would ask him if her theory was correct.

Deep down, in the darkest recesses of her mind, Merry entertained yet another possible scenario, one that had caused her to sit straight up in bed in the middle of the night awakened by the nightmarish possibility, a scenario where Peter Wells was not a naïve dupe in a devious game, but instead, one of its corrupt architects, who'd played her as only a brilliant ringleader can.

Greyeyes, in an uncharacteristic act of sharing, had quietly disclosed to Merry something further, something that would not appear in the press release. Livingsky's deputy mayor would be taking the reins of the city for the next couple of weeks while the Durabonts took a long overdue vacation to Oahu. Merry didn't want to think too much about whose idea the trip was and what purpose it served.

Merry slipped a second paper, face down, across the table toward Drover.

"There's more? What's this one about?" he asked, picking it up and studying the words and numbers. Lots of numbers.

"It's your final bill."

Merry sniggered at the exaggerated sourness developing on Drover's plasticine face.

Drover dove into full complaint mode, directed at Roger. "You said you were consulting on my case—well, consult me on this, Mr. Consultant—where's the friends and family discount I so richly deserve?"

Merry was happy to sit back and half-listen as the two men playfully bickered while she sipped beer and considered her future. Thanks to Drover she had money coming in, not much but enough to allow her to keep living at the Junk House. Her very first case didn't end with the tidy conclusion she preferred, but it had been solved to her client's satisfaction. Under any other circumstances, a successful first case would have convinced Merry that more work would soon be on the way. The Drover case, however, had blown up into something bigger and more complex than she'd ever anticipated. The resolution had affected the highest level of city government, a government run by a woman who at that very moment might be sitting on a beach in Hawaii ruminating over the fact that private detective Merry Bell had nearly caused the disintegration of her world.

It was clear that Merry had been on Durabont's radar for some time. The tenants of 222 Craving Lane hadn't been invited to the Mayor's Gala because of Alvin Smallinsky. She hadn't been singled out that night by happenstance. She couldn't ignore the fact that, by way of Gerald Drover, she'd managed to plaster a huge target on her back. What did it mean for her career and the future of LSI? What would life be like living in a city whose mayor had it in for you?

And then there were her complicated feelings for the mayor's husband. And Gerald Drover. The decision to return to Livingsky had made Merry's life cheaper, but definitely not simpler.

222 Craving Lane was quiet and mostly dark when Merry slowly mounted the two flights of stairs to the third floor. It was the last day of her first case and she wanted to end it in her office. A symbolic act. Reaching the final landing, she noticed a thin line of light beneath the door of Designs by Brenda. Of course she was here, probably laying in wait hoping to catch Merry doing something that contravened tenancy bylaws. Tiptoeing to her office, she unlocked the door and was about to make good on not arousing the attention of her nosy neighbour when she saw it. A single sheet of paper, plain white, just like the previous one. She picked it up and inspected it. Written in exactly the same handwriting as before was the message: "I still know it's you."

"Oh, for crying out loud!" Merry shouted into the empty office. "What is with this woman?"

Making a hasty decision she'd probably regret, Merry turned face, marched out of her office, down the hall, and knocked on the door of Designs by Brenda.

After a short wait, there came a strained but sing-songy reply: "Come in."

Merry threw open the door and led with: "Sauvignon blanc time?"

Brenda's face lit up like a plate of firecrackers.

If she hadn't been trained by Nathan Sharpe to always "pay attention to people's faces for what they aren't telling you out loud," Merry might have missed the redness in Brenda's eyes. She was either suffering from bad allergies, lack of sleep, or she'd been crying.

"Absolutely!" was Brenda's enthusiastic response. "Pull up a seat." She fluffed up some fabric swatches on her desk that hadn't moved since the last time Merry was in the room. "I could use a break from all of this. It's endless."

As Merry sat, Brenda pulled a half-empty wine bottle and two crystal glasses from a mini fridge handily situated next to her desk. "I love a chilled wineglass, don't you?"

As Brenda launched into beigey chit-chat, Merry noticed the waste basket next to the desk was filled with balled up Kleenex. Something was wrong. Merry knew what it was. "Brenda, are you okay?"

Brenda's eyes widened. "What do you mean? Of course I'm okay. A little tired maybe, overworked, you know how it is."

"You've been crying. It's not the first time I've seen you with red eyes. Is it because of Roger?"

Brenda's eyelids flickered. She began to speak, then stopped cold. Then, carefully, she asked, "What about Roger?"

"I know you and I haven't really talked about it, about the podcast, about…Stella, but I know you know I know. I know you spend a lot of time here, after hours. It's almost like you don't want to go home."

A small smile tickled Brenda's expertly rouged cheeks. "You think this is about Stella? About Roger being a crossdresser?"

Merry bit the inside of her cheek. "Uh, yeah."

"It's true that our lifestyle is…not exactly what other people have, and yes, it's not always easy, but Merry, I wouldn't trade it for the world."

This was not at all what Merry expected to hear and her face said so.

"Do you know why?"

"Uh uh."

"Because without it, I wouldn't have Roger, and I wouldn't trade Roger for the world. He's the best person I know. He's a wonderful husband and father, a good provider, he's smart and funny, which I'm sure you already know now that he's your assistant."

"He's not my assistant." *Jeez!*

"You're right about one thing though. I have been, let's say, a bit teary lately. But not because of Roger. If anything, he's the only thing keeping me sane."

Merry held up her hands as if to stop the flow of words coming in her direction. "You don't have to say another thing. It's none of my business. I just wanted to make sure you were okay."

Brenda gave Merry a strange look.

Merry suddenly felt something—was it sympathy?—for the other woman. Other than her husband, did anyone ever check in on Designs by Brenda, to ask how she was doing, or make sure she was okay? Everyone—Merry included—probably assumed she was perma-happy. For good reason. Brenda Brown worked hard at making sure that was exactly what people saw when they looked at her. No one looked hard enough to see behind the façade.

"That's very kind of you," Brenda murmured.

Merry nodded, anxious to move on to the topic she really came to discuss. With Brenda pouring herself a second glass of wine, the time was nigh.

"You were right about another thing too," Brenda added.

"Oh?"

"I have been spending a lot of time here in the office. I know this will come as a surprise, but Designs by Brenda is not quite as busy as I make it out to be."

Merry did her best to look surprised. The poor woman deserved that much.

"I do look for reasons not to go home, but it's not because of Roger. It's because of my mother."

Could the well-dressed, older woman she'd briefly met in Brenda's kitchen be such a monster that her own daughter was afraid to go home at night? She'd learned in her years as a private eye to never judge a book by its cover. "She seemed pleasant enough."

"We built a big house on purpose; so Mom could move in and help us take care of the children. We both have busy careers, and with Roger's podcast and my spin classes, it made sense. But as soon as she moved in, I could tell something was off. She was acting funny, not being herself. I thought she just needed time to settle in, get used to new routines. But that wasn't it."

"She didn't like your kids," Merry said with a mockingly sympathetic nod, hoping it might elicit a chuckle or lighten the mood. It didn't.

"Merry, I think my mother has dementia. I suppose we've been living with it for years, but in the last six months it's gotten much worse. Mainly for me."

Merry immediately regretted her insensitivity. "What do you mean?"

"She's mostly okay with the kids, and Roger, but with me she's a fucking troll..." Brenda stopped there, as if shocking herself with the words she'd just used, out loud, to describe her mother.

Merry shifted her chair a little closer and laid a hand on the desktop, near Brenda's but not touching. "It's okay, Brenda. I won't say anything to anyone about this. Your mother's a fucking troll. What else?"

Brenda nodded, reaching for the stash of Kleenex she kept in the desk's top drawer. "She's so mean. She accuses me of all sorts of horrible things. She doesn't understand me. I don't know how to handle it, so I stay here as much as I can. It's wrong, I know it. I should be dealing with the problem instead of hiding from it. But for now, this office, and a few glasses of Sauvignon blanc every night, is my refuge, my escape hatch. Roger tells me he doesn't mind, that he's okay dealing with her and looking after the kids while I'm here. I know he means it. But sometimes, like tonight, I can't help feeling guilty. I can't help feeling I'm a lousy wife, a lousy mother, a lousy daughter."

"Brenda, I'm so sorry." Merry truly was. Designs by Brenda was dealing with a lot. A demented mother, a crossdressing husband, two young children, a (faltering?) business, all while desperately trying to present herself to the world as Little Miss Perfect. Merry knew plenty about trying to convince people you were someone you weren't. It was exhausting and, ultimately, soul-crushing. So then why, on top of all of that, was this woman expending so much energy busting her balls about having broken a few tenant rules? Especially now that all previously broken rules had been repaired by Merry moving into the Junk House.

Merry pulled the note out of her pocket and handed it to Brenda. With a smile she hoped gave off an I'm-your-wine-drinking-gal-pal vibe, she said, "I think we should talk about this." She knew the timing might not be the best, but if nothing else it might take Brenda's mind off her mother problems and, if they could reach some sort of détente, Merry knew she could be a more sympathetic shoulder to cry on.

Brenda studied the note then glanced up at Merry. With convincing innocence that unnerved Merry, she said, "What's this about?"

"You wrote this note and slipped it under my door." *Again.* "I thought we should clear the air."

"No, I didn't." Looking back at the note Brenda read the words out loud, "I still know it's you." She turned the note over to see if there was more on the back. "Merry," she said, "this sounds like a threat. Who in the world would threaten you like this?"

Merry's cheeks burned red. "I don't know." She took back the note and stared at it. Her clever handwriting analysis ruse had resulted in a false positive. "It's a mystery."

Fortunately, Merry Bell, owner and operator of Livingsky Sharpe Investigations, liked nothing better than having a good mystery to solve.

ACKNOWLEDGMENTS

I believe many writers would agree there are a great many unique experiences we have by virtue of doing what we do. I suppose the same might be said for any career. Most of these experiences are wonderful. Some are educational, some are funny or heartwarming or zany, others are downright bizarre. And—if you're lucky—there may be one or two that can only be described as transformative. I had one of those while preparing this book.

If someone were to ask me why I write, I would tell them I write to tell stories about underrepresented people and underrepresented places in an accessible and (hopefully) entertaining way. The place I favour writing about is my home province of Saskatchewan, certainly underrepresented in the mystery genre. The underrepresented people I often feature are members of the LGBTQ+ community. Keeping all of that top of mind, when I began thinking about writing this book, the possible start of a new series, I knew I wanted to work with a main character who is transgender. I wanted to create a new kind of protagonist, much in the way that, twenty years ago, I wrote about Russell Quant, a main character who was the first and perhaps only half-Irish, half-Ukrainian, ex-cop, ex-farmboy, world-traveling, wine-swilling, wise- cracking, gay, Canadian, prairie PI being written about anywhere by anyone. And so, Merry Bell was born. Apparently, that wasn't enough for me. It was serendipity that added another dimension to my cast of characters. Over a fine meal shared with good friends an idea was born with one simple question: have you ever written about a crossdresser? Without going into detail, one thing led to another and then another and eventually the above-mentioned transformative experience. Over a period of several months, I had the privilege of interviewing a crossdresser and their spouse. During those hours, oftentimes mid- afternoon in a sunny room, they (separately) revealed themselves, their lives, their ups and downs, their worries, sorrows, joys, their challenges and, overwhelmingly, their love story. All along it was made clear that although any characters I created would not be based on them, their input would be used to inform, humanize, make richer, make true, to the best of my abilities, the content of this book. The characters of Brenda and Roger Brown are probably as far from my new friends as can be, but the confidence I felt in creating the Browns is all thanks to them. You won't read much about the Browns in Livingsky, but the beginnings are there and, with any luck, there will be more to come. However things go, my deepest thanks goes to this couple for their forthrightness, humour, and generosity in sharing their life, so far, with me. You left me better, you left me inspired.

At a splendiferous after-launch-party in Calgary hosted by Lisa Murphy-Lamb (someone who really knows how to throw a party—the appetizers were inspired by our books!), Netta Johnson of Stonehouse Publishing told me that her primary goal as a publisher was to publish books that needed to be out in the world. What's this? Could such a lofty, selfless goal be true, or was it the scotch talking? Turns out, it was true. Some months later, the words were barely out of my mouth describing what I wanted to do with this book before Netta said yes. Thank you, Netta Johnson, I love being a Stonehouse author.

Speaking of Stonehouse authors, a special place now resides in my heart for our group of "Stoners", the 2022 Stonehouse Publishing authors: S. Portico Bowman, Kelly Kaur and Joanne Jackson. Over a period of several months we toured together, exchanged a great many group emails, planned and plotted promotional pursuits, and brought up our babies, our books, together. But mostly we supported one another, held each other up, and made the sometimes challenging process of delivering a book into the world much, much better. Thanks Stoners!

Speaking of book touring, I need to say an extra big thank you to all the people who came out to events from Vancouver to Toronto, Palm Springs to Minneapolis, Saskatoon to Moose Jaw. Your presence and exuberant support truly makes it all worthwhile.

Kudos to comma-loving Rhonda Sage for agreeing to give this book one last read before the printer hit the button. And thanks to Herb for reading it and loving it because that's what good husbands do. And to my sorely under-celebrated community of supporters: book reviewers, bloggers, journalists, interviewers, social media friends, the Beautiful Bunch, and fellow authors (I have the best colleagues), thank you for saying nice things—in public—about my books, putting them on lists, mentioning them in posts, writing reviews and blurbs. You are the lifeblood of a book's success.

ANTHONY BIDULKA

In 1999 Anthony Bidulka left his career as a corporate auditor to pursue writing and never looked back. His books have been nominated for several awards and Bidulka was the first Canadian to win the Lambda Literary Award for Best Men's Mystery. When he isn't writing or busy volunteering on boards, Bidulka loves to travel the world, collect art, walk his dogs, obsess over decorating Christmas trees (it's a thing) and throw a good party. His motto: life is short, so make it wide!

Please visit his website at www.anthonybidulka.com for further information about Anthony and his books. Anthony lives just outside Saskatoon, Saskatchewan.